Rancher
to the Rescue

—

STELLA BAGWELL

HARLEQUIN
SPECIAL
EDITION

HARLEQUIN®
SPECIAL EDITION™

Recycling programs for this product may not exist in your area.

ISBN-13: 978-1-335-59415-0

Rancher to the Rescue

Copyright © 2023 by Stella Bagwell

For questions and comments about the quality of this book, please contact us at CustomerService@Harlequin.com.

Harlequin Enterprises ULC
22 Adelaide St. West, 41st Floor
Toronto, Ontario M5H 4E3, Canada
www.Harlequin.com

Printed in U.S.A.

After writing more than one hundred books for Harlequin, **Stella Bagwell** still finds writing about two people discovering everlasting love very rewarding. She loves all things Western and has been married to her own real cowboy for fifty-one years. Living on the south Texas coast, she also enjoys being outdoors and helping her husband care for the animals on the small ranch they call home. The couple has one son, who teaches high school mathematics and coaches football and powerlifting.

Books by Stella Bagwell

Harlequin Special Edition

Men of the West

A Ranger for Christmas
His Texas Runaway
Home to Blue Stallion Ranch
The Rancher's Best Gift
Her Man Behind the Badge
His Forever Texas Rose
The Baby That Binds Them
Sleigh Ride with the Rancher
The Wrangler Rides Again
The Other Hollister Man
For the Rancher's Baby

Montana Mavericks: Brothers & Broncos

The Maverick's Marriage Pact

Montana Mavericks:
The Real Cowboys of Bronco Heights

For His Daughter's Sake

Visit the Author Profile page
at Harlequin.com for more titles.

With love to my son, Jason,
a dedicated coach and educator.
You've always made me proud.

Chapter One

Grace Hollister was wearily slipping one arm out of her lab coat when a voice called to her from the open doorway of her office.

"I hate to be the messenger to bring you bad news, Doctor, but you have one more patient to see before we shut the doors."

Grace turned a questioning look at Cleo, one of two nurses who assisted her throughout the busy days at Pine Valley Clinic.

"I do? I thought Mr. Daniels was the last one."

Cleo stepped into the small space and Grace shrugged the white garment back onto her shoulder.

"Harper scheduled a last-minute walk-in," the nurse explained. "Guess she was feeling softhearted."

In spite of being bone-tired, Grace managed to chuckle at Cleo's explanation for the clinic's receptionist. "Harper is always softhearted. And her tongue refuses to form the word *no*."

"In this case, I don't think you would've wanted Harper to turn this patient away. She's five years old and as cute as her father."

Sighing, Grace reached for a stethoscope lying on the corner of her desk and motioned for the petite brunette to precede her out of the office. "Since when have you started eyeing married men?"

The two women started down a short hallway to where three separate examining rooms were located. As they walked, Cleo answered in a hushed voice, "If there's a wife, she's not listed on the patient's information sheet."

Grace rolled her eyes. Being twenty-five and single, Cleo was always looking for Mr. Right. So far, she'd not found him. But it wasn't for lack of trying.

"Hmm. I suppose it was necessary for you to take a peek at the parent-guardian information."

The nurse slanted a guilty glance at Grace. "My eyes just happened to land on that part of the paper."

"You're hopeless, Cleo."

"Yes, but this place would be boring without me."

No, without her two nurses, Cleo and Poppy, the flow of patients going in and out of the clinic would be reduced to a crawl, Grace thought.

"Like watching grass grow," Grace joked, then quickly switched to serious mode. "Is the child in room two?"

That particular examining room was referred to by Grace and the staff as the kid-friendly room. The walls were adorned with playful paintings of animals and clowns, while colorful balloons floated from the handles on the cabinets.

"Yes. And her dad is with her." Cleo followed Grace to the next closed door. "If you can handle this patient without me, I'll help Poppy finish tidying up three."

Grace pulled a clipboard from a holder on the wall and began to scan the patient's information. "I'll call—"

Her words broke off abruptly as she stared in disbelief at the signature at the bottom of the paper. The cursive writing was barely legible, yet the name seemed to leap off the page.

Mackenzie Barlow!

"Doc, is anything wrong? You look sick!"

Tearing her gaze off the signature, Grace glanced over at Cleo. The nurse was studying her closely.

"Uh…no. Nothing is wrong." Even though she was trying her best to sound normal, she could hear a tremble in her voice. "I'm tired, that's all. Go help Poppy. If I need you I'll find you."

Cleo cast her a skeptical look before she walked on down the hallway and entered room three. Once the nurse was out of sight, Grace drew in a bracing breath and passed a hand over her forehead.

You're a physician, Grace. A professional. It doesn't matter that you once planned to marry Mack. You've been taught to turn off your emotions. So turn them off and go do your job.

Determined to follow the goading voice going off in her head, Grace straightened her shoulders. Then, after giving the door a cursory knock, she stepped into the room to find a small, dark-haired girl sitting on the edge of the examining table.

Purposely keeping her focus on the patient, Grace smiled at the girl, who was dressed in a fuzzy red sweater and blue jeans that were stuffed into a pair of sparkly pink cowboy boots. A single braid rested on one shoulder, while her arms were hugging protectively against her midsection. The heels of her boots were thumping rhythmically against the vinyl padding on the end of the table.

To her immediate right, Grace sensed Mack rising from a plastic waiting chair, but she didn't acknowledge his presence. Instead, she closed the short distance between her and the patient and introduced herself.

"Hello, young lady." She held her hand out to the girl. "I'm Dr. Grace. And I believe your name is Kitty. Is that right?"

The girl hesitated for only a moment, and then, with an affirmative nod, she placed her hand in Grace's. "I'm Kitty Barlow. And I'm five years old."

Grace gave the child a reassuring smile. "Five. I'm going to guess you're in kindergarten."

Kitty nodded again, but she didn't look a bit proud of the fact.

A couple of steps behind her, Mack said, "Hello, Grace."

Slowly, she turned and faced the man who'd once held her heart in his hand. As her gaze settled on his face, everything around them turned into a dim haze. "Hello, Mack. How are you?"

Over the years Grace had often imagined how she

might react if she ever saw Mackenzie again. But none of those scenarios came close to matching this moment. Pain, joy and longing were flashing through her as though their parting had only happened yesterday.

He offered her his hand, and as she reached to wrap her fingers around his, she hoped he couldn't detect the cataclysmic effect he was having on her.

"Fine, thanks," he replied. "And I want to apologize for showing up at such a late hour. I imagine you normally shut the doors before now."

Her throat was so tight she was surprised her vocal cords could form a sound. "Normally. But not always."

Fourteen years. That's how much time had passed since Grace had seen this man. The long years had changed him, she realized, but only for the better. The nineteen-year-old she'd been so in love with had evolved into a rugged hunk of man with broad shoulders, a lean waist and long sinewy legs. Beneath a battered gray cowboy hat, his dark hair was now long enough to curl over the back of his collar. Yet it was his face that had appeared to change the most, she thought. The youthful features she remembered were now hardened lines and angles carved from a weathered, dark brown skin that matched his deep-set eyes.

He said, "I appreciate you taking the time to see Kitty. My schedule has been pretty hectic here lately. But I'm sure you're accustomed to hectic schedules."

"Doctors are busy people," she said, then cleared her throat, withdrew her hand from his and turned back to his daughter.

"Well now, Kitty, I'd like to hear how you've been

feeling. This paper on my clipboard says you've been having tummy aches. Can you tell me how your tummy feels when you get sick?"

Kitty's big brown eyes made an uneasy sweep of Grace's face before she finally nodded. "It hurts a lot— like it squeezes together."

Grace fitted the stethoscope to her ears. "Well, I'm going to do my best to make all the squeezing go away," she said gently. "Can you tell me when your tummy hurts? Before or after you eat? When you go to bed or go to school?"

"In the mornings—when I get ready for school. And it hurts at school. I want to put my head on the desk, but teacher says if I feel bad I need to go home. So Daddy comes and gets me."

Grace turned a questioning look at Mack and she didn't miss the lines of worry on his face.

He said, "I've had to pick her up at school a couple of times in the past two weeks and then again today."

"I see." She turned back to the child. "Okay, Kitty, I want you to lie back on the table for me. I'm going to figure out what's causing these tummy aches."

For the next few minutes Grace gave the girl a slow, methodical examination. Throughout the inspection of Kitty's physical condition, Mack remained standing, but thankfully he didn't interrupt Grace with questions. Even so, with his watchful presence, it was a fight for Grace to remain focused on her job.

"Do you think her appendix needs to come out?" Mack asked. "Or does she have a hernia? I know kids her age can get them and she's always climbing and jumping."

"I don't believe we're dealing with anything along those lines," she told him as she gathered up her clipboard. "Wait here. We'll talk in a minute."

Grace left the room and headed down the hallway in search of Cleo. She found the nurse in the storage room, restocking a cabinet with paper gowns.

"Cleo, I want you to keep our little patient occupied while I talk with her father in my office. I'll try to make the consultation as quick as possible. I realize everyone is waiting to go home for the night."

Cleo joined her in the open doorway. "Quit worrying about your staff staying late. We know the score around here. Are you feeling better?"

The nurse's question caused Grace's eyes to widen. "Better? There wasn't anything wrong with me."

Cleo shook her head. "You could've fooled me."

Grace did her best not to smirk. "Send Mack...uh, Mr. Barlow to my office."

The nurse's eyebrows arched, but she didn't say anything as she took off in long strides toward the examining room.

In her office, Grace took a seat behind a large desk and resisted the urge to run a hand over her hair, or look to see if any of the lipstick she'd applied earlier in the day was still on her lips. How she looked to Mack Barlow hardly mattered. He'd been out of her life for years now. And, anyway, he wasn't here to see her. This was all about his little daughter.

She barely had time to draw in a deep breath, when a knock sounded on the door.

"Come in," she called.

Poppy ushered Mack into the room, then closed the door behind her. Grace forced a smile on her face and gestured for him to take a seat in one of the padded armchairs in front of her desk.

"Please make yourself comfortable, Mack."

He lifted the cowboy hat from his head, then ran a hand over the dark waves before he eased his long, lanky frame into one of the chairs. As he settled back into the seat, she noticed for the first time this evening that his clothing was splotched with dust and manure. Apparently he'd come straight here from the feedlot.

"I'm sure you're wanting to kick me in the shins right about now," he said.

Surely he didn't think she was harboring a grudge about their breakup all those years ago, she thought. Yes, he had stomped on her heart, but she'd survived and moved on. Besides, her parents had always taught her, and her seven siblings, that carrying a grudge wasn't just harmful, it was sinful.

"Oh. Why? For yanking my ponytail in chemistry class?" she asked impishly. "Don't worry. I've forgiven you."

Grinning faintly, he raked a hand over his hair for a second time and Grace couldn't help but notice how a thick dark wave fell onto the right side of his forehead.

"Actually, I was referring to a few minutes ago," he said. "I shouldn't have asked you to explain Kitty's health in front of her. I know better than that—but I've been worried about her. I, uh… It's not always easy trying to be both mother and father. Especially now that I have so many things going on with the ranch and my vet practice. I…don't get to spend as much time with her as I should."

So there wasn't a mother in the picture, Grace thought. What could've have happened? A divorce? His wife died? She could pose the question as a medical one. Kitty's lack of a mother could possibly be affecting her health. But given their past history, Grace doubted Mack would view the question as a professional one.

Instead, she said, "I heard about your father's death. Will was a special man. Everyone in the area thought highly of him."

"Thanks. Losing him—it's still a shock. I have to keep reminding myself that he's really gone. Especially now that I'm living on the Broken B. I expect to look around the house and see him. Or find him down at the barns, or spot him riding across the range."

About two months ago, Mack's father had died unexpectedly from a sudden heart attack. Grace hadn't gone to the funeral. At the time, her appointment book had been crammed full and she'd mentally argued that trying to reschedule patients would've been a nightmare for Harper. Plus, closing the clinic for the day, for any reason, always caused double loads of work for the staff later on. Yet in all honesty, Grace had skipped saying a public farewell to Will because she couldn't summon the courage to face Mack. And she'd regretted it ever since.

"I'm sorry I wasn't at the funeral. But I—"

He interrupted her with a shake of his head. "No need to explain. I'm sure you were busy. And, anyway, your parents and brothers were there. That meant a lot to me."

Grace felt like a bug crawling across the hardwood floor of her office. "My family always thought highly of your parents. As did I."

He gave her a single nod. "I've not forgotten."

No, Grace thought. There'd been too much between them to forget completely. She cleared her throat, then steered the conversation back to his daughter.

"Well, regarding Kitty, it's perfectly natural for you to be concerned and ask questions. But in your daughter's case, I think you need to quit worrying. She's going to be fine…in time."

His dark eyebrows arched upward. "In time? What does that mean?"

Grace was amazed that she could sit here talking to him in a normal voice, while inside she felt as if a tornado was tearing a path from her head to her feet.

"First off, let me say I'm not detecting anything seriously wrong with Kitty's stomach. There's no bloating, bulges, lumps or bumps or sensitive spots that I could detect, and her digestive sounds are normal. She told me she doesn't throw up. Is that true?"

"No. Her meals stay down. She just holds a hand to her stomach and says it hurts."

Grace thoughtfully tapped the end of a pen against a notepad lying on the desktop. "Hmm. When did these stomachaches start?"

"About two weeks ago—after she started school."

Grace nodded. "Does your daughter like school?"

"When we lived in Nevada, she loved nursery school and all her friends. She adored her teacher. But now that we moved up here everything is different for her. She says the other kids look at her funny and the teacher is always telling her to be quiet. Which is understandable. At times, Kitty can be a chatterbox." Frowning, he leaned forward in his seat. "Do you think my daughter is pretending to be sick so she won't have to go to school?"

"No. I believe she's honestly experiencing stomach pains and I have a notion they're all stemming from the stress of moving to a strange place and leaving her friends behind. Tell me, has Kitty lived in multiple places or is this the first move for her?"

He shook his head. "Ever since she was born, we've lived on the KO Ranch, not far from Reno. That's the only home she's ever known. I was a resident vet there."

Grace couldn't contain her interest. "Oh. Must've been a huge ranch. Stone Creek can't afford a resident vet. Although, Dad often wishes he could."

He shrugged. "It was a good place to live and work. And a nice place to raise Kitty. But with Dad's death… well, I want to keep the Broken B going. And I'm hoping the ranch will come to be a good home for her."

She nodded. "I've not forgotten how hard your parents worked to make the Broken B profitable. I'm sure the ranch is very important to you."

He cleared his throat and glanced to the wall on his right, where a wide window was shuttered with woven blinds. "Mom and Dad wanted that place for me. I guess—" His gaze settled back on her face. "Now that I have Kitty, I understand what it actually means to build a legacy."

More than once in their young romance, they'd talked about the children they would have and their plans to build their own ranch, together. Unfortunately, some dreams were meant to die, she thought sadly.

The stinging at the back of her eyes caused her to blink several times before she could focus clearly on the prescription pad lying on the desktop.

"Well, uh, I think the issue with Kitty's stomach will take a little time. Once she gets more settled she should begin to feel better. In the meantime, I'm going to prescribe something mild to soothe her tummy. And don't worry, it's nothing she can become dependent on."

"So how long does she need to take this medication? And if she doesn't get better soon, how long should I wait to bring her back to see you?"

"Give her two more weeks, at least. And then if you don't see an improvement, bring her back to see me and we'll take things from there. Right now, I'd rather not put her through a bunch of unnecessary testing. It would only put more stress on her."

"Yes, I agree."

"Do you want a paper prescription? Or I can call your pharmacy?"

"You still do the paper thing?"

Even though her nerves were rapidly breaking down, his question put a smile on her face. "I do. Some of my elderly patients feel more at ease when they have a piece of paper in their hand. And anything I can do to make them feel better is my job. I'm sure you feel that way about your patients, too."

He smiled back at her and she thought how different it was from the carefree grins he gave her all those years ago. Now she could see the everyday strains of life etched beneath his eyes and around his lips.

"Only my patients can't talk to me. At least, not in words. A kick, or bite or scratch pretty much tells me what they're thinking about Dr. Barlow."

She chuckled. "Sometimes I wish my patients couldn't talk."

She reached for the prescription pad and hurriedly scratched out the necessary information. Once she was finished, she stood and rounded the desk. At the same time, Mack rose from the chair.

She handed him the small square of paper. "Here's the prescription. If you have any questions about the dosage, just call the office," she told him. "Now, I'll go say goodbye to Kitty and the two of you will be ready to go."

"Thank you, Grace. I, uh, already feel better about Kitty."

She gave him an encouraging smile. "Have faith. Time heals."

He shot her an odd look and then a stoic expression shuttered his face. "I'll keep that in mind."

As Grace followed him out of the office, she realized her remark had struck some sort of chord with him. Perhaps she should have made it clear that she was referring to Kitty's problem, she thought. He'd lost so much in his life already. His mother and father. And somehow, he'd lost Kitty's mother, too. Maybe he'd considered Grace's comment as being trite or even insulting.

Why should it matter if you've bruised Mack's feelings? Toughen up, Grace. It hadn't bothered him to stomp all over your hopes and dreams.

As the two of them walked down the hallway to the waiting area at the front of the clinic, Grace tried to push away the nagging voice in her head. And for the most part, she succeeded. However, she didn't have any luck at ignoring Mack's tall presence.

The way he walked, the lanky way he moved and the scent of the outdoors drifting from his clothes all reminded her of how much she'd once loved having his arms crushing her close to him, his lips devouring hers.

Oh, Lord, how could those memories still be so vivid in her mind? she wondered. She'd just told Mack that time heals. And yet time had done little to wipe him from her memory bank.

When they reached the waiting room, Cleo was reading a story to Kitty from a children's book, but as soon as the child spotted her father, the story was forgotten. She jumped from the short couch and ran straight to his side.

Grabbing a tight hold on his hand, she asked, "Can we go home now, Daddy?"

"Yes, we're going home. As soon as you thank Dr. Grace for taking care of you."

Grace squatted to put herself on the child's level and as she studied Kitty's sweet face, she could see so very much of Mack in her features. She had his rich brown eyes and dark hair. And her little square chin and the dimple carving her left cheek was a miniature replica of her father's.

"It was nice meeting you, Kitty. And I hope your tummy gets better really soon. I'm giving your daddy some medicine to give you so you won't hurt. Will you take it for me?"

Kitty wrinkled her nose as she contemplated Grace's question. "Does it taste awful?"

Numerous children passed through the clinic on a weekly basis and they all touched Grace's heart in one way or another. But none of them had pulled on her heartstrings the way Kitty was yanking on hers at this very moment.

Smiling, Grace said, "Not at all. It tastes like cherries."

"Oh, I guess it will be okay then."

"That's a good girl. And there's something else I'd like for you to do."

Kitty's eyes narrowed skeptically. "What? Take a shot?"

Grace glanced up to see a look of amusement on Mack's face, and without thinking, she gave him a conspiring wink. He winked back and suddenly the tense knots inside Grace begin to ease.

Turning her attention back to Kitty, she said, "No. You don't need a shot. I want you to promise me that when you go to school tomorrow you won't be afraid that your tummy is going to hurt. And you'll try your best to make friends with your classmates."

As soon as Grace spoke the word *friends*, Kitty's lips

pursed into a pout. "But the other kids don't like me," she said with a shake of her head.

"Do they really tell you that they don't like you? Or do you just have a feeling that they don't?"

Kitty glanced up at her father as though she wanted him to rescue her. When he didn't, her chin dropped against her chest. "No. They don't tell me that," she mumbled. "But they won't talk to me—that's how I know."

Grace patted the girl's little shoulder. "Maybe they're waiting on you to talk to them first. Why don't you try it tomorrow? I'll bet you'll find out they'd like to talk to you. Do you have a horse or a dog?"

Her head shot up and she nodded eagerly. "I have both! My horse is Moonpie and my dog is Rusty."

"That's nice. So you can talk to them about Moonpie and Rusty and tell them all the things you and your pets do on the ranch. Do you think you can do that?"

To Grace's relief, Kitty gave her a huge nod.

"Good girl!"

After giving Kitty another encouraging pat, she straightened to her full height and turned to Mack.

"Thank you, Grace."

His gaze was roaming over her face as though he was trying to read her thoughts. The idea caused a ball of emotion to suddenly form in her throat.

"You're welcome," she said, barely managing to get out the words. "And if Kitty has any more problems, let me know."

"I will," he assured her.

Father and daughter started toward the door and as Grace watched them go, she was struck by a sense of loss.

"Goodbye, Kitty."

The girl turned and gave Grace a little wave. "'Bye, Dr. Grace. Thank you."

Once the pair had stepped outside and the door closed behind them, Cleo immediately jumped to her feet.

"You knew that man! Why didn't you tell me?"

Grace felt her cheeks growing warm. Which was a ridiculous reaction. She shouldn't feel awkward about being acquainted with Mack.

"I hardly thought it mattered," Grace said.

"Grace! He's hot! Hot! Of course, it matters!"

"To you, maybe. Not to me."

Turning away from the nurse, Grace walked over to a low counter separating the waiting area from Harper's reception desk. The young woman with short, platinum-blond hair was busy typing information into a computer, but glanced up as soon as she noticed Grace's presence.

"Shut everything down, Harper," Grace told her. "I'm sorry you stayed so late. You should've gone home before this last patient."

The young woman shook her head. "No problem, Doctor. I thought I'd stay, just in case you needed to schedule the girl another appointment."

"Thanks for being so thoughtful, Harper, but that won't be necessary. At least, not for now."

A few steps behind her, Cleo let out a wistful sigh. "Grace, I don't understand why you didn't suggest a follow-up. You could have included the cost with this visit."

Rolling her eyes toward the ceiling, Grace turned

to the nurse. "Cleo, if you weren't so indispensable, I'd fire you."

Cleo giggled. "Oh, come on! I can't help it. It's not every day we get to see a guy like Mr. Barlow. So where did you know him from?"

Not wanting to overreact and cause the nurse to be suspicious, she answered in the most casual voice she could summon. "He's an old classmate. That's all."

"Oh. I thought —"

"What?"

Grace's one-word question must've sounded sharp because Cleo suddenly looked a bit shamefaced.

"Uh…nothing. If you don't need anything else, I'll go tell Poppy we're closing up."

"I'd appreciate that, Cleo. It's been a long day," Grace told her. "And right now I just want to pick up Ross and go home."

She started down the hallway to her office and Cleo walked briskly at her side.

"Grace, I'm sorry if talking about Mr. Barlow offended you. I never thought it would make you…well, angry with me."

Holding back a sigh, Grace said, "Forget it, Cleo. I'm not angry. And if I sounded cranky, just chalk it up to exhaustion."

"Is Kitty going to be okay, you think?"

"Yes. In time."

"That's good. She's an adorable little girl. Too bad she doesn't have a mother," Cleo said,

"How do you know she doesn't have a mother?"

"Because she told me so. While I was sitting with her in the waiting room."

Pausing in midstride, Grace shot the sassy nurse a look of disbelief. "Oh, Cleo, don't tell me you pumped the child for personal information!"

"No! I promise, Grace, I didn't. She asked me if I had any kids and I told her no. That's when she told me she'd never had a mommy."

Never had a mommy. Grace could only wonder what that possibly meant.

"I see. Well, you know how children are. They say things in different ways. Hopefully she has one somewhere. Because right now she could certainly use one."

Before Cleo could reply, Poppy stepped out of a nearby storage room. As she joined them in the middle of the hallway, she glanced pointedly at her watch. "Should I go ahead and call the Wagon Spoke for four orders of eggs and toast? Someone at the café might take pity on us and deliver it here to the clinic."

Grace released a good-natured groan. "I'm definitely starving. But, no. Let's turn off the lights and get out of here."

Twenty minutes later, Grace picked up her seven-year-old son, Ross, at the babysitter's house, which fortunately was located only two doors down from her own home.

Ross was accustomed to his mother's erratic work hours, but this evening as she unlocked the front door, he was complaining. Grace could hardly blame him. Tonight she was an hour and a half behind schedule.

"Gosh, Mom, I didn't think you were ever going show up! I'm starving!"

"Didn't Birdie make dinner for the twins?"

Besides babysitting Ross after school on weekdays, Birdie held down a computer job that allowed her to work from home. Divorced and in her early thirties, she had twin boys two years older than Ross. Normally, if Grace was working late, Birdie would have Ross eat dinner with them.

"Birdie had a lot of extra work to do. So she's just now cooking dinner," Ross explained. "She gave us cookies and milk when we got home from school, but I'm starving now."

With a hand on his shoulder, Grace guided her son into the house. As they passed through the living room, Ross tossed his schoolbooks into an armchair and Grace placed her purse and briefcase on a wall table.

"I've had a long list of patients today, honey," Grace explained as she tiredly raked a loose strand of blond hair away from her face. "That's why I'm late."

Ross paused to look at her, and as Grace took in his slim face, blue eyes and wavy blond hair falling across his forehead, Mack's words came back to her.

Now that I have Kitty I understand what it actually means to build a legacy.

Yes, Grace understood, too. She was Ross's sole parent. It was her responsibility and deepest concern to provide her son with a good home and a solid future.

It's not always easy being a mother and father to Kitty.

No, Grace thought, sometimes it was achingly hard

to be a single parent. She could've told Mack she knew all about being both father and mother, but she'd kept the personal information to herself. He hadn't brought Kitty to the clinic in order to learn about Grace's private life. In fact, she doubted he cared one whit about her marital status.

"Mom, why are you looking at me so funny?"

Ross's question interrupted her thoughts and she let out a weary breath and patted him on top of the head.

"Sorry, Ross. I was just being a mommy and thinking how much I love you."

He groaned and scuffed the toe of his athletic shoe against the hardwood floor. "Aww, Mom. That's mushy stuff. Boys don't want to hear mushy stuff."

Chuckling now, she playfully scrubbed the top of his head, then shooed him out of the room. "Okay. No more mushy stuff. Go change and wash and I'll see what I can find in the kitchen."

Ross started down the hallway to where the bedrooms were located, then stopped midway to look back at his mother.

"Can we have pizza?" he asked eagerly. "Just for tonight?"

Being a doctor, Grace had tried to instill good eating habits in her son. But that didn't mean she was a strict prude and never allowed him, or herself, to eat something simply because it tasted good.

"Sure we can. As long as you eat some salad with it."

"Okay! Thanks, Mom!"

He raced on down the hallway and as Grace headed to the kitchen, her thoughts unwittingly drifted to Mack and Kitty. The drive from town to the Broken B consisted of more than fifteen miles of rough dirt road. And once they arrived at the big old ranch house, it would be empty. Just like this one.

Maybe he preferred living a solitary life, she thought. But Grace couldn't help but wonder if he might think of her as he went about his nightly chores. Moreover, had she ever crossed his mind since that awful day fourteen years ago when he'd told her their romance was over? Had he ever felt a twinge of regret?

No. Mack wasn't the sort to have regrets, she thought. She remembered him as being the type of guy who, once he made a decision, plowed forward and never looked back. And that was the same way she needed to deal with her own life. Plow forward and forget she ever knew Mack Barlow.

Chapter Two

"Daddy, why don't I have a mommy to braid my hair?"

In Kitty's bedroom, Mack stood behind his daughter, who was sitting on a padded bench in front of the dresser. Braiding her long, dark hair was something he'd done since she was a toddler and the chore came as natural to him as bridling a horse.

"Because you have a daddy to do it for you instead of a mommy," he told her.

From the corner of his eye, he could see her image in the dresser mirror, and the frown on her face said she was far from satisfied with his answer. The fact hardly surprised Mack. The older that Kitty got, the more questions she had. Especially questions concerning her mother.

"But why don't I have a mommy? The kids at school have one."

"All of them?"

"Yes! Every one of them!"

He made a tsking noise with his tongue. "Kitty. I've told you to always tell the truth. Are you telling me the truth now?"

She huffed out a heavy breath. "Oh, Daddy— Okay. I don't know for sure if they *all* have mommies. They say they do."

He fastened the end of the braid with a red scrunchie, then gave her shoulders a pat. "Well, you don't have one because she—"

When he paused, Kitty twisted around on the dressing bench and looked up at him. "'Cause why? 'Cause she don't love me?"

Oh, God, I'm not equipped for this, Mack thought. And he especially didn't need this sort of father-daughter talk this morning. If they didn't leave the house in fifteen minutes, she was going to be late getting to school and Mack's veterinary clinic would be overrun with patients before he ever got there.

With his hands on her shoulders, Mack gently turned his daughter around to face him. "Don't ever think such a thing, Kitty. She loved you and that's why she gave you to me—so I could take good care of you."

Frowning with confusion, Kitty's head tilted to one side. "Why couldn't she take care of me?"

From the moment Kitty had begun to talk and form whole sentences, Mack had learned that one question always led to another. Most of the time his daughter's quest for answers was amusing. But not this morning. Talking about Kitty's mother was like prying the scab off a wound. Not that he regretted having a child with the woman. No. He wouldn't trade Kitty for anything in his life. He only wished, for Kitty's sake, that their relationship had been something more than a meaningless affair.

"Well, because your mommy was different. She was like a bird. To be happy, birds have to fly free—to far-off places."

"But she can't be a bird, Daddy. She can't fly."

Mack bit back a sigh, while at the same time admiring his daughter's ability to see the reality of the situation.

Mack said, "No. She doesn't have wings or anything like that. I only meant that she has to keep traveling. But I promise that she thinks about you."

To his relief a smile spread across her face. "Really?"

"Yes. Really." He patted her cheek. "Now go find your boots and get your red coat. It's going to be colder today."

She jumped off the dressing bench. "Can I wear my red cowboy boots, too? The ones with the stars on the tops?"

"Sure. But don't drag your toes on the concrete."

"Okay." She started toward the closet, then halfway there, turned to look at him. "Daddy?"

"Yes."

"Will I get to see Dr. Grace again?"

The question caught him off guard. Last night after they'd left the clinic, she'd talked briefly about the examination Grace had given her, but after that, she'd not mentioned Grace or anything about the doctor's visit.

Mack had assumed his daughter had already dismissed the whole experience.

"I don't think so. Unless you get sick again. And you don't want that to happen, do you?"

"No! I'm going to do like Dr. Grace told me. I'm not gonna think about my tummy!" Momentarily forgetting her father's order to fetch her boots and coat, she took a few steps toward him. "She was really nice and pretty. Did you think so?"

Unfortunately, he'd been thinking those very things and a whole lot more he shouldn't have been thinking. "She's a nice doctor," he said.

Kitty nodded emphatically. "And she smelled extra good, too! I wish I could smell like her."

Oh, yes, Mack had noticed the soft, sultry scent floating around Grace. He'd also noticed how her silky blond hair brushed the tops of her shoulders and the way her black slacks and sweater had clung to her feminine curves. The passing years had been sweet to her, he thought. Even under the harsh fluorescent lighting, her ivory skin had appeared flawless, her blue eyes bright and her pink lips just as full and luscious.

Damn it, he had to be a glutton for punishment, Mack thought. Instead of taking Kitty to one of the other physicians in town, he'd taken her to a doctor he'd been in love with for all of his adult life.

That thought brought him up short. He wasn't still in love with Grace! That part of his life had ended years ago. Now, she was nothing more than a book of bittersweet memories. One that he hadn't cared to open for a long, long while.

He said, "When you get older I'm fairly certain you'll smell as good as Dr. Grace."

Kitty's smile grew wider. "And be smart like her, too."

"Don't worry, Kitty, you're going to be as smart as you need to be. That is, if you get to school on time." He gestured to the closet, where a pile of clothes spilled out of the small enclosure and onto the bedroom floor. "Now, hurry. Get your boots and coat. I'll wait for you in the kitchen."

Thirty minutes later, Mack dropped off his daughter at Canyon Academy, a private elementary school located in the heart of the small town of Beaver. Then he drove to the western edge of the community where for the past six weeks, carpenters, electricians and plumbers had been working nearly nonstop to transform the old feed and grain store into Barlow Animal Hospital.

Before Mack had purchased the vacated property, the large building with lapboard siding had sported peeling, barn-red paint and a rusty tin roof. Now the siding was a soft gray color and the roof was white metal. Corrals and loafing sheds had been erected at the back of the structure to house large animals, while the interior of the building had been partitioned into smaller rooms, consisting of a treatment area with an adjoining recovery room, two kennel rooms and a break room. At the front entrance of the clinic, there was a large waiting area with a tiled floor and plastic chairs, along with a reception counter.

Mack parked his pickup truck at a gravel parking area at the side of the building, then quickly strode toward a private entryway located at the back.

He was stepping beneath the overhang that sheltered the door, when a tall, sandy-haired cowboy with an anxious look on his face hurried to intercept him.

"Man, am I ever glad to see you!" Oren exclaimed. "There's already a row of vehicles parked out front. Two of them have stock trailers with about eight head of cattle in each one. If we try to do first come, first serve, we'll probably have a riot on our hands."

Three weeks ago, Mack had hired Oren Stratford as his one and only assistant. The young man, who was in his midtwenties, lived in the nearby town of Minersville and had been working for a well-established veterinarian in Cedar City. Because he'd been looking for a chance to shorten his commute, he'd answered Mack's ad for an assistant. Knowledgeable and friendly, Mack had already developed a good bond with him. But they needed more help in the worst kind of way.

The number of patients passing through the animal clinic each day was growing at a rapid pace and Mack had yet to hire anyone to fill the job of receptionist. So far Mack and Oren were trying to deal with answering the phone and scheduling appointments, along with treating animals.

"We're going to deal with one thing at a time," Mack told him. "The most critical comes first and then on down the line." He opened the door and headed into a narrow hallway with Oren walking alongside him. "Have any idea who arrived first?"

Oren spoke as he followed Mack into the space he'd designated for his office. "Actually, I can tell you that much. A lady with a cat. He has a cyst on his back and at first glance it looks like it's going to need to be cleaned surgically."

Mack switched on a row of overhead fluorescent lights, then flicked on the computer on his desk. "Okay. We'll begin with the cat. Sedate and prep him. Have you turned up the thermostat to the rest of the building?"

"Yes. It's already warm. And I've let the customers into the waiting area. I've taken down names, but that's as far as I gotten with the paperwork."

Mack let out a long breath. "Thanks, Oren. I'd be in a heck of a mess without you. Kitty was dawdling this morning or I would've been here sooner. Once you have kids, you're going to understand what that means."

Oren chuckled. "I get it, Mack. Mom said as a kid I was the world's worst at dawdling."

"Thank God you grew out of it," Mack said with an amused grin, then quickly shifted gears. "What about the cattle? What's the reason for their visit to the vet?"

"Two separate owners. Vaccinations for one bunch."

Mack groaned. "Doesn't anyone work their own cattle anymore?"

"It's an old man who walks with a cane. Said he couldn't find anybody to come out to his place and help him do the job."

"That's not surprising," Mack said with a grimace. "And the other trailer load?"

"Cow-calf pairs. Looks to me like they might have shipping fever. The guy hasn't had them long. Said he bought them over in Sevier County. But you're the doctor, Mack—you might have a different diagnosis."

"Lord, help us. If that's the case, we'll have to keep

them contained and away from the rest of the animals. I'll look them over while you get the cat ready. Anything else?"

"A dog with a torn ear. Doesn't look like it's worth saving to me."

Mack shot him a stunned glance. "The dog?"

"No. The ear. But I could be wrong."

"I hope you're wrong about the ear and the cattle." The phone began to ring and as Mack reached for the receiver, he jerked a thumb toward the door. "Go on and get the cat ready. I'll deal with this."

More than five hours later, the two men had managed to successfully treat the morning patients and send all of them home except for the cattle with the shipping fever. After they had treated the cow/calf pairs with shots of strong antibiotics and corralled them safely away from the adjoining pens, Mack suggested they take advantage of the time and eat lunch at the Wagon Spoke Café.

Wedged between a saddle shop and an antique shop, the Wagon Spoke had been in business in Beaver for nearly a century. Although, according to the town's history, the eatery moved to its current location after the original building burned down in 1936 from a fire that many old-timers say originated in the kitchen.

Some of Mack's earliest memories were those of his parents bringing him to the café on Saturday nights to eat dinner. Simply furnished, with wooden tables and chairs and one long bar with a green Formica top and matching stools, the place only served ordinary food, but to Mack the outing had always been special for him.

Presently, the front of the old building was sided with

a mixture of corrugated iron and asphalt shingles and one large plate glass window overlooking the street. A wide wooden door painted bright green served as the entrance.

As the two men stepped into the busy interior, a cowbell clanged above their heads. To the right, standing behind a long bar, an older waitress with fire-engine-red hair waved to them.

"Seat yourself, boys. Laverne will be with you in a minute."

The two men worked their way through a maze of tables, most of which were occupied with late lunch diners. A couple of men Mack had been acquainted with for years lifted their hands in greeting, while a pair of young women at a nearby table smiled and waved at Oren.

Mack slanted him a sly look. "You obviously have friends here in Beaver."

Oren grinned. "Beaver is only about twenty minutes away from Minersville. And a guy has to do a little socializing. You remember how that is, don't you?"

Mack certainly remembered when he and Grace had been dating. Every minute he'd spent with her had been like a slice of paradise. But after they'd parted, dating or partaking in the social scene had meant little to him.

"I may act old to you, Oren. But I'm not *that* old."

Oren chuckled. "You don't act old, Mack. Just disinterested."

Mack grunted. "Well, Kitty gets what little spare time I have."

The two of them found a vacant table located near the wall at the back of the long room. Once they were seated, Oren looked over at him. "I haven't had a chance to ask you how Kitty is feeling. You were going to take her to the doctor yesterday evening. How did that go?"

If a man liked having scabs ripped off old sores, Mack supposed the appointment had been successful. But he'd not made the visit to Pine Valley Clinic for himself. It was all for Kitty's health and nothing else.

Mack said, "It went better than I thought. The doctor prescribed a mild medication and suggested the problem was the stress of being away from her friends and having a new teacher. This morning she seemed to feel perfectly fine and since I've not gotten any calls from school yet, I'm keeping my fingers crossed that she's going to remain that way."

Oren said, "Moving can be tough on a kid. When I was about ten Dad moved us up to Spanish Fork. My brother and I hated living in town. We were used to roaming outside and being with our best friends. Thank goodness we weren't there long before we moved back to Minersville."

"Yeah. Moving to a new place is tough on kids. Tough on adults, too." Mack shrugged out of his denim jacket and hung it on the back of his chair.

"You almost sound like you regret moving back here to Beaver. What's wrong? I thought you liked it here," Oren said.

"Getting into the swing of things here hasn't been as easy as I'd hoped." Especially now that he'd come face-to-face with Grace again, he thought ruefully. He'd held the notion that seeing her would be no more than seeing any other old acquaintance. Hell, just how stupid could he get? Just looking at her had been like a hard wham to the side of his head and he still wasn't sure he'd recovered from the blow. "You've heard the old adage you can't go home again? Well, I think that aptly applies to me. I...well, if Dad was still alive it would be different—better."

"If your father was still alive you wouldn't be here, period," Oren reminded him. "You told me you moved back here to take over the Broken B."

"Yeah. That's true. Mom died several years ago, so I'm the only one left now to run the ranch. And for a long time I've been wanting to start my own veterinary business. This move gives me the chance to do both."

Oren opened his mouth to reply when Laverne, a middle-aged waitress with salt-and-pepper hair and a weary smile, walked up to their table and placed plastic-coated menus in front of them.

"You guys look like you could use some coffee," she said.

"Make it hot, Laverne. It's getting colder outside," Oren told her.

"Coming right up."

She left to get the coffee and Mack picked up the menu. A small square of paper with the details of today's special was clipped to the front. As soon as he spotted the words *meat loaf*, he dropped the menu back on the table.

Oren lifted off his cowboy hat, and after placing it in the empty chair next to his, he raked both hands through his hair. "How long has it been since you lived here in Beaver?" he asked.

"About twelve years. Before then, I'd been commuting back and forth from here to college in Cedar City. But after I got my associate degree there, I decided to attend a college in St. George for the rest of my education, so I moved down there. I decided I couldn't do a long commute, attend classes and work a part-time job. I've lived away ever since then. Until Dad died a couple of months ago."

"So you never had the pull to come back here until now?"

Mack supposed most people wouldn't understand his reasoning for staying away. But for a long time he'd associated his hometown with Grace and he'd wanted to forget that idyllic time he'd spent with her. Then later, when his father had told him she'd returned to Beaver from Salt Lake City, he could only think how gut-twisting it would be to see her from afar. At that time he'd never imagined his father would die an early death and send Mack back here to take over his inheritance.

"Kitty and I were just fine down in Nevada," Mack answered. "But we'll be just fine here, too."

Laverne arrived with their coffee and two glasses of ice water. As she placed the beverages on the table, she looked questioningly at Mack.

"Have you hired anyone to be your receptionist?"

No doubt the waitress probably saw an endless number of people pass through the café on a daily basis and heard just as many stories. Mack was surprised the woman remembered he'd mentioned he'd been on the hunt for someone to fill the job of receptionist for his animal hospital.

"A few persons have inquired about the position. But

none were suitable," he told her. "You have someone in mind who'd be good at the job?"

"As a matter of fact, I think I do. I don't know why it didn't cross my mind before now. Eleanor Shipman. She retired from her job about three months ago. Worked twenty years as a receptionist for Denver Garwood over at Independent Insurance. I'd say the woman would know how to answer the phone and schedule things. And I know she's as bored as heck sitting home. No husband or kids to keep her busy, you see."

Mack exchanged hopeful looks with Oren.

"Sounds like she might be the answer," Oren said.

"You have her number?" Mack asked. "I'll give her a call."

"I'll get it when I turn in your orders." She pulled out a pad and pencil. "You two decided on what you want?"

"The special for me," Mack told her.

The woman scribbled down the information, then looked pointedly at Oren. "What about you, scrawny? Looks like you could use a double-plate special."

From the very first day Oren had walked into the café with Mack, Laverne had teased him mercilessly and Oren was always trying to get her back. Now he playfully pulled a face at her.

"No meat loaf for me, Laverne. Give me a double-meat, loaded burger, fries and a piece of rhubarb pie."

"We don't have rhubarb today," Laverne said. "We only serve it on Tuesdays and Wednesdays."

"Okay. What do you have on Thursdays?" he asked.

"You want the meringue choices or the fruit?"

"Fruit."

The waitress named off a list of pie flavors until Oren held up a hand to halt her.

"Blueberry, that's it," he told her, then gave her a sassy wink. "And for your information I'm not scrawny. If you saw me without any clothes on, you'd know so."

Mack watched the waitress sweep a skeptical gaze up and down Oren's tall frame.

"Not interested," she said blandly. "But those girls at the table across the room probably would be."

Oren's face turned red and Mack couldn't choke back a laugh.

With her pen still poised above her pad, Laverne asked, "Is that all?"

"That's plenty," Mack told her, then continued to chuckle as the woman turned and headed toward the kitchen.

"Guess I asked for that, didn't I?" Oren muttered.

"Don't try to get ahead of Laverne. It'll never happen. She's been here for years and heard it all. Besides, she picks on you because she likes you."

"I'd hate to hear what she'd have to say if she didn't like me," Oren muttered.

Mack picked up his coffee cup, but only managed to lift it halfway to his mouth when the cell phone inside his shirt pocket began to vibrate.

"An emergency?" Oren asked as Mack pulled out the phone and scanned the screen.

"I don't think so. I wanted to make sure it wasn't the school informing me that Kitty was sick again. Thankfully, it's not the school, so I'll let voice mail deal with the call. Otherwise, I'll not get much of lunch break."

"Yeah. You need to fix the way you operate, Mack. The vet I worked for down in Cedar City let the receptionist deal with all the business calls. Only family or close friends had his personal number."

Mack enjoyed a few sips of coffee before he replied. "You don't need to remind me how we're hurting for help. It would be great if the woman Laverne recommended works out."

Oren didn't reply and Mack glanced over to see he was focused intently on something at the front of the room. In fact, the young man's jaw had dropped to leave his mouth partially gaped.

"Who is *that*?"

The wonderous tone to Oren's question told Mack the object of his attention had to be a woman. "I'm sure I wouldn't know."

"Well, I'd sure like to!"

Curious, Mack gave a cursory glance over his shoulder to see a young, slender woman with short blond hair moving into the maze of dining tables. She looked vaguely familiar and then it dawned on him as to where he'd seen her.

With a wan smile, Mack looked back at Oren. "What a coincidence. We were just talking about receptionists and one walks in."

"You know *her*?"

Mack nodded. "She works the front desk at Pine Valley Clinic. I think her name is Hailey. No, it was Harper...or something like that. I wasn't paying much attention."

He'd been too busy worrying about Kitty and wondering where he was going to find the nerve to face Grace again, Mack thought ruefully.

Oren playfully grabbed one side of his rib cage. "Oh! I just felt an awful pain in my side."

"The blonde doesn't treat patients," Mack pointed out. "She only makes appointments for them."

"Well, in that case I need one." He leaned forward eagerly and snapped his fingers. "Mack, she's the sort of woman you need to hire! Your office would be overrun with male customers."

"Sure! And I'd be spending most of my time chasing my assistant out of the waiting area." Above Oren's shoulder, he spotted Laverne coming their way with a loaded tray of food. "Here comes our lunch. Maybe Laverne can tell you whether Eleanor is a raving beauty."

"Ha! I'm not giving her another chance to make me look like a fool," Oren said.

Years ago, Mack had made a mighty big fool of himself when he'd fallen in love with Grace. But since then he'd learned to never hand over his heart to a woman and, so far, he'd managed to hold fast to the difficult lesson.

Mack grunted. "Women tend to do that to us men, Oren. It's just a fact of life."

Each year on the Monday night before Thanksgiving, the town's business owners provided a free dinner to anyone who wanted to attend. Ever since Grace had returned to Beaver after living a few years in Salt Lake City, she'd always contributed to the charity meal by giving food and helping in the kitchen.

Tonight was no exception. Except that she and Ross were running late as she steered her SUV into the large parking lot located next to the town's civic building. A huge number of vehicles were already taking up the parking slots, forcing Grace to settle for a spot at the far end of the area.

"Gosh, Mom, we're going to have a long walk from here," Ross said as he unsnapped his seat belt. "Couldn't you get any closer?"

"Sorry, lazy bones," Grace told him. "This is the only space left and it won't hurt you to walk."

He groaned. "Yeah, but we have to carry all this food."

Grace climbed out of the vehicle and hurriedly pulled on a gray trench coat to ward off the cold wind sweeping across the parking lot. "That's right. So hurry and jump out and make yourself useful."

Shrugging on a puffy nylon coat, the boy joined his mother at the back of the SUV. "We must be the last ones here. Do you think they've started eating yet?"

"Probably. But don't worry," she told him as she opened the hatch on the SUV. "There will be plenty to go around. Just remember we're here to help others, not ourselves."

She placed a cardboard box holding a ham into Ross's arms, then picked up a two large plastic shopping bags loaded with bakery goods. After closing the hatch and locking the vehicle, mother and son walked toward the redbrick building.

"I imagine you're going to see some of your classmates here tonight," she told him.

"Bobby said he'd be here tonight. And Trevor said he might get to come. I hope he does," Ross said. "It's more fun when you get to eat with friends."

He glanced curiously up at his mother. "Mom, do you have any friends?"

Grace was accustomed to having Ross ask her all kinds of questions, some of which were a bit weird. But this one brought her up short. "Of course, I have friends, Ross. What makes you ask such a thing?"

"'Cause I never see you with any."

She said, "All the women I work with are my friends. And the people we attend church with are all friends."

"Yeah," Ross said. "But you don't have a friend you go places with or do things together."

Her son had noticed that about her? He was definitely growing up, she thought.

"Hmm. Do you mean like a boyfriend?"

"Sorta something like that," he agreed.

And why had Ross been thinking about this sort of thing? Grace wondered. When he'd been smaller, he had often begged her to get him a father. However, now that he'd gotten older and understood a daddy wasn't something his mother could pluck from a tree, he'd quit asking.

"Ross, I don't want a boyfriend. At least, not right now. I'm too busy being a doctor."

He frowned as though her reasoning didn't make sense. "But, Mom, you're always going to be a doctor."

"Yes. I will always be a doctor," she replied, while thinking she'd already tried being a girlfriend and a wife. Neither had worked out the way she'd planned.

Yes, she wished more than anything that Ross had a father, but Bradley had been dead five years now and even before his death, she'd obtained a divorce. No. The only father Ross could hope to have now would be a stepfather and so far she'd not met anyone here.

To Grace's relief, they finished the walk to the building without Ross throwing any more dating questions her way, and by the time they stepped into the busy kitchen he'd turned his mind back to eating.

After turning the food over to a pair of kitchen helpers, Ross asked, "Mom, is it okay if I go out to the dining room?"

"Not yet. Just wait over there by that far wall while I speak to Dorothy about helping with the serving. I'll come tell you."

Ross left to do as she instructed and Grace made her way through the bustling workers until she reached a middle-aged woman with a messy bun and harried smile. Grace didn't know how the woman managed to do it, but every year Dorothy successfully orchestrated this whole event for the townspeople.

"Happy Thanksgiving before Thanksgiving!" she said with a little laugh. She gave Grace a brief hug. "I'm glad you could make our dinner tonight."

"I wouldn't have missed it for anything, Dorothy. And I'm ready to help serve," Grace told her. "Just show me what you want me to do."

The woman shook her head. "Honestly, Grace, we already have more help than we need. People are tripping over each other back here. And you've done more than enough by donating food. You and Ross go on and mingle with the townsfolk. We're almost ready to begin serving."

"Are you sure, Dorothy? I'm more than happy to do my part."

With a laugh of dismay, Dorothy patted Grace's arm. "Oh, my, you're one of the hardest-working persons in Beaver, Grace. And believe me, we all appreciate you. So scram. Go enjoy the meal."

Seeing there was no point in arguing with the woman, Grace thanked her and made her way over to where Ross was impatiently shifting his weight from one cowboy boot to the other.

"Dorothy says I'm not needed," Grace told him. "So let's go out to the dining area, where everyone is gathering. Maybe you'll spot Bobby or Trevor."

"Yay! Let's go!"

At the far end of the room, they passed through a pair of open doors and were suddenly faced with a thick crowd blocking the entryway.

"Gosh, Mom, I think everybody in town is here," Ross commented as he tried to peer around a group of men standing in front of them. "Reckon there will be room for us to sit down?"

Going home and cooking a meal for her and Ross might actually be easier than fighting their way through the crowd, Grace thought. But they were already here and she didn't want Ross to view her as a party pooper. Especially since this event was primarily given for the needy townsfolk.

"We'll see how things are after people start going

through the serving line," she told him. "Right now let's find a quieter spot to stand."

They were slowly working their way along the wall toward an open space at the back of the room, when Grace felt a hand come down on the back of her shoulder.

Expecting to see a coworker, she was stunned when she turned and found herself staring straight into Mack Barlow's face.

"Hello, Grace."

Nearly two weeks had passed since he and Kitty had come to the clinic. She'd not seen or heard from him since. But that hadn't stopped her from thinking about him. To be honest, she'd thought about little else.

"Good evening, Mack."

As she met his gaze, her heart gave one hard thump, then leaped into such a fast pace that the rush of blood caused her ears to roar.

"Hi, Dr. Grace! My tummy is really good now. Are you gonna eat turkey with us?"

Grace's gaze dropped from Mack to Kitty, who was standing at her father's side, clutching a fold on the leg of his jeans. She was wearing a blue velvet dress with a white Peter Pan collar, and a pair of silver cowboy boots with sparkling rhinestones on the shafts. A wide velvet headband the same color as her dress held her dark hair away from her sweet little face. She looked so adorable that bittersweet tears pricked the back of Grace's eyes.

"Hello, Kitty. I'm very happy to hear your tummy is feeling well. But I—I'm not sure if they'll be enough room for all four of us to sit down together."

"I imagine we can find room enough somewhere," Mack said.

Did he want her and Ross to sit with them? More importantly, did she want to spend this evening in his company?

The questions were running through her mind when she felt Ross tugging on her hand to catch her attention.

Taking him by the shoulders, she said, "Ross, this is Mr. Barlow. He's the new veterinarian in town. And, Mack, this is my son, Ross."

"Nice to meet you, Ross." Mack reached down and shook Ross's hand, then urged Kitty to take a step forward. "This is my daughter, Kitty."

The girl gave Ross a long, critical look. Then she shot her father an inquiring glance. "Is it okay for me to shake Ross's hand, too?"

Mack nodded. "If it's okay with Ross."

The girl held her hand out to Ross and the hearty shake he gave it put a wide, smile on her face.

"My name is Kitty and I'm five," she told Ross. "How old are you?"

"I'm seven," Ross told her. "Do you go to school?"

Kitty gave him a proud nod. "I'm in kindergarten— at Canyon Academy. Do you go to school?"

Ross shot his mother an amused grin before he answered Kitty's question. "Sure, I do. I go to Canyon Academy, too. I'm in second grade."

Kitty's expression said she was properly impressed. "You must be awful smart."

Ross's face turned a light shade of pink. "I don't

know." He cast a doubtful glance at his mother. "Am I, Mom?"

Grace and Mack both laughed.

Clearly amused with his daughter, Mack said, "Kitty admires smartness in a person."

Grace said, "Well, I might have a biased opinion, but I think Ross is smart. He makes good grades."

"I'm gonna make good grades, too," Kitty announced, then directed her next statement to Ross. "I have a horse and a dog. And two cats. Do you have any animals?"

He nodded. "I have a horse. Her name is Penny, 'cause she's red and she's a mare. She stays at my grandpa's ranch. And I have two cats, too. George and Ginger."

Kitty giggled and Grace was a bit surprised that Ross appeared to be totally charmed by the girl's reaction.

"George and Ginger," Kitty repeated. "Those are funny names. I just call my cats *Cat*."

"Why?" Ross asked.

Tilting her head to one side, Kitty contemplated his question. "Because they live in the barn and when I try to play with them they run from me. So I don't think they want names."

Ross stepped closer to Kitty and the children went into a deeper conversation about their cats. While the two of them continued to talk, Grace looked at Mack and smiled.

"Kitty must love animals as much as Ross."

"When we're home on the ranch, I can hardly keep her inside," Mack admitted. "She wants to live at the barn."

"Sounds like she takes after her father. Remember

the baby goats you raised on a bottle? You took them on our picnic, just so you wouldn't miss their feeding time. I knew then that you'd be caring for animals the rest of your life."

Mack's gaze met hers and suddenly she was transported back to when the two of them were very young and very much in love. They had spent many days riding and exploring the Broken B and dreaming about making their home on his family ranch. When she thought of those days, she always viewed them through a warm, golden haze of sunshine. Even now, after all these years, it was hard for her to believe he'd wanted their relationship to end. But where Mack was concerned, she'd always been a bit blinded.

A wan smile touched his lips. "Actually, both of those goats are still on the ranch," he told her. "Mildred and Morris are old now, but in good shape for their age."

At least the goats had survived all these years, even if Mack's love for Grace hadn't, she thought.

"Wow. Your father must've taken good care of them."

He shrugged. "Dad made sure they were pampered. Now Kitty loves seeing after them."

As he spoke, his expression shifted subtly and Grace found herself staring at him and wondering. Was that regret she was seeing? Sadness?

No. He'd been talking about goats and nothing else. She needed to quit weighing every expression that crossed his face, each word that rolled out of his mouth.

"I'm sure she does," she said. Then, realizing her voice had taken on a husky tone, she cleared her throat and glanced toward the front of the long room. Thankfully, she spotted Dorothy stepping out of the kitchen and ringing the dinner bell.

"Looks like they're going to start serving," Grace announced as the milling crowd began to slowly migrate toward the buffet tables.

Overhearing his mother, Ross exclaimed, "Yay! I'm hungry!"

"Me, too!" Kitty added with eager excitement.

Ross turned to the girl with an all-important question. "Are you going to eat turkey or ham?"

Her little eyebrows pulled together as she contemplated the two choices. "What are you going to eat?" she asked him.

"Ham!"

"Then I'll eat ham, too!" she said happily.

Ross looked hopefully at his mother. "Can we get in line now?"

Grace glanced at Mack. "Are you ready?"

"From the looks of this crowd, better now than later," he agreed.

As the four of them began to head toward the side of the room where a line was already forming, Grace was more than surprised to see Ross reach for Kitty's hand.

"You'd better hang on to me, Kitty," he said to the girl. "Or you might get lost."

Kitty gave him a beaming smile. "I'll hang on real tight," she promised.

While the children moved a few steps in front of their parents, Grace cast a look of amazement at Mack.

"I've never seen him behave this way," she said in a

voice too low for Ross to hear. "Does Kitty normally take this quickly to boys?"

He let out a short laugh. "She never takes this quickly to any kid, girl or boy. And that's the biggest smile I've seen on her face since we moved here."

"I'm glad. Hopefully Kitty will get more than a meal out of this evening," Grace said. "She'll get a new friend."

He slanted her a wry smile. "Maybe I'll get more out of this evening, too."

Grace very nearly stumbled. What was he talking about? Spending time with her? No! Her imagination was working far too hard, she thought. She and Mack had been more than friends...once. She'd be silly to think they could ever be more than friends again.

Yet as they maneuvered their way toward the long line of waiting diners, she felt Mack's hand lightly rest against the small of her back. And foolish or not, she realized the contact felt just as good as it had all those years ago.

Chapter Three

Mack hadn't planned on seeing Grace tonight. He figured her contributions to the community were usually made by writing a check whenever the occasion warranted. Not personally attending an event for needy folks. When he'd spotted the back of her tall figure and golden-blond hair weaving through the crowd, he'd been surprised. But he'd been even more stunned when, without a second thought, he'd automatically started after her.

What was he doing? Just trying to get his heart broken all over again?

Who are you trying to fool, Mack? Yourself? Grace didn't break your heart. She's not the one who wanted to call it quits. You did that. You kicked her in the teeth with that story of yours. It's a miracle she's even speaking to you now.

Pushing back at the goading voice in his head, he

glanced across the table to where his daughter and Grace's son were sitting with their heads together. He'd not counted on Kitty taking an instant liking to Ross. Or that the boy would be so attentive and kind to his daughter. Mack was grateful for that much. As Grace had suggested, Kitty needed new friends to fill the void made by their move here to Beaver.

Mack was grateful, too, that the unexpected link between the two children had given him a chance to spend time with Grace. If that made him a glutton for punishment, then he was guilty. As a teenager, he hadn't been able to resist her, and now that he was back in Beaver as a grown man, he was still finding her impossible to resist.

From a chair next to his, Grace said, "Looks like Ross and Kitty are enjoying the food. What about you?"

Her question drew Mack's gaze across the table to the children. Throughout the meal, Kitty had been chatting and giggling nonstop with Ross. It was like a happy switch had been flipped on inside his daughter.

He looked over at Grace and thought once again how lovely she looked tonight in a chocolate-brown dress that skimmed her curves and made her rich, blond hair resemble the color of pure gold.

"I never get tired of turkey and stuffing," he answered. "Occasionally, the Wagon Spoke serves it on Sundays throughout the year. I always try to stop in whenever they have it on the menu."

Her eyebrows arched with interest. "I wasn't aware of that. I'll have to try it. Although, on most Sundays I drive out to Stone Creek. Sunday dinner with the family, you know."

Yeah, he used to have a family, he thought dully. Going home and experiencing the warm love of his parents. Feeling as if he truly belonged to a family unit. He'd had all of those things for a while, but he'd never have them again.

"Yes, I know."

Something in his voice must have struck a chord of empathy in her. Or maybe she was seeing a strained look on his face. No matter the reason, he was a bit jolted when she reached over and rested a hand lightly on his forearm.

"Forgive me, Mack. I spoke without thinking. It can't be easy for you going into the holidays without your dad."

His throat was suddenly blocked with a ball of emotions and the hell of it was, he knew only a part of the grief pouring through him was for the loss of his father. The touch of her hand was a heavy reminder of how much he'd given up over the years.

He took a sip of coffee in hopes it would ease the tightness in his throat. "It won't be the same, that's for sure. But I have to think of Kitty now and try to make things good for her."

She gave his arm a little squeeze, then eased her hand away from him. "Yes. That's my main focus, too. To make things good for Ross. Without spoiling him," she added on a lighter note. "If you can tell me how to manage that, I'd be eternally grateful."

He let out a short laugh. "I'd be grateful if someone would tell me the secret to child-rearing."

She was about to make a reply when an elderly man with a head of curly white hair paused at the end of their table.

"Well, hello Dr. Hollister. You're looking mighty pretty tonight."

Smiling with genuine pleasure, she rose and gave the tall, stately figure of a man a brief hug.

"It's good to see you, Ira. How are you feeling?"

He affectionately patted Grace's shoulder. "Now, now, Doctor, tonight is for pleasure, not work. But since you asked, if I felt any better I couldn't stand myself."

"That's music to my ears," she told him. "Tells me I must be doing something right."

"You're my favorite doctor," he said with a sly chuckle.

Grace laughed. "Probably because I'm your *only* doctor."

Ira agreed, then inclined his head toward Mack. "Aren't you going to introduce me to your friend?"

"Absolutely." She looked at Mack and gave him a conspiring wink, then returned her attention to the older gentleman. "Ira, this is Mack Barlow. He's a doctor, too. A veterinarian. And, Mack, this is Ira Nelson. He's been a family friend to the Hollisters for years."

Mack rose and shook hands with the man.

Grace said, "You might be interested to know that Ira loves animals. He has something of a petting zoo on his property just south of town. Everything from rabbits and chickens to goats, cows and horses."

Ira's bushy white eyebrows lifted with interest. "A

veterinarian, eh? You must be the one who took over the old feed store," he said. "You've made some nice changes on the property."

"Thank you, sir. I'm trying."

Ira cast him another long, meaningful look. "You wouldn't happen to be looking to hire more help, would you? I could clean cages or do other janitor work. And Grace can tell you that I'm pretty good at handling animals. Giving them baths—things like that."

Mack did need more help at the clinic and in the past week he'd been approached by several young people looking for a job. However, none of them had come across as being knowledgeable or responsible enough. Before now, he hadn't considered hiring an older person to help with the never-ending tasks that popped up throughout the day. But Ira's sturdy appearance and honest face were giving Mack reason to pause and reconsider.

"I do need someone to help in the kennel area. And outside with the larger animals," Mack admitted. "You'd need to be prepared to be a jack-of-all-trades."

Ira said, "I'm not an expert at any one job, but I'm fair at doing several."

"If you're worried about Ira's physical ability, don't be," Grace said. "He can go circles around a younger man."

Since Ira appeared to be closer to eighty than seventy, Mack found her comment hard to believe, but she was an MD. She ought to know about the man's physical condition.

"Well, Ira, you might be just the man I need. Can you come to the clinic in the morning?"

A wide grin split the older man's face as he reached to give Mack's hand another shake. "Sure can! I'll be there before you open. Thank you, Mr. Barlow."

"Call me Mack."

"As long as you keep calling me Ira," he said.

"That's a deal, Ira. I'll see you in the morning."

Ira gave Grace a one-armed hug, then went on his way. Mack looked at her and chuckled.

"Did I just hire someone?"

"I believe so." She grabbed his upper arm and gave it a grateful squeeze. "Thank you, Mack. Ira is such a good man and since his wife died a couple of years ago, he gets lonely. He needs more than just his animals. And I'm positive he'll make a great employee."

"Well, the receptionist working for me is hardly a spring chicken. I got her out of retirement. You might know her. Eleanor Shipman."

She shot him a crafty smile. "Oh, yes. I know Eleanor. She's a lovely woman. And—" She paused and chuckled. "Ira is going to be a happy camper when he sees she's working the front desk."

Mack groaned. "I think I need to sit down on that one," he said.

They returned to their seats and as the two of them resumed eating, Grace said, "Don't worry, Mack. If Ira gets too flirty with Eleanor, she'll put him in his place. I'm sure you've already seen for yourself that she's a straight shooter."

Mack grunted. "My assistant tiptoes around her and

I stay at least ten feet away from her desk when I talk to her," he joked.

Chuckling, Grace started to reply when Kitty directed a question at him.

"Daddy, Ross wants to know if we're going to eat turkey at our house on Thanksgiving?"

Mack looked at her and the boy. "I don't know, sweetheart. We'll see when that day gets here."

Kitty's head tilted to one side and then the other as she explained to Ross. "See, I told you. We don't do stuff like that since Grandpa went to heaven."

"Oh. That's too bad," Ross told her. "You're missing all the fun."

Kitty shrugged, then grinned at him as if to say she wasn't going to let anything dampen her spirits tonight. "Well, I'll help my daddy make macaroni and cheese. That's my favorite meal. And we'll have fun."

Kitty's words smacked Grace right in the middle of her chest. Yes, there were plenty of people at this dinner tonight who'd lost loved ones, who were poor, or alone and in need of companionship. Kitty was neither poor nor alone and yet Grace's heart hurt for the little girl. This was Mack's daughter. It wasn't fair or right that she should be without a family during the holidays, or any other days for that matter.

Where was her mother? Grace asked herself for the umpteenth time. Even if the woman was dead, there would most likely be a set of grandparents somewhere. The questions burned her tongue, but she kept them to herself. Mack hadn't been throwing personal questions about Ross's father at her, she reasoned. And the maternal side of Kitty's family was none of Grace's business.

"You're probably thinking macaroni and cheese is the only thing I can cook for my daughter."

Mack's voice had her glancing over to see that his brown eyes were making a leisurely inspection of her face, and she'd be lying if she said she wasn't affected by his gaze.

Grace shook her head. "I wasn't thinking anything of the sort. Actually, I've never met a child who didn't love mac and cheese. Ross makes a pig of himself whenever I fix it," she told him. "But I was thinking...no, to be honest, I was wondering what you are going to be doing on Thanksgiving Day. Are you planning on having guests out at the Broken B?"

After darting a quick at the children, he answered in a lowered voice, "I am closing the hospital on that day. But, no, having guests out would mean cleaning up the place, buying food and all that sort of thing. Getting the clinic going makes it hard for me to plan anything outside of work. Hopefully I can make it up to Kitty later by doing something special."

She pushed away her empty plate and reached for her coffee. "I understand. When I first set up my practice here in town, I felt like I was being pulled in a thousand different directions. To make things even harder, Ross was only a toddler at that time. Leaving him with a sitter while I worked long hours made me feel like a bad mother. To be honest, I stayed in a state of exhaustion."

"I try to tell myself I'm doing it all for Kitty's future," he said as though he needed to defend himself.

Grace thoughtfully sipped her coffee as an idea began to form in her head. "Mack, uh, what would you say to joining me and my family out at Stone Creek this Thursday?"

He looked at her, and from his expression she could see that her invitation had caught him off guard. He couldn't know just how much it had taken her by surprise, too. The invite had simply rolled off her tongue before she could stop it.

"Why are you asking?"

Dropping her gaze to the tabletop, she absently picked up a spoon and slowly stirred her coffee. How could she answer without making herself sound ridiculous?

"Well, because it's a holiday and I think Kitty would enjoy spending the day with Ross. If the weather is decent, the two of them would have a great time exploring the outdoors together. And I'm fairly sure you'd enjoying eating Mom's turkey and stuffing."

"I...don't imagine your family would appreciate me showing up. I—I've not been to Stone Creek since..."

When he didn't go on, she lifted her gaze back to his face. Doubt shadowed his brown eyes and it was clear he was thinking back to the last time they'd been together before she'd left for Salt Lake City. It was true they'd parted on a bad note, but they'd been so very young. Too young to maintain a serious romance with hundreds of miles separating them. Plus, each of them had been facing years of difficult college classes. And, anyway, she wasn't trying to rekindle any of the old flames that had once burned between them. She was simply extending an olive branch of friendship to him.

"Since our college days," she said, finishing for him. "We're not going to dwell on that, Mack. It's in the past. We can be friends now. And everyone needs those."

Obviously relieved that she wasn't going to dredge up their broken past, he let out a long breath.

"Friends. Yes," he said. "That would be nice—for me and for Kitty."

She couldn't believe how happy his response made her and before she could let herself consider the consequences, she gave him a warm smile. "It would be nice for Ross and I, too. So it's all settled. I'll contact Mom tomorrow and let her know she'll need to add two more plates to the dinner table."

He studied her for a long moment. "Okay, Grace. I'll accept your kind invitation. Thanks."

"I'm glad," she said. "Now let's tell the kids what we've planned. I think they're going to be happy."

A wry grin curled up one corner of his lips. "In case you haven't guessed, Grace, you've made me happy, too."

Thursday morning started out cold and gray, but the weather was hardly enough to dampen her son's spirits. From the moment Ross had sat down at the breakfast table, he'd been chattering nonstop about the day ahead. Now, as Grace maneuvered her SUV over the graveled road leading to Stone Creek Ranch, he continued to talk, with the bulk of his conversation revolving around Kitty and Mack.

"Mom, do you think me and Kitty can walk down to the creek after we eat? Uncle Quint says all the sheep are in the valley now. We might see some of them. Kitty would like that, don't you think? 'Cause she likes animals, just like I do."

She glanced over her shoulder to where Ross was safely belted in the back seat and, as always, the sight of his boyish face, with its spattering of freckles and the gap where his two front teeth used to be, left her heart spilling over with love. No matter the problems that had occurred with her and Bradley during their short marriage, she was grateful she'd given birth to a son. Especially one that regarded the feelings of others.

"I imagine Kitty would enjoy seeing the sheep," Grace told him. "But you'll have to have an adult with you and Mack will have to give Kitty permission. So maybe. We'll see."

He looked at her. "Well, you and Mack could come with us. He might like seeing the creek and the sheep."

Given the fact that Mack dealt with animals from sunrise to sunset and later, she wasn't sure he'd consider visiting a flock of sheep on his day off as fun. But she wasn't going to burst Ross's bubble before the day ever got going.

"You like Kitty very much, don't you?" Grace asked as she steered the vehicle around a washed-out spot in the road.

Ross grinned. "Yeah. She's funny and nice. It'd be fun to have her for a little sister."

A bit stunned by his statement; Grace studied him from the corner of her eye. From time to time, he'd mention how much he'd like to have a brother, but he'd never once talked about wanting a sister.

"You'd like to have a sister?" Grace asked casually.

"You bet! One like Kitty, I would. We could do all sorts of things together. She can ride her horse all by herself. Did you know that?"

Clearly he considered that an impressive feat for a five-year-old girl, which it was. What amazed Grace was that he so gladly acknowledged Kitty's accomplishments.

"I didn't know Kitty could ride. That's good. Maybe you two can go riding together someday on Stone Creek. That is, if Mack will allow it. Would you like that?"

"Oh, boy, would I! That would be cool!" he exclaimed.

For the next two minutes he fell quiet, and she was about to glance back to see if he'd fallen asleep when he suddenly spoke.

"Mom, do you like Mack?"

Her fingers tightened slightly on the steering wheel. "Yes, I like him. He's a friend."

"Like a boyfriend?"

How did a child his age think of such things? "Not exactly."

"Why not? He seems nice and you smile at him a lot, and he smiles back at you."

Ross's simple observation caused a pang of regret to swirl in a spot between her breasts. "That's because a long time ago Mack was my boyfriend. Now we're just friends."

"Oh. Well, why can't he be your boyfriend now?"

Grace wasn't about to ask Ross if he'd like for his mother to get friendlier with Mack. Because she had

the feeling her son would be all for the idea of Grace
and Mack getting together, and it would be impossible
to explain to Ross why such a thing couldn't happen a
second time.

"Because…well, we're both grown-up people now
and we don't feel that way about each other anymore."

Dear God, just saying the words caused tears to sting
the back of her eyes. What was wrong with her, anyway? She'd gone for years without pining over Mack.
Now, just because she'd seen him, heard his voice and
felt the touch of his hand, it was like all the feelings
she'd ever held for him had come rushing back to her.

*You've placed yourself on a slippery slope, Grace.
One meeting with Mack led to another. Now, here you
are eager to see him again. When will it end? When
he's broken your heart a second time?*

"Yay! We're here!"

Ross's excited announcement was enough to silence
the dismal voice in her head and she gazed ahead to the
large two-story house, where she and her seven brothers
and sisters had grown up and where some still resided.

Stone Creek Ranch had first come into existence
around 1960, when Grace's grandfather, Lionel, and his
wife, Scarlett, purchased the land and began to stock
it with cattle and sheep. Since that time, the property
had steadily evolved and grown into one of the largest
and profitable ranches in southern Utah. It was a fact
that filled Grace with pride. Her father, Hadley, and her
five brothers had all worked hard to build the Hollister
legacy into what it was today.

"I see smoke coming out of the chimney," she said.

"Your grandfather must have built a big fire in the fire-place this morning."

"Do you think Grandpa will want to play checkers with me?"

"I imagine he will. If he's not busy," Grace answered.

Her father and brothers were all super about spending time with Ross whenever he was on the ranch. Grace was grateful to them for giving her son the male guidance he missed from not having a father.

"I'll ask him," Ross said. Then, after a moment, he added, "No. I changed my mind. I don't want to play checkers. I'm going to sit on the porch and watch for Kitty to get here."

He was clearly excited about seeing the girl again, Grace thought. And for the most part, Grace was glad he'd made a new friend. But what was she going to do or say if he started asking to visit Kitty on the Broken B? Or what if Kitty wanted to come to Grace's house to play with Ross? She wouldn't be able to say no to either child.

And why should she? she asked herself. Both children only had one parent and no siblings. If spending time together helped to fill a bit of those voids in their lives, then Grace was all for it.

She said, "Ross, you don't have to wait on the front porch for Kitty to arrive. I'm fairly certain when Mack and Kitty arrive, they'll ring the doorbell. Then you can run to the door and let them in."

"Yeah, but that wouldn't be the same, Mom."

Grace tossed a smile over her shoulder. "No. It wouldn't be the same," she replied. "But I'd like for you to go in the house and say hello to the family before you go to the porch."

"I will. Thanks, Mom!"

A few minutes later, after saying hello to her father and brothers, Grace entered the spacious kitchen, where her mother, Claire, twin sisters, Beatrice and Bonnie, and two sisters-in-law, Vanessa and Maggie, were already busy preparing for the big meal.

The room was filled with the delicious aroma of rising yeast dough, roasting turkey and baking pumpkin pie. The yummy scents, coupled with the affectionate hugs and greetings from her family, had Grace thinking how truly thankful she was for this day and every day she spent with her loved ones.

"I'm glad you drove out early, Grace. I saved this job for you." Her mother took her by the arm and led her over to one end of the cabinet counter. "Making the deviled eggs. I didn't get around to peeling the eggs, but I've already gathered everything you'll need to put them together."

Grace grabbed a checked pinafore apron and slipped it over her sweater and jeans. "Mom, you might want these eggs to be edible," she joked.

"Don't try to weasel out of the job," Bonnie teased. "Everyone says your deviled eggs are the best."

Grace walked over and rinsed her hands at the sink. "I wish the rest of my cooking received a bit of praise. Ross complains that I burn everything."

Standing at the opposite end of the work counter,

Beatrice asked, "Where is our nephew? Conning Dad into a game of checkers?"

Grace cracked a cooled egg and began to peel away the shell. "He's out in the front yard. Waiting for Mack and Kitty to arrive. She's his new little friend."

"Aww, that's sweet," Bonnie said. "Except, I didn't know Ross liked girls that much."

Grace let out a short grunt. "I didn't, either. Until he met Kitty."

Maggie chuckled as she placed a pair of mixing bowls into a sink of sudsy water. "Sounds like Ross is starting young. He obviously carries the same genes as his Uncle Cord."

Across the room, Vanessa let out a groan of amusement. "I was thinking the little guy is taking after his Uncle Jack."

Both of her sisters-in-law had originally resided in Arizona, where another branch of the Hollisters lived on the massive Three Rivers Ranch. Vanessa had taught high-school history in the town of Wickenburg, while Maggie had worked as an RN in the hospital's ER unit.

The Arizona Hollisters had first introduced her older brother, Jack, to Vanessa about a year and a half ago and after a brief courtship the couple had eloped to Las Vegas. A short while later, Maggie had traveled up to Stone Creek to attend Jack and Vanessa's wedding reception and once she'd met Cordell, the fireworks had started. The couple had fallen in love and, following Jack and Vanessa's example, they'd had a quick, private wedding back in January. By July their baby daughter,

Bridget, had arrived and next to Ross, she was only the second grandchild to be born to Claire and Hadley.

Grace adored Maggie and Vanessa. Especially because they'd made her brothers so ecstatically happy. Yet, God help her, there were times, such as this morning, when she looked at both women and felt a slice of envy. Grace wanted what they had—a spouse who loved her madly and a chance to give Ross a sibling or two. She wanted that same eternal bond her parents shared. Yet now that she was thirty-three years old, she was beginning to think love and a lasting marriage was going to elude her completely.

"Grace, I want to know why you've been holding out on us."

Grace glanced down the long work counter to where Beatrice was pouring boiling water into a teapot.

"I wasn't aware that I'd been hiding anything," Grace said to her.

Beatrice shot her a clever look. "Until Mom told us about you inviting Mack out for dinner, we didn't know you'd been seeing him!"

Everyone who knew Beatrice was well aware that the younger of the twins, by a whopping ten minutes, was the polar opposite of Bonnie. Beatrice had men on the brain and was always on the lookout for the next boyfriend. Especially now that she'd broken up with Jeremy, her latest love interest.

"I haven't been *seeing* Mack," Grace assured her sister. "Not in the way you're thinking. We just happened to run into each other and I decided to invite him out for dinner. Since his father died not long ago, I felt it was the right thing to do."

"It was the perfect thing to do," Claire said as she peeked into the oven at the last of the pumpkin pies. "After all, Mack and his daughter are our neighbors."

"Jack tells me the entrance to the Broken B is about fifteen miles east of here," Vanessa said, while carefully spooning black olives onto a sectional salad plate. "I remember Will was a guest at mine and Jack's wedding reception. He seemed like a really nice man."

"I remember Will at the reception, too," Maggie added. "Hadley introduced me to him. I thought he was a good-looking man for his age, not that a person in the midfifties is old. Far from it."

Claire carefully placed one of the pies on a cooling rack. "Well, I always believed Will needed to find himself a wife. After Dayna passed away, he was never the same. But I suppose he never met anyone he wanted to get close to. And in the end maybe it was best that he didn't. What with him dying so young and unexpectedly."

Grace had gathered from a few of Mack's remarks that he'd never planned to be taking over the Broken B at this stage of his life. But Will's untimely death had forced him to change his plans. Otherwise, the chance of Grace seeing him would've been rather slim. Unless by some sheer accident she bumped into him whenever he returned to Beaver County to visit his father and during the past five years she'd been living here, such a chance meeting had never happened. Now she had to wonder if fate had stepped in to throw the two of them back together.

Beatrice walked over to the double sink, where Maggie continued to wash several pots and pans that Claire had used to make the stuffing.

"Maggie, what you and Vanessa probably don't know is that Mack was once Grace's steady beau. Everybody in the county expected them to get married."

Grace gasped. "Bea! Do you have to be such a big mouth? And what could you know about it, anyway? You and Bonnie were only ten years old when Mack and I parted ways."

"Bea and I were old enough to remember you crying your eyes out," Bonnie said to Grace in a rare defense of her twin. "And you might not know it, but we plotted ways to get back at him. Bea wanted to go over to the Broken B and slash the tires on his truck, but we found out he was wasn't staying there. He'd moved to St. George."

"Bea! How could you have been so malicious!" Claire scolded. "Thank goodness your father and I didn't hear about this back then."

Beatrice giggled. "Well, Bonnie wasn't exactly a sweet little innocent. She wrote a letter to Mack basically calling him a snake and warning him to never come back to Beaver County, then signed it, from the citizens of Beaver. But we didn't know his address, so we had to nix that plan, too."

Claire groaned and shook her head in dismay. "What were you girls thinking?"

"We wanted him to hurt the way he'd made our big

sister hurt, that's what we were thinking." Beatrice walked over and gave her mother a one-armed hug. "Don't worry, Mom. Since then we've learned that revenge will get you nothing."

"And we imagine Mack has paid for his mistakes," Bonnie added, then cast Grace a tiny smile. "Grace has obviously forgiven him."

Yes, Grace had forgiven Mack. She'd even forgiven her late ex-husband for deceiving her with false promises. But forgetting was another matter. Memories of past hurts were hard to push from the mind and the heart, she thought.

"Please. Would you all just talk about something else," Grace insisted. "Like where is my little niece? I haven't seen her since Ross and I got here."

Maggie let out a good-natured groan. "Believe it or not, Cord took Bridget upstairs to change her clothes. I put her in a romper this morning, but he thought she should be in a party dress. She's not yet five months old. It's not like she can dance around and twirl her skirt."

"Not yet," Vanessa said with a chuckle. "Just give her a few more months."

"In a few more months Cord will have her sitting on a pony," Maggie replied. "He can't wait for her to grow into the cowboy boots he's already bought for her."

She can ride her horse all by herself.

The conversation about baby Bridget caused Ross's comment about Kitty to suddenly drift through Grace's mind. Had the girl's mother ever taken part in her daughter's life? When Kitty was an infant had the woman been there to feed her in the middle of the night, to change her diapers and rock her to sleep?

She was trying to push the unsettling questions out of her thoughts when the doorbell suddenly chimed, causing everyone in the room to look up.

"That must be Mack," Claire said to Grace. "You need to go greet him."

"But I'm just getting started with the eggs," Grace protested, even though she was itching to run to the front door.

"I'll finish the eggs for you," Bonnie kindly offered. "You go meet your guests."

Grace hurriedly slipped off her apron, and after pecking a grateful kiss on Bonnie's cheek, she rushed out of the kitchen.

By the time she made it to the front of the house, her father was ushering Mack through the short foyer that opened into a formal living room. Carrying his gray cowboy hat in his hand, he was dressed in a sherpa ranch jacket and dark, blue jeans that somehow made his long legs appear even longer.

For long seconds, her gaze lingered on his handsome image before she moved her attention to Kitty and Ross, who were walking hand in hand directly behind the men.

As Grace grew near, she heard her father as he said, "We're awfully glad you and your daughter could make it today, Mack. I just hope you can deal with all the noise."

"Thanks for having us," Mack told him. "And trust me, having Kitty has gotten me used to plenty of noise."

Hadley chuckled. "Just wait until you have eight of 'em, Mack. You'll need plenty of headache tablets."

"Dad!" Grace scolded with a laugh. "All of your children are grown now. We don't make noise."

"Ha! Just go to the den and tell that to your brothers. The bunch of them are in there now arguing, loudly I might add, over how to spend *my* money."

Grace exchanged a pointed grin with Mack. "I can settle that argument easily. They should spend *your* money one dollar at a time."

"Oh, you're a big help, Gracie," her father joked, then turned to Mack. "Come on down to the den, Mack. We've all gathered there. Since it will be a while until dinner, I'm sure Grace will be glad to get you something to drink."

"Of course." Grace looked at him and smiled, then glanced back at the children. "What about you two?"

"We want to go out to the patio," Ross answered. "Grandpa says the cats are out there and I want to show them to Kitty."

"It's all right with me if it's okay with Mack," Grace told him. "As long as you put on your coat and don't wander away from the backyard."

Kitty rushed to her father's side and gazed eagerly up at him. "Is it okay, Daddy?"

His smile indulgent, he nodded. "Sure. As long as you stay with Ross. And keep your hood on your head."

"Yay! Come on, Kitty!" Ross grabbed her hand and tugged her along after him. "We go this way!

"Don't run," Grace called after him. "And don't forget your coat."

"I won't!"

Hadley chuckled as he watched the two children hurry from the room. "I think those two are a little excited."

"Just a little," Mack agreed. "Having a big Thanksgiving Day is something new for Kitty."

"Let's hope she enjoys herself," Hadley said, then glanced at Grace and Mack. "If you two will excuse me, I need to go upstairs for a minute."

Grace said, "Go on, Dad. We'll be fine."

Hadley disappeared through an open doorway and as Grace turned to Mack she tried to ignore the fact that they were alone in the room. But she failed miserably. Her heart was tripping over itself and in spite of the coolness of the room, her palms felt damp.

"It's nice to see you again, Mack." The greeting was trite, but maybe he could see it was sincere, she thought. "I hope you aren't dreading today."

An amused look crossed his face. "Why would I be dreading it? Your father didn't meet me at the door with a bullwhip."

Smiling wanly, she shrugged one shoulder. "Well, when my large family is gathered together in one spot, we can be a bit overwhelming."

To her relief, he looked anything but worried.

"In case no one ever mentioned it to you, during the years you were living in Salt Lake City, I often returned to Beaver County to visit my parents. On most of those occasions I ran into your brothers and sometimes your dad."

"No one ever mentioned that to me," she told him.

"Where did you cross paths with them? Here on the ranch?"

"No. Usually at the feed store or at the Wagon Spoke Café. Beaver is a small town, you know. It's hard not to bump into old acquaintances."

Curious now, she paused. "So what happened when you ran into my family members? I hope they were civil to you."

His smile was wan. "Your family has always been warm and friendly with me. As far as you and I go, I don't think they ever wanted to…uh, take sides. Which was pretty damned generous of them, I'd say. But I think they saw us for what we were—just two starry-eyed kids."

Starry-eyed kids. Yes, Grace supposed as a couple they had been living in a romantic dream world. Even so, she would always believe there had been a deep and special bond between them, one that transcended physical attraction. If not, she would've already forgotten the joy of being *his girl*, and the deep crushing pain she'd endured when their relationship had ended. But apparently, his feelings about the past were far different than hers, she thought.

"I'm glad to hear my family has remained on good terms with you," she said.

"I am, too. Although, I can't say how your twin sisters feel about the matter," he conceded. "I've not seen them since they were kids."

She chuckled knowingly. "The twins used to hate you, but they've grown out of those feelings. They're twenty-four now and pretty, like Mom," Grace told him.

"Before you go to the den to join the men, would you mind stopping by the kitchen and saying hello to them and my sisters-in-law?"

"I wouldn't mind at all. It'll give me a chance to say hello to your mother. I wouldn't want her to think I'm ignoring her."

She hadn't realized she'd been holding her breath, until a rush of air passed her lips. "Uh, let me take your coat and hat. I'll put them away for you."

He slipped out of the garment, then handed it and his hat to her. After Grace hung them in a small coat closet, she returned to his side and, because it felt so right, linked her arm through his.

"You might get lost," she said impishly.

A slow grin curved his lips. "I've not forgotten my way around this house," he told her. "But it's nice of you to guide me."

Her soft laugh was full of guilt. "Actually, all we need to do is follow the delicious smell of roasting turkey."

"Mmm. It's tempting my appetite. That's for sure."

And he was definitely tempting the woman in her, she realized. And to make matters worse, he wasn't even trying.

Chapter Four

Thanksgiving dinner was served later that afternoon in the formal dining room. Two long tables were required to accommodate the entire family of twelve adults and one baby, plus the only guests, Mack and Kitty.

After lingering over plates of rich food, everyone migrated to the den, where Hadley piled more logs onto the fire in the fireplace and folks made themselves comfortable.

Ross and Kitty were sitting on a large braided rug playing a board game, while four of the Hollister brothers were lounging on a pair of long leather couches. Mack had taken a seat in a stuffed armchair not far from the fireplace, and directly across from him, Hadley and Claire sat cuddled together on a love seat. A few steps to the left side of Mack, Cordell sat in a wooden rocker, gently rocking his daughter.

Watching Cordell interact with the baby brought back a wealth of memories to Mack. Those early days of caring for a newborn had been especially trying for a young man who'd not even known how to hold a baby, much less tend to her needs around the clock. There had been times he'd wondered if he and Kitty would survive. And when his father had practically begged him to return to the Broken B so that he could help care for baby Kitty, Mack had been tempted. But in the end, he'd decided Kitty was his responsibility. Not only that, but his love for her was also boundless and he'd wanted to do everything for her himself.

"I remember those days, Cord," he said to the new father. "I thought they'd go on forever. Now Kitty is five years old. Time marches on."

His expression full of love and pride, Cordell gently rubbed a hand against his daughter's back. "Maggie says I'm obsessed with holding Bridget, but you know how things are, keeping a ranch running smoothly. I don't have enough time to spend with her."

"I hate to tell you this, Cord, but it doesn't get any better. Makes me wonder how your parents dealt with eight of you."

Cordell cast a fond glance over at Claire and Hadley, who were presently absorbed in conversation with each other.

"Mom is a hero," he said. "That's how I see things."

Mack's mother had definitely been a hero to him, also. Dayna hadn't just worked at her husband's side to keep the Broken B going, she'd also made sure Mack remained steadily on the right path to become a responsible man. His mother had been the first one to notice Mack had an affinity for healing animals and she'd encouraged him to follow his dream of becoming a veterinarian. When things had gotten rough with studies or lack of money, she'd always been there to bolster his spirits and to prod him onward.

His mother would've adored Kitty. But he wasn't sure how she would've viewed Mack being a single father. She'd not been a prude by any means, but she would've wanted her grandchild to be brought up in a traditional family.

"Mothers are heroes," Mack thoughtfully replied.

As though Cordell was following Mack's thoughts, he said, "Will told Dad that ever since Kitty was born you've raised her on your own. I was blown away when I heard about you caring for your little one, Mack. You're to be admired."

Mack shook his head and wondered if anyone had ever told Grace about Kitty never having a mother. If so, what had she thought about it? That he couldn't hold on to his woman? Or he'd balked against marrying the mother of his child? The idea that she might believe either of those scenarios bothered him. And yet, the truth of the matter really wasn't much better.

"You're giving me too much credit, Cord."

The baby began to fuss and Cordell shifted her around so that she was lying against his shoulder. When that didn't seem to satisfy her, Mack rose from the chair and walked over to father and daughter.

"Would you mind if I held her?" Mack asked. "I'm an old hand at quieting baby girls."

"I imagine you are." Chuckling, Cordell handed the baby up to him. "Go right ahead. I'm not having any luck."

Mack carefully propped the baby's red head in the crook of his left arm and with his other arm supporting her little body, he swayed her gently from side to side. She hushed almost instantly and Cordell let out a good-natured groan of surrender.

"Okay, Mack, I'll concede. You have the magic touch."

Mack smiled as he gazed down at the baby's angelic face. With Maggie's vivid red hair and Cordell's bright blue eyes, Bridget resembled both her parents. No doubt they were over the moon with joy at the arrival of their daughter.

"Nothing magical about it," he said to Cordell. "I'm just different to her and she's momentarily fascinated."

The precious weight of the baby in his arms had him thinking back to when Kitty had been an infant, and even deeper into the past, when he'd first fallen in love with Grace. At that time, he'd dreamed of having several children with her. He'd imagined them with a boisterous family, all loving and working together. But ultimately, he'd struck out on those dreams, too.

"Daddy, why are you holding baby Bridget?"

Mack glanced away from the baby in his arms to see Kitty and Ross were standing a few steps away. Both children were staring at him as if he'd turned into a stranger.

He looked over at Cordell and gave him a conspiring wink. "Well, Cord told me that we could take baby

Bridget home with us and keep her for a week. What do you think? Think you'd like that?"

Ross cast a stunned look at his Uncle Cordell, while Kitty carefully pondered her father's question. "What would we do with her?" she asked.

Mack and Cordell both laughed.

Mack said, "We'd take care of her. You know, like you take care of your baby doll. We'd change her diapers and feed her. And when she cried, we'd have to make her happy."

Kitty's expression was dubious as she continued to eye the baby in her father's arms. "We might not be able to make her happy."

Cordell chuckled. "Mack, I don't think Kitty is quite ready to share her daddy."

Deciding he'd teased his daughter enough, Mack said, "Don't worry, sweetheart. I was only teasing. Cord wouldn't let us take his little girl."

"Oh. Well, it might be fun until she cried," Kitty conceded.

Ross rolled his eyes. "Bridget cries all the time."

Cordell and Mack laughed just as Grace walked up. "Am I missing a good joke?" she asked.

Cordell said, "Your son thinks his little cousin is a crybaby, that's all. Maybe we ought to tell him he used to howl like a lost coyote when he was a toddler."

Laughing, Grace leveled a pointed look at her son. "Maybe we should."

"Aww, Mom. I'm too big to cry now. And, anyway, me and Kitty want to walk down to the creek. Can we go now?"

Grace arched an eyebrow at Mack. "What do you think? Feel like a hike to the creek?"

Mack hardly wanted to disappoint the children and he'd be lying to himself if he tried to pretend he wasn't looking forward to spending a bit of private time with Grace.

He said, "After the big dinner we just had, I need to do some hiking. I'll be ready as soon as I hand this precious bundle back to her father and fetch my hat and coat."

"I'll get them for you. We'll meet you out back on the patio," she told him, then motioned to the children.

With shouts of excitement, they followed her out of the den and Mack walked over to where Cordell was still sitting in the rocker and handed Bridget down to him.

"Thanks, Mack," Cordell said as he carefully cradled the baby in his arms.

Mack dismissed his words with a wave of his hand. "I'm the one who should be thanking you. Holding Bridget was a treat for me."

Cordell shook his head. "I wasn't thanking you for quieting Bridget's fussing. I was talking about you being with Grace. She needs, uh, to remember she's more than a doctor."

Cordell's remark surprised him, although it shouldn't have. Cordell and the whole Hollister family were probably assuming Mack was here on Stone Creek Ranch today to be with Grace. And the hell of it was, they'd be right.

"I understand, Cord. Sometimes I need to remember I'm more than a doctor, too."

Mack left the den, and as he made his way to the back of the house, his footsteps grew light. For the first time in a long, long time, his spirits lifted like a bird flying high on a spring morning.

Yes, being with Grace under any circumstances gave him joy. Proof that some things never changed.

Most of the dogs on Stone Creek Ranch were working cattle and sheep dogs and rarely, if ever, ventured near the ranch house. However, a few months ago Maggie rescued two Australian shepherd pups from a local shelter, and since then both dogs had grown into hopeless pets. They were constantly roaming back and forth between the main ranch house and Cordell and Maggie's house, which was located about a quarter of a mile north.

Now, from her spot on the patio, Grace watched the brown-and-white dogs zoom in wild circles around Ross and Kitty, who were doing their best to try to catch them.

Laughing, she called to them, "You kids aren't nearly fast enough on your feet to catch those dogs."

"Just guessing, I'd say we're going to have two more going along on our hike."

At the sound of his voice, Grace glanced around to see Mack had walked up behind her and the smile on his face filled her with a warmth that had nothing to do with the wintery sun slanting across the patio.

Handing him his coat and hat, she said with a chuckle, "I don't think Jasper and Jimmy will stay behind while we walk to the creek. Those two dogs roam all over the ranch. Even over the hill to Hunter's house."

"Do they belong to Hadley?" He eyed the playful dogs as he pulled on his coat and hat.

She shook her head. "No. But you might as well call them Dad's dogs. He takes them around with him most everywhere he goes. They're really Maggie's dogs. She rescued them from a shelter."

"I'm happy to hear it," he said, then inclined his head toward a weathered stone fence surrounding two sides of the yard. "I see Claire has something covered with tarps. Are your late grandfather's roses still growing there? Or has she cultivated some other kind of flowers now that he's passed away?"

Lionel Hollister had been a crusty character who hadn't made friends easily. But for some inexplicable reason, her late grandfather had actually gotten on well with Mack.

"Grandfather's roses continue to grow and Mom makes sure she keeps them as beautiful as ever. During the winter months if she thinks the temperatures are going to dip too low, she sets up heat lamps to warm the tarps."

His gaze moved from the covered garden to Grace's face. "I've noticed something today," he said.

She'd noticed several things, too, Grace thought. Like how being near him sent little spurts of joy rushing through her and how looking at him made her thoughts drift to a dreamy place. None of her reactions to him made sense, but just for today, she didn't care. For once, in a long time, she wanted to think and feel like a woman.

She slanted him a coy glance. "I imagine you've decided it would have been far more restful to have stayed home and kicked back in a recliner in front of the TV?"

"You're describing some other guy, Grace. Not me." He jammed his hands into the pockets of his ranch coat. "What I've noticed is how everything here on the ranch has stayed the same."

His remark left a bittersweet ache in her throat. "Except that we've all gotten older," she said huskily. "And Cord and Jack are both married. Hunter is divorced and I'm…single again."

He studied her for a long moment and Grace practically held her breath in fear he was going to ask her why or how her marriage to Bradley had ended. The fact that she'd divorced her husband shortly before his accidental death was hardly a secret within her family or close friends. Even so, it wasn't something she was ready to explain to Mack.

His head moved negligibly from side to side. "I was talking about the house and the surrounding grounds. It's exactly the way I remembered."

"Mom and Dad aren't big on change," she explained.

"No. They're still the same warm and loving couple I knew years ago," he replied. "I hope they'll never change."

"I'm lucky to have them," Grace admitted, then added gently, "I only wish— Well, it would have been nice if your parents had been able to give you siblings."

He glanced across the yard, to where Ross and Kitty had turned the tables on the dogs and were now chasing the animals in merry circles.

"Nice, yeah. But Mom never was able to carry any more babies to full term."

"I remember," she murmured.

Mack's mother had suffered her third miscarriage when Mack and Grace had been juniors in high school. After that, the Barlows had ended their attempts at more children. During that time, Mack hadn't said much about his mother's fertility problems, but Grace understood it had saddened him greatly.

His gaze turned back to her and Grace gave him a cheery smile. "You gave me a surprise back there in the den. You looked perfectly natural holding Bridget."

His lips took on a mocking slant. "There's an old saying that guys who are good with animals are also great with kids."

Her smile turned impish. "I've not heard that one. Is there any truth to it?"

"I don't believe so. When I was finishing up my vet training, I worked with a veterinarian that couldn't have been any better with treating animals, but as a father, he stunk. He yelled and ordered his kids about like they had no feelings at all."

Mack hadn't kept his promise to remain true to Grace. But she could honestly say, he didn't have a mean bone in his body. "Kitty is lucky she has you."

"Thanks, Grace. Coming from you that means a lot."

Was he saying he admired her? For what? she wondered. Becoming a doctor? Managing to raise her son on her own? She wanted to ask him, but she feared the question might pry into feelings better left buried.

Deciding that now was a good time to change the

subject, she said, "I thought we'd follow the cattle trail past the old barn. It's the shortest route to the creek. I don't want to wear out Kitty's little legs."

Mack chuckled. "Don't worry about Kitty. She can follow me around the ranch for hours."

"In that case, maybe it's me I should be worrying about. I'm like the shoe cobbler with the barefoot kids. I'm a doctor, but rarely follow my advice to my patients on getting the right exercise—I just can't find the time."

"You don't look like you're falling apart to me. Not yet, anyway," he told her.

Was he flirting? The notion warmed her cheeks and she purposely turned toward the north wind in hopes it would cool her face and her thoughts.

"We haven't made it to the creek and back yet," she said in a joking manner, then gestured to the kids. "If you're ready, we should probably head out."

"I'm ready. Let's go round up the youngsters. And the dogs," he added.

"Right," she said. "The dogs need a hike, too."

After giving Kitty and Ross the rules of everything they could or couldn't do, the four of them set out on a narrow dirt trail headed north. In spring and summer, the sweeping meadows in the valley were normally green and dotted with colorful wildflowers, but now that the last part of November had arrived, frost had turned the grass brown. Even so, there was still plenty of color to be found in the ribbon of evergreens that lined the creek banks and the forest-covered mountains that stretched out to the distant north and west of the ranch house.

Grace had grown up roaming and riding the thousands of acres that made up Stone Creek Ranch, and to this day, she never took its beauty for granted.

"Is Lionel's old cabin still standing up there on the mountainside?" Mack asked as he and Grace followed the children at a slower pace.

"Sure is. Every now and then Maggie and Cord ride up there. And during the summer months Quint uses it as a shepherding camp. In case you didn't know, about a year ago, Dad made Quint the head of the sheep division. They're planning to increase the flocks. That is, if Quint can hire a full-time sheep herder."

"Yes, they were telling me all about the sheep plans before dinner. Quint thought I might run in to someone at my clinic who might be interested in the sheepherding job. Right now, I can't think of anyone. But I promised to keep my eye out for him."

"So what about Ira? Did you end up hiring him?"

"Sure did. And I'm glad I hired him. He's a hard worker. Oren likes him and Eleanor *loves* him."

Grace chuckled. "I'm glad they're working out for you. It's chaos when you don't have enough help." She glanced at him. "Do you have enough help now, or do you plan on hiring more?"

He shook his head. "Right now, I need one more assistant for sure. And later, if things get busier, I'll probably need a third one." He looked at her. "Do you have much turnover in employees at your clinic?"

"Surprisingly, the three women who work with me have been there from the first day I opened the clinic. Sometimes I wonder how they handle the hectic pace and everything else that involves dealing with sick folks. But Cleo, Poppy, and Harper are all very dedicated. And honestly, I don't know what I'd do without them."

They walked a few more steps down the trail before he reached over and broke off a twig from a waist-high clump of sage growing nearby. "Do you remember when we used to talk about becoming doctors?"

The spot between her breasts twinged with a pain of regret. "Oh, yes. I remember," she said, trying hard to keep a husky note from creeping into her voice. "We thought we were going to do great things. Me with people and you with animals."

He rolled the sage between his fingers. "I think you could say that we have done great things in a small way. And that's what counts, don't you think?"

Yes, but their accomplishments would've counted so much more if they'd shared their personal successes together, she wanted to tell him. But voicing her regrets to him would ruin this day and probably any other chance she might have to be in his company. And she didn't want that to happen for any reason.

"As long as we're able to help people and animals, we're doing what counts," she told him.

Up ahead, Kitty stopped and looked back at the adults, then pointed to the distant mountains.

"Daddy, see way up there? Ross says the sheep and cows go up there when it's summertime. How do they get up there?"

As Grace and Mack caught up with the children, he answered Kitty's question.

"The sheep and cows climb up there with their four legs. Like you climb up a hill with your two legs."

"See, Kitty, I told you right," Ross said smugly.

"Okay," the girl conceded even though she cast a doubtful gaze at the mountains. "But that's so high. What keeps them from falling off?"

Kitty's question caused Ross to giggle and Mack and Grace to exchange amused glances.

"A thing called gravity, Kitty," Mack explained to his daughter. "You'll learn all about it in science class someday."

Ross grabbed Kitty's hand. "Come on, Kit! The dogs are getting way ahead of us!"

The kids took off in a jog after the dogs and Grace said, "I think I'd be wasting my breath if I told them not to run."

"They're having a great time."

Before giving herself time to think, she reached over and clasped her hand around his. "Are you having fun yet?"

He laughed. "I'll use Ira's quote. If I was having any more fun I couldn't stand myself."

She wasn't sure if it was the sound of his laughter or the warmth of his hand enveloping hers that was sending joy rushing through her. Either way, he was the reason her heart suddenly felt like it had wings. Which didn't make sense. How could a man who'd caused her so much misery in the past give her so much pleasure now?

"I'm glad. I didn't like to think of you and Kitty spending Thanksgiving Day alone."

"And eating sandwiches, or something out of a can?" he asked dryly.

"No. Doing without roasted turkey isn't nearly as bad as not having anyone to share your dinner with. But I—" She paused and regarded him thoughtfully. "I think I need to apologize to you, Mack. I've been assuming you don't have anyone in your life—like a special woman. If you do, I—"

"I don't," he bluntly interrupted. "Do you have a special man in your life?"

The question sounded inane to her, even though it shouldn't have. After all, she was single and still a young woman. Dating should be a normal part of her life. But it wasn't. To think of trying to negotiate a meaningful relationship with a man left her exhausted, not to mention disillusioned. She'd had two attempts at love and both had ended up being painful experiences. Why should she want to try for a third installment?

Somehow, she made her groan a playful sound. "Mack, do I look like a woman in love?"

His steps slowed as he glanced over at her. "I couldn't say. I don't know what a woman in love looks like."

Now that was a strange remark, she thought. Surely, Kitty's mother had been in love with him. Moreover, Grace had been in love with him. But apparently he didn't he remember how her eyes had sparkled when she looked at him, or how her face had held a perpetual glow whenever he was near.

"Uh, well, I don't have a special guy. And honestly, I haven't been looking for one."

"Do you ever think about looking for one?"

Refusing to believe his question was anything more than normal curiosity, she said, "Not really. I think if there's a man meant to be in my life, he'll show up—without me looking for him."

He didn't say anything to that and although the remainder of their walk to the creek passed in silence, his hand remained tightly clasped around hers. As sweet as the physical connection was, it made Grace remember too much, feel too much. And yet she couldn't find the will to pull away from his touch.

With the children safely within reach, Mack and Grace strolled along the edge of the creek until they found a spot where the shallow water splashed over large boulders. Near the edge of the steep bank, the gnarled trunk of a juniper tree created a natural bench. Mack brushed it clean with his hand.

"This looks like a good place to sit while the kids explore," he said. "Unless you want to explore with them."

She let out a short laugh. "Are you kidding? I'm going to rest while I can. We still have to walk back."

He handed her down to the makeshift bench, then took a seat close to her side.

"There isn't much room," he said as he tried to make himself comfortable without invading her space. "If you think I'm getting too close, just elbow me in the ribs."

"There's plenty of room for both of us. Besides, you're not contagious."

He gave her a lopsided grin. "How can you tell, Doc? I might be coming down with the flu?"

Her mouth formed a perfect O and as his gaze slipped

over the moist pout, he wondered how she would react if he leaned closer and touched his lips to hers. Would he discover she still tasted like wild honey? Would her lips be just as soft and giving?

"Are you serious?" She placed her palm on his cheek as if to check him for a fever. "Is your throat getting scratchy?"

He chuckled. "No. I'm only joking, Dr. Hollister. But thanks for your concern."

She reached over and gave his forearm a playful pinch. "You'd better tell me that you've had your flu shot. Otherwise, you need to stop by the office tomorrow and get one."

"I got my shot last month. What about you? If you don't have your latest rabies vaccine, you need to stop by my clinic tomorrow," he teased.

She chuckled. "I think I'll be fine without one of those."

At that moment, a gust of wind blew down from the mountain and smacked her directly in the face. She shivered slightly and he looked over to see her tightening the blue woolen scarf wrapped around her neck.

"Cold?" he asked.

"A little."

He slipped his arm across her back and snugged her closer to his side, then scanned a bank of blue clouds gathering over the mountaintops.

"Clouds are moving in. We might be in for wet weather," he said. "But I'm guessing it will hold off until we make the walk back to the house."

She followed the line of his gaze. "I hope so. It's been

a long while since I've had a chance to enjoy getting outdoors on the ranch like this." She lifted her nose to the wind. "I love how fresh and clean the air feels here in the valley. It smells like evergreen and sage and the scent of snow lying in the shadows. It's a lovely fragrance you can't find in a bottle."

He could say the same about her, Mack thought. There was nothing manufactured about the unique scent emanating from her hair and skin. If there was one thing Mack had learned these past few years, it was that Grace was one of a kind. He'd never crossed paths with any woman quite like her. Maybe that's why he was still single and Kitty was without a mother.

"The kids are certainly enjoying this outing," he commented as he looked over to where Ross and Kitty were both laughing and shrieking as they played tag among the fat trunks of cedar and pine trees growing along the creek bank.

"I'm not sure who's enjoying it more," Grace said. "The kids or the dogs."

She'd barely had time to get the words out of her mouth when the children skidded to a stop a few steps away from where Mack and Grace were sitting.

As the pair eyed the dogs splashing happily across the creek, Kitty said to Ross, "Boy, it would be really fun if it was warm. We could take off our boots and go wading with Jasper and Jimmy. See, we could go way over there and climb up on that big rock."

Ross followed the direction of Kitty's pointed finger. "Yeah! We could probably catch a trout. Mom would cook it for us. She cooks it good!"

Grace gave Mack a hopeless grin. "Ross is a bit biased," she said in a voice meant only for him. "I'm not much of a cook."

"What does that matter? You can treat a tummy ache," he told her. "Or a case of the flu."

Her grin turned into a soft little smile and something inside his chest tightened as once again she placed her palm against his cheek. Only this time, she wasn't checking his temperature. She was simply touching him, and it felt so intimate and sweet that he could hardly stop himself from dragging her into his arms and kissing her.

"I, uh, try my best."

Clearing her throat, she dropped her hand back to her lap and Mack thought how he'd gladly endure a 103-degree temperature to feel her gentle hands touching him, soothing him.

Kitty's voice broke into Mack's thoughts and he glanced over to where the kids were sitting together on the top of a pile of boulders.

"How do you catch a trout?" Kitty asked Ross. "With your hands?"

Expecting Ross to cackle with laughter, Mack was pleasantly surprised when the boy didn't poke fun at Kitty's lack of fishing knowledge. Instead, he gently began to explain all about rods and hooks and bait.

"Guess you can tell Kitty has never been fishing," Mack said to Grace. "I hate to admit it, but she's five years old and there are still plenty of recreational pastimes I haven't exposed her to."

"It takes time," Grace reasoned, then added wryly,

"Anyway, she's too young for some recreational pastimes."

He grimaced. "How do you manage with Ross? He seems well-rounded. Especially since he's only seven."

"I can't take all the credit for Ross's development," she said. "He has grandparents and a slew of aunts and uncles to show him things and take him places. Without their help, I'd be lost."

His gaze returned to her face, and as he watched the wind flutter a golden tendril of hair against her cheek, he wondered how fate had maneuvered them both back to Beaver County at the same time. It was as if they were supposed to be sitting here together as if they had never parted.

And yet they had parted. Years had passed, during which he'd moved on and had a child with Libby. Grace had married and given birth to a son. Mack had never imagined their paths would cross again. At least, not this closely.

And now you're wondering what it all means? I'll tell you what it means—you're a fool, Mack. This woman doesn't want you. Not the way you want her to. Not the way you're wanting her. She feels sorry for you because your father is dead. Because you're alone and emotionally pathetic.

Cursing at the mocking voice going around in his head, he reached over and wrapped his hand tightly around Grace's.

The contact caused her to look at him, and as he gazed into her blue eyes, he felt like an avalanche was going off inside him.

"Grace, why did you really invite me here to the ranch today?" he asked gently. "I get that it's Thanksgiving. But I…have a notion there was more behind your invitation."

Her eyebrows lifted, while one corner of her lips curled up faintly. "You're right. There was something more. I was curious to find out if you're still as sweet as you used to be."

He studied at her for a moment more before he threw back his head and laughed. "Sweet? Oh, Grace. You are so—"

"Silly?" she said, finishing for him.

"No. I was thinking…there's no one else like you."

Her eyes softened as a dimple appeared in one of her cheeks. "Was that meant to be a compliment?"

His fingers tightened on hers. "You are unique, Grace. In all the good ways."

Something flickered in her eyes before she turned her face away. Though she didn't say anything, he saw her swallow. Was she trying to down a bitter remark? Did she really want to tell him what a lying hypocrite he was? He couldn't blame her if she did harbor some resentment toward him. He deserved it, he supposed. He could hardly expect her attention or kindness. But, dear God, he wanted it.

"Mom! Mom! I hear sheep bells! Over there!"

Ross's voice scattered Mack's dismal thoughts and he looked over to see the boy pointing to a spot on the opposite side of the creek. A few seconds later, he spotted several sheep emerging from the underbrush.

Grace shot him a helpless smile. "Looks like the dogs have rounded up a flock and headed them this way."

By now the children had scampered down from the rocks and were racing toward the edge of the creek bank for a better glimpse at the wooly animals.

"We'd better go join them." He stood, then reached down and helped Grace to her feet.

Standing close to his side, she said, "Well, it was nice while it lasted."

Was she talking about these past few minutes they'd sat together on the juniper trunk? Or was she referring to the young, tender romance they'd shared so many years ago?

Damn it, Mack! You need to snap yourself back to reality. Grace isn't thinking of the past. Her thoughts are focused on the present and the future.

Shaking away the nagging voice in his head, he said, "Well, we couldn't expect it to last very long."

Her gaze lifted to meet his and for a split second, Mack thought he saw longing in the blue depths. But then, being close to Grace was causing him to imagine all sorts of things.

"Come on, Mom! You're going to miss seeing the sheep crossing the creek," Ross called out.

Kitty yelled, "Daddy, come look! The lambs are jumping!"

Grace smiled at Mack. "Duty calls."

Where he and Grace were concerned, duty would always be calling. That's why he needed to simply enjoy this day and forget about any chances of making a future with her.

Yet, as they begin to walk over to join the children, he couldn't stop his arm from wrapping against the back of her waist. Or wishing that when he went home to the Broken B tonight, Grace would be going with him.

Chapter Five

During the next two weeks, colder weather arrived, along with enough snow to pack the streets and turn the sidewalks into slushy ice. As a result, the clinic had seen an uptick in patients, not only from colds and flu, but also from frostbite and injuries acquired from falling on the ice.

Grace didn't mind the extra work. Serving the people of her hometown area was the very reason she'd first decided to become a doctor. Even when she'd agreed to marry Bradley, she'd made sure he understood that she ultimately intended to return to Beaver and build her own private practice. And during their short engagement, he'd been more than willing to agree with her plans.

Yet when Grace had finally finished her schooling and become a full-fledged doctor, Bradley had done an about-face. Why should he leave Salt Lake City? he'd argued. He had a thriving practice as a cardiac surgeon and Grace could do just as much good working as a general practitioner in one of the many clinics throughout the city as she could in Beaver.

Bradley had considered her noble reasons for becoming a doctor as old-fashioned, even downright stupid. He'd argued how he'd not gone through eight years of exhausting studies to bury himself in a one-horse town, where he wouldn't earn a fraction of the money he'd earn in Salt Lake City. Grace had understood his way of thinking up to a point. However, she could never give in to his self-centered ideals. She hadn't become a doctor to make money. Her job was to improve and save lives. Ultimately, the stark differences between them had eventually caused her to seek a divorce.

She'd never regretted ending a marriage that was obviously doomed from the very beginning. Yet there were times, like this evening, when fatigue and a sense of melancholy struck her and she wondered if she'd ever be given the opportunity to have love in her life and to make her family complete.

"Hey, Grace, what are you doing about shopping for the holiday? Buying everything online and praying your orders arrive on time?"

Halfway down the hallway to her office, Grace paused and glanced over her shoulder to see Poppy rapidly approaching. The tall, shapely nurse had a head full of long, bright red curls that she kept contained in a loose bun on the top of her head. In spite of the long hours the young woman put in at Pine Valley Clinic, she never complained or quit smiling.

Grace waited for the woman to catch up to her before she answered. "I've already ordered a few things for Ross. So hopefully, those gifts won't be late. But unless there's a letup in patients, I doubt I'll get to do any in-store shopping."

"Aww, that's a bummer," Poppy replied. "Cleo and I are considering a drive down to St. George over the weekend. But we're about to nix the idea. If we go to the mall we'll end up spending too much."

Grace chuckled knowingly. "Isn't that what we're supposed to do when we go to the mall to shop?"

A cheery smile crossed the nurse's face as she snapped her fingers. "You're right. And the holidays only come around once a year. To heck with saving money. I'm going to convince Cleo we need to make the trip this weekend. Want to come along?"

"Thanks for asking, but if I do end up getting some extra time for shopping, I'd rather do it here in town. I like to support the local businesses."

"Then you should make time and treat yourself, Doc. Take an extra-extra-long lunch hour," Poppy suggested. "And when you do, be sure and pop into Canyon Corral. Maybe your sister Bea has mentioned some of the new things they've gotten in the past few days. There's a maxi-denim dress that would look fab on you, Grace. Especially with that pair of brown boots you have. It would be a great outfit for dancing."

Grace laughed. "Poppy, you need to make a U-turn and go to examining room three. I need to give you a thorough checkup. Me, dancing? You're clearly hallucinating."

Shaking her head, Poppy leveled a serious look at her. "Grace, you're a young, beautiful woman. And don't scold us for gossiping, but Cleo told me you invited the new veterinarian in town to have Thanksgiving with you. Don't you plan on seeing him again?"

Stifling a groan, Grace started walking on down the hallway. The nurse remained stubbornly at her side.

"How do you know I haven't seen him again?" Grace asked coyly.

Her brown eyes wide, Poppy turned a stare on her. "Oh! I didn't think— Well, you've worked late nearly every evening since Thanksgiving. I don't believe you've had time for a date."

By now they'd reached the doorway to Grace's office. She opened the door and, as expected, Poppy followed her into the small space.

After pulling off her lab coat, Grace hung it on a coatrack in the far corner of the room. "You're right, Poppy. I've not seen Mack or heard from him since Thanksgiving. But I wasn't planning to, really."

Even so, she'd spent every day of the past two weeks thinking about the man and wondering if he'd thought about her and the time they'd spent together on Stone Creek Ranch. She couldn't deny that being close to him had stirred old longings in her. Especially when she'd walked him out to his truck to tell him and Kitty good-night.

For a moment the expression on his face had given her the idea that he'd wanted to kiss her. Everything inside her had certainly been begging him to. Every part of her had been longing to discover if kissing him after all these years would still ignite a fire inside her. But he hadn't kissed her. The most he'd done was give her hand a fond squeeze. Now she was trying to face the fact that Mack merely wanted to be her friend and nothing more.

Poppy tapped a forefinger thoughtfully against her chin. "Uh, Doc, in case you didn't know, women have evolved. We don't have to sit around and wait on a guy to call us. Nowadays, it's perfectly acceptable for a girl to call a guy…if she wants to."

Grace picked up a stack of test results she needed to study tonight and stuffed the papers into a leather briefcase.

"I'm not following my mother's dating guidelines, Poppy. It's just that Mack and I have busy lives. And it's, uh, sort of complicated."

"Because you knew him a long time ago? Sorry. Cleo told me you two used to be…friends."

She gave the nurse a rueful smile. "Something like that."

"Oh." Clearly disappointed, Poppy turned and started out of the room. "Sorry for being so nosy, Doc. I only want you to be happy. Everyone here in the clinic wants that for you."

Knowing Poppy was being sincere rather than meddlesome, Grace walked over and gave the nurse's shoulder a gentle squeeze. "I understand, Poppy. And I'm grateful that all of you care that much about me. But I'm truly okay as I am. When the right man comes along,

I'll make an effort not to let him slip away. And even if he never comes along, I'll still be happy. Now let's finish up here and call it an evening. Okay?"

"Right."

Poppy gave her a bright smile and headed out the door. Grace turned back to her desk and picked up a pair of manila folders that needed to be filed away in the record room. Three years ago, Grace had begun putting patient medical history in computer files rather than keeping everything on paper. But there were still occasions when she wanted the information to actually be in her hands.

Carrying the files, she started out of the office, but before she could make it through the open doorway, her cell phone rang.

She turned on her heel and returned to her desk. After dropping the folders to one side, she reached for the phone.

Mack! Why was *he* calling? Was Kitty suffering stomachaches again?

Her hand trembled as she punched the button to accept the call. Then she answered in the breeziest tone she could muster. "Hello, Mack."

"Hi, Grace. Did I catch you at a bad time?"

She scurried over to shut the office door. "Not at all. I was just getting things organized to close up shop for the day."

"I just finished doing surgery on a horse's foot. He's my last patient for today."

She covered the bottom half of the phone and released a breath she'd been holding far too long. "I hope everything went well with the surgery."

He said, "Better than I hoped. Recuperation will take some time, but he's going to be okay."

"That's good."

There was a long pause and Grace's mind began to spin with questions.

"So how have you been?" he asked. "And Ross?"

With her knees feeling like two wet sponges, Grace sank into the executive chair situated behind her desk. "We're both good," she told him. "What about you and Kitty?"

"Fine. Except Kitty is driving me crazy asking me the same question over and over. She wants to know when she'll get to see Ross again."

The low, masculine timbre of his voice was like the stroke of warm fingers across her skin. "I'm not surprised. I'm hearing the same question from Ross. I'm amazed at how close he's grown to your daughter."

"Same here. Usually it takes Kitty a while for her to put her trust in someone, but she thinks Ross is pretty much the cat's meow. I might as well tell you—she calls him her big brother. I hope that doesn't bother you."

The connotation of their children calling each other brother and sister brought up all sorts of images to Grace's mind. But she figured the best way to handle the situation was to make light of it.

"I hope this doesn't worry you, but Ross says Kitty is his little sister. However, I believe this is just a play-like thing to them and nothing to get bent out of shape over."

The connection went quiet for a moment and then he

said, "Right. They're just young kids who happened to enjoy being with each other. They like the same things and I think Kitty sees Ross as her big protector. And he seems to enjoy the role."

She chuckled. "Most men do."

After another short pause, he said, "I imagine you're wondering why I called."

Her heart felt like it was doing backward flips in rapid succession. In fact, it was beating so hard the front of her blouse was shaking.

"Actually, I've been wondering why you haven't called before now," she said frankly.

"Really? I didn't mention that I would call. Did I?"

She rolled her eyes while wishing this was a Face-Time call. She'd love to see his expression right now.

"No. But I thought you would. I thought...well, nothing," she said. "So why are you calling?"

"I wanted to ask if you'd like to come out to the Broken B and have dinner tomorrow night. And bring Ross with you, of course," he quickly added.

The invitation stunned her, but she tried to keep the sound of surprise from her voice. "Are you cooking?"

He chuckled. "Worried you'll be eating fried bologna sandwiches."

She felt her smile spreading from ear to ear. "No. And don't tell any of my patients, but I love fried bologna sandwiches."

He made a tsking noise with his tongue. "Shame on you for eating all that fat and cholesterol. I'd never put anything like that in my body," he joked.

Just by looking, she could believe he didn't consume anything that wasn't healthy. He was nothing but lean, hard muscle. Yet she knew from watching him eat Thanksgiving dinner that he was human enough to treat himself to tasty food.

"Okay. Are you going to be cooking? Or are you going to stop by the Wagon Spoke and pick up a bunch of takeout?"

Fatigue laced his laughter. "Will my answer make a difference in whether you agree to come or not?"

"No. We'll be there."

"Good," he said. "I'll make sure I cook something nice."

Her heart had stopped its backward flips. Now it was singing like a spring bird. "What time should we be there?"

"Just whenever you can make it. If you get there early, I'll put you to work in the kitchen."

Grace wasn't going to ask herself what this might mean, or where it could lead. Or if it would mean anything more than eating a meal with an old friend. She was simply going to enjoy the fact that Mack wanted her company and she wanted his.

"Daddy, do you think Dr. Grace and Ross will like roast? You should've cooked spaghetti. Everybody likes that."

Mack turned away from the cabinet counter to see Kitty carrying out the task he'd given her—placing silverware next to the four plates on the varnished pine table. His daughter always liked helping him in the kitchen. Even when he was preparing a meal that was far from her favorite. But tonight she was especially eager to help her father make everything special for their guests.

When he'd told her about Grace and Ross coming for dinner, she'd hardly been able to contain her excitement. And now, as the time grew closer for their arrival, she'd been chattering like a magpie and hopping from one end of the kitchen to the other.

A big part of Mack felt like hopping with joy, too. Since the day he'd spent with Grace on Stone Creek, he'd thought of little else but her. Yet he'd been reluctant to give in to his desire to see her again. Spending time with Grace was only going to make him want to deepen their relationship. And there was a definite chance she might throw that idea right back in his face. She might view their fractured past as a wall that would always stand between them.

Darn it, he couldn't allow such dour thoughts to take hold of him tonight and ruin the evening. And, anyway, Grace had seemed happy to accept his invitation. For now, that had to be enough, he decided.

He carried salt and pepper shakers, and a sugar bowl over to the table, before he glanced pointedly at Kitty. "Spaghetti is your favorite. That's why you think I should've made it. But most people like roast just as much," he told her. "And I'm a fair hand at cooking roast."

She let out a dramatic sigh. "Well, the brownies will be good. Cause they came from the Wagon Spoke."

"Sssh! Kitty, we're not supposed to mention where the brownies came from, remember?"

She placed the last piece of silverware on the table, then, with a deep frown on her face, marched over to him. "Why, Daddy? They're yummy."

"Yes, they're extra yummy. But I told Grace I'd be doing all the cooking tonight," he explained.

She scowled at him. "Daddy, it wouldn't be right to fib to Dr. Grace. You always tell me not to fib to anyone."

If only he'd followed his own advice years ago and been truthful with Grace about his reason for ending their relationship, she might not have considered him a snake in the grass. And he would've felt a hell of a lot better about himself. But that was water under the bridge. He couldn't go back and change the choices he'd made. He could only go forward and pray he'd grown wiser.

Patting the top of Kitty's head, he said, "You're right, sweetheart. Fibbing is wrong. So if you want to tell Grace where the brownies came from, go right ahead."

Smiling with approval, she hugged his waist and Mack realized that at this point in his daughter's life, it was fairly easy for him to make her happy, to be a father she could be proud of. But he often wondered if later, when she grew into adulthood and learned the truth about her mother, she would still view him as a good and loving father.

Stepping back, she fastened a wishful look on him. "Daddy, after we eat, can me and Ross go down to the barn? I want to show him Rusty and the cats and the goats."

Since Rusty, their Collie, was more than content to

be an outdoor dog, he spent his winter nights snuggled in the barn with the rest of the animals. And if Mack would let her, Kitty would spend every waking hour in the barn with them.

"I understand you want to show Ross all your animals. But not tonight. It's too cold for you two to be traipsing around the barn. You'll have to find something to do here in the house."

"Aww, we can put on our coats and gloves," she protested. "We'd be warm."

"Even if you were as warm as toast, you're still not going," he said firmly.

Her mouth flopped open and Mack was expecting to hear another loud protest, but she suddenly turned and tilted her head thoughtfully to one side.

"I hear a car! They're here, Daddy!"

Before he could respond to her announcement, she raced out of the kitchen. Mack hurriedly switched off the oven and followed her through the house to the front entrance.

By the time Mack caught up to Kitty, she'd already ushered their guests into the house and was shutting the door behind them. Both were bundled in heavy coats and woolen scarves to stave off the bitterly cold wind.

His smile encompassing both mother and son, Mack said, "Hello, you two. Welcome to the Broken B."

"Hello, Mr. Barlow," Ross politely replied.

Mack patted his shoulder. "You know, Ross, I'd like it fine if you'd call me Mack. As long as that's okay with Grace."

Ross glanced at his mother and she acquiesced with a nod and a smile.

Looking back at Mack, he grinned. "Okay, Mack. And thanks for inviting us. I've never been here before. Your house is nice."

"Thanks, Ross. I'm glad you and your mother could make it," he said to the boy, then turned his attention to Grace. The smile on her cherry-colored lips warmed him far more than the fire he'd built in the fireplace.

"Hi, Mack. I'm afraid we have snow on us." She glanced down at the icy specks spotting her coat. "We should probably leave our coats at the door instead of dripping on your floor."

"Nonsense. Everything gets tracked onto the floors in this house," he told her, then turned to Kitty. "Sweetie, take Ross's coat and put it in the closet for him. Then you two can go on to the kitchen."

"Yeah, come on, Ross!" Kitty grabbed him by the arm and led him away from the adults. "We're going to have brownies. Big fat ones!"

With the children hurrying out of the room, Mack turned back to Grace. "She's excited about dessert."

A guilty smile tilted her lips. "I don't blame her. I'm always excited about dessert."

Although he was trying his best not to stare, he couldn't stop his gaze from taking a slow survey of her appearance. Dressed in a dark blue woolen coat with a white muffler knotted at her throat, her blond hair was lying loose upon her shoulders. Snowflakes were scattered over the silky strands, and beneath the overhead light, the bits of ice glistened like tiny diamonds.

"I'm glad you're here," he said simply.

That adorable dimple appeared in her cheek. "I'm glad I'm here, too."

His gaze met hers, and for a split second the connection caused his breath to catch in his throat. "You look very pretty."

Her smile turned a bit coy. "Thank you."

She handed him a red tin container decorated with holly and silver bells. "Butter cookies. If you'd rather not break into them after dinner, they'll be good for later on."

"This is nice. But there was no need for you to bring anything," he told her.

"My pleasure. Just don't eat the whole tin in one sitting." She pulled a playful face at him. "Doctor's orders."

"I always follow doctor's orders."

She unbuttoned her coat and Mack stepped behind her to lift the garment off her shoulders. The scent of spices and warm vanilla swirled around her, and all at once he was overcome with the urge to bury his face in her tumbled hair, to hold her soft body next to his, even for just a moment.

"It feels nice and toasty in here," she said.

To avoid the temptation, he stepped back and draped her coat over his forearm. "I followed your dad's example and built a fire tonight in the fireplace. I thought you might enjoy the extra warmth. The weather has been brutal the past few days."

She migrated to the middle of the room and waited while he put her coat away.

"Very," she agreed. "We've been quite busy at the clinic. And I'm sure you're seeing more patients, too. Human or animal, the weather places extra stresses on our health. Unfortunately, Dad has several heifers that could drop calves any day now. Cord is keeping them sheltered in the barn."

Rejoining her, he said, "We've been exceptionally busy. We have people waiting with their animals in the parking lot early in the mornings before I even get the door open. As for your father's heifers, Cord mentioned them to me when I was at Stone Creek on Thanksgiving. I told him if he has any trouble or needs me, just to call—there'd be no charge."

Surprise crossed her face. "That was more than generous of you, Mack. But Cord would never take advantage of you like that. If you did help him, you'd be paid for your services."

"I don't call it being taken advantage of if you're doing something you want to do." He slipped his hand beneath her elbow and began guiding her out of the room. "For example, if we go to the kitchen and I cut my hand on a butcher knife, would you charge me to stich it up?"

She laughed. "I get your point. But to answer your question, whether I charged you would depend on how good a patient you were."

"Oh, I'd be the perfect patient."

Slanting him a sly look, she said, "I wouldn't expect anything less of you."

He couldn't decide whether the impish expression

on her face meant she was teasing him or flirting with him. Either way, she was making him want to get closer.

"I have to admit I'm a little nervous," he said. "Kitty tells me I've made a mistake cooking roast for dinner. She says I should've opted for spaghetti."

His admission was met with a tinkling laugh. "I love roast and so does Ross. But really, Mack, you shouldn't have gone to so much trouble."

"No trouble. Dad left a freezer filled with cuts of beef and I've been trying to steadily make use of it. I even donated some to the senior-citizens center in town. On weekdays they serve lunches for a minimal cost to the elderly."

As though she was reading his thoughts to get closer, she looped her arm through his and snuggled herself to his side.

"Good for you, Mack. It saddens me to think how many geriatric patients I see who are actually malnourished. They either don't have the money to buy proper food, or they aren't physically able to prepare a nutritious meal for themselves."

He cast her a wry smile as they turned a corner and stepped into the kitchen. "Once you taste my cooking, you might put me in that latter group."

She laughed softly, and her gaze swept up and down the length of him. "You're going to have to come up with a different excuse. As a physician I can say you're not elderly and you look physically able for just about any task."

So did she, Mack thought. But cooking wasn't one of them.

He said, "If that's the case, you'd better check everything before we sit down to eat."

She squeezed his arm and if the children hadn't been taking notice of their entrance into the room, Mack would've been greatly tempted to pull her into his arms and kiss her.

"Don't be silly," she told him. "Everything will be perfectly good."

Everything was perfectly good, Mack thought. Now that she was here.

"Mack, I'm glad you chose for us to eat in the kitchen. Not that the dining room in this house isn't nice," she said after dinner as she scraped scraps from a dirty plate into the garbage disposal. "Your mother loved that room. Especially after your dad got the china hutch she wanted to match the table. But it's warmer and cozier here in the kitchen."

Standing next to her, he dropped a granite roasting pan into a sink of sudsy water. "Kitty and I haven't used the dining room," he said. "Actually, I don't think the room has been used since Mom passed away. Dad never had the heart for it. And after Kitty and I moved back, I guess…" Pausing, he shook his head. "I don't have the heart for it, either."

From the corner of her eye, Grace could see a somber expression had crept over his face. When Mack's mother had died, Grace had been in Salt Lake City, finishing her college education. By then, five years had passed since she and Mack had parted ways. Even so, when Grace had heard the news of Dayna Barlow's death, her heart had ached for Mack. He'd been very close to his mother and his father. Now they were both gone and she couldn't imagine the emptiness he must feel.

"Maybe someday you'll enjoy the dining room again, Mack. When you have a whole family."

Turning slightly, he leveled a skeptical look at her. "A whole family?"

Darn it! She shouldn't have said such a thing to him. Now he was probably thinking she was digging for clues about his future plans. But he'd be wrong. Maybe a part of her was curious about what he wanted for himself and for Kitty, but her major concern was his happiness. Which hardly made sense. Fourteen years ago, he hadn't cared the least bit about her happiness.

She said, "Yes. You know. Having a wife and more kids to go with Kitty. When that happens, you'll feel different about this house."

He studied her for a few seconds, then turned his attention back to scrubbing the roast pan. "Is that what you want for yourself, Grace? A whole family?"

She drew in a deep breath and blew it out. "I used to think I didn't. But something about being back in Beaver has made me look at things differently. I realize I want Ross to have a father. And I don't mean just having a man in the house. He deserves a real, loving father."

He glanced at her. "And you deserve a real, loving husband."

Oddly enough, she'd thought Bradley had truly loved her. Yet toward the end of their marriage, he'd admitted that he didn't have any room in his heart for love. He'd conceded that he'd been physically attracted to her, and with both of them being doctors, he'd believed they'd make a compatible couple. He'd not counted on Grace's deep sense of loyalty to her hometown, and her family and friends.

Not wanting Mack to think she was getting serious notions in her head, she laughed softly. "I've learned that real loving husbands don't grow on trees. But if a man comes along that would make Ross a good father, then I'd consider getting married again. Otherwise, I'm a single parent trying to do my best."

He didn't reply, so Grace figured the talk of family and marriage was making him uncomfortable. Which only made her wonder even more about Kitty's mother. What had happened to end his marriage? He'd never so much as mentioned the woman's name in Grace's presence. But to be fair, she'd never talked to him about Bradley, either. Admitting that she'd made such a horrible mistake by marrying the wrong man was not something she wanted to discuss with anyone.

Grace placed the last plate into the dishwasher and was shutting the door when the patter of running footsteps sounded behind her.

She looked around to see Kitty and Ross coming to a skidding halt a few feet behind her and Mack. Both children had sheepish smiles on their faces.

"What are you two up to?" Grace asked. "I thought you were going to play a video game."

"We are," Ross quickly answered, while darting an uneasy look at Kitty. "But Kitty is still hungry."

"Ross is hungry, too," Kitty stated, then walked over to her father. "Daddy, can we have another brownie to take with us to the den? I promise we won't leave crumbs on the floor."

Turning away from the sink, Mack exchanged a knowing smile with Grace before he looked down at his daughter's pleading face.

"Hmm. Another brownie. Well, since you both ate all your roast and vegetables I think it would be okay," Mack told her, then glanced at Grace. "What do you think?"

"Oh, I think this is definitely a two-dessert night."

While the kids celebrated with handclaps and happy jigs, Grace crossed the room to a baker's rack, where Mack had placed the container of leftover brownies.

After wrapping the treats separately in paper napkins, she handed them to the kids. "Here you go. Just make sure you don't make a mess everywhere."

After assuring her they'd clean up after themselves, the pair raced out of the kitchen and Grace walked over to where Mack was hanging a dishtowel on a rack at the end of the cabinet.

"That ought to give them a sugar buzz for a while," he said with wry humor. "Good thing it's Friday night and no school in the morning."

She sighed. "No school. But I had to schedule some appointments for tomorrow morning. I just couldn't fit all my patients in this week. So Ross has to go to the sitter's house."

"Same here. I'm working tomorrow, too. So Kitty will have to go to day care. I have several house calls to make that I couldn't fit into my schedule this week," he told her. "But let's not think about that now. What do you say we take our coffee out to the living room and get comfortable by the fire?"

"Sounds good."

A few minutes later, after making sure the children were settled in the den with their video game, Grace and Mack sat down on a short leather couch positioned a few feet away from the fireplace.

"If you'd like I could turn on some music or the TV," he offered.

She crossed her legs and smoothed her black suede skirt over her knee. "No thanks. The soft crackle of the fire is music enough for me."

"I noticed you don't keep your phone close," he said. "Do you not do nighttime emergency calls at your clinic?"

Shaking her head, she said, "No. Since Ross only has one parent, I'm not going to drag my son out of bed to be dumped off with a sitter. While he's still so young, I want his nightly routine to be as normal as possible. So all my patients understand I won't reopen the clinic if they have an emergency after I close for the night, they're to go to the hospital ER for treatment." She sipped her coffee, then turned slightly toward him. "What about you? Are you taking after-hour emergencies?"

"Thankfully, I've not had any yet. But I expect the phone to start ringing soon. When that happens, I'm not sure how I'll handle it. I'm in the same situation you are. I can't leave Kitty. And I can hardly drag her around with me at all hours of the night."

Glancing thoughtfully at him, she asked, "When you

lived on the ranch down in Reno, how did you manage your job and Kitty? I'm sure there were occasions you were called out at night."

He grunted. "You know, I used to think juggling work and being a parent was hard. Now, I realize I was clueless. Compared to being up here on my own, I had it great on the KO."

As she studied his rugged profile, she wondered what had stopped him from marrying again. It couldn't be for lack of female admirers. With his dark good looks and lean, athletic build, he could easily turn a woman's head.

"So you had help with Kitty there?"

He nodded. "The owner of the ranch and his wife had two younger children and a live-in housekeeper. They would care for Kitty while I had to be out on a job."

Still no mention of a wife, Grace thought. Maybe the woman had died, or they'd divorced before he took the position of resident vet? "I see. That was convenient."

"Yes. A perk of the job," he said.

She finished the last few sips of her coffee and placed the cup on the low table in front of them. "Mack, you can tell me if this is none of my business and I'll understand. But I've been wondering about Kitty's mother. Is she…dead?"

Surprise swept over his face, but his expression quickly changed to an odd look of cynicism. "I guess you have a right to ask about Kitty's mother. And the answer to your question is no. She's not dead. At least, I don't think so."

Grace frowned with confusion. "You don't think so? You mean—"

Before she could go on, he interrupted, "It means I have no idea where she is or what she's doing."

A shocked gasp very nearly passed Grace's lips, but somehow she managed to stop it. "Oh. I guess that means she doesn't interact with her daughter."

"No."

The one word wasn't spoken bitterly, but there was a fatal sound to it that sent a chill through Grace. "That's so sad, Mack. Kitty is such a beautiful, darling child. I'd be thrilled to have a daughter like her."

His dark brown eyes made a slow survey of her face and then he said, "Yes. But you're different, Grace. You have that mother instinct. You possess that loving nature it takes to be a good mother. Libby didn't have any of those things. She had no interest in being a parent. She didn't even want to have a baby. She only carried it to full term because she understood I wanted my child and she was decent enough to comply with my wishes."

With each word he spoke, Grace grew more astounded. No, she thought, she was more than shocked— she was horrified that he could've ever been hooked up with such an uncaring woman.

Breathing deeply, she said, "So, I guess that means you two got a divorce. Was that after Kitty was born?"

His face was like stone as he leaned forward and placed his cup next to hers on the coffee table.

"We didn't get a divorce," he said flatly. "Libby and I were never married."

Chapter Six

Stunned by Mack's admission, Grace squared around on the couch and stared at him. "Never married? I don't understand."

He shot her a droll look. "Why don't you understand? People have affairs all the time."

"Yes, but you...well, with Kitty coming, didn't you want to be married?"

"Marrying Libby would've been like jumping off a cliff. Not that she would've consented to marrying me, even if I'd asked her. No. She wasn't the marrying kind. And at that point in my life, I don't suppose I was the marrying kind, either. Anyway, all we had between us was a brief affair and the connection didn't take long to burn itself out."

If he wasn't the marrying kind then, Grace could hardly expect him to be the marrying kind now. Or had he changed? Her mind was suddenly spinning with all sorts of questions and doubts.

"I didn't think…" Pausing, she shook her head. "I'm still confused, Mack. Wasn't Kitty's mother the reason you ended everything with me?"

The question pulled a deep groan from him. "No. She wasn't. I met Libby shortly after Mom passed away. I was at a very low, vulnerable point in my life. I needed something to fill the ache. I was well aware that Libby was a free spirit. But she was full of life and fun was her middle name. For a while she was just what I needed. It wasn't until after I'd come to my senses and ended things with her that I learned about the baby. And… well, no matter how Kitty was conceived, I felt I needed to be responsible."

Before now, Grace had imagined all sorts of situations as to why Kitty's mother wasn't a part of her or Mack's life. But none of them had come close to the truth of the matter.

"Okay. I understand a bit better now about Kitty and her mother. But what happened to the other woman? The one before Libby. The one who came between you and me? She had to have been important to you. All these years, I figured you had married her and—"

She broke off as he suddenly scooted closer and reached for her hand. "I should've told you this earlier— when we were together on Thanksgiving Day," he said. "But I— That day was special. At least, it was for me. And I didn't want to spoil it with rehashing a bad time in our lives."

She tightened her fingers around his. "I don't want

to spoil this evening, either," she said gently. "And for what it's worth, I've forgiven you for falling in love with someone else. You were very young and we were apart. After a while I could understand how it happened. I don't want to blame you or judge you over any of that. I'm just curious as to what happened with her."

He let out a heavy sigh. "Nothing happened with her, Grace. Because there was no other woman."

If the roof had suddenly crashed in on them, she wouldn't have been more stunned. "What…are you talking about?"

His brown gaze locked with hers. "I made up all that stuff about falling for another woman. I couldn't think of any other way to convince you that we needed to go our separate ways."

Each word he spoke was like a stone striking her chest and she pressed her hand between her breasts in an attempt to ward off the pain. "You made up the whole thing! But why? If you were that desperate to break ties with me, why didn't you just tell me the truth? Instead of making up some fictitious romance?"

Regret, or something like it, flickered in his brown eyes before he turned his gaze away from her and settled it on the fireplace.

"Because I was fairly sure you wouldn't have accepted the real reasons. Letting you think I wanted someone else was the only way," he said ruefully.

How could something that happened so long ago affect her so deeply now? The question was racing through her brain even as she tried to breathe around the pain in her chest. "And what were those reasons, the real ones?" she asked in a low, strained voice. "You were tired of being saddled with me?"

His groan was a helpless sound. "No. You're not even close to being right. With you going to college in Salt Lake City and me forced to settle for a college down in Cedar City, more than two hundred miles stood between us."

She scowled at him. "I'm fairly certain you remember how hard I worked to earn a full scholarship. Should I have tossed it away? My parents weren't poor, but at that time they were already bearing the bulk of Hunter and Jack's college expenses. It would've been even more costly for them to send me to a prestigious university."

"You don't need to remind me of the situation. I told you back then that I'd never allow you to throw away your scholarship. Not for my sake. How do you think I could've lived with myself?"

"Then I don't know what—"

"Oh, Grace, can't you see? Six long years of college studies, plus internships. That's what we were going to be facing. And if that wasn't enough of a load, you were in the northern part of the state and me in the southern. With any luck, we might've seen each other maybe three times a year."

Grace darted a glance toward the open doorway leading out of the living room. She hoped Kitty and Ross were still absorbed in the video game they were playing in the den. It wouldn't be good for them to walk in and overhear this intense conversation. Especially about things they couldn't understand.

She turned her gaze back to him. "That's true. But

in between three visits a year, we could've stayed connected. Yes, it would've been hard, but I believed we were worth it."

He shifted closer to her side and Grace's heart was suddenly skipping and tripping over itself. How did he expect her to focus on his words when all she wanted to do was touch him? To throw herself in his arms and forget everything?

His hand came to rest on her shoulder. "It wasn't just the being apart, Grace. I was looking at the future. It was going to take years for me to become a veterinarian. Years until I could afford to give you a home and the security you deserved. I decided it wasn't fair of me to ask you to wait."

The hand on her shoulder was like a branding iron still hot from the fire. The heat from his fingers was penetrating her silky blouse and shooting fiery splinters deep into her flesh. The distraction made it doubly hard to digest what he was saying.

She gently cleared her throat, but her voice still came out on a husky note. "Don't you think it would've been better to let me in on the decision about what was fair? I believed we were a couple. I believed we would plan and save and sacrifice for our future, and that we'd do it all together. But you left me out of the decision—you took it upon yourself to end everything!"

Remorse shadowed his brown eyes. "Believe me, Grace, it didn't take long for me to realize I'd messed up in a big way. I shouldn't have expected to have everything perfectly laid out before we could marry. And I

was especially wrong when I told you I'd found someone else."

She swallowed, then lowered her head and said, "It
was a cruel thing to do, Mack. I can't begin to count
the times I cried myself to sleep because you'd chosen
some other girl over me. I blamed myself." Her eyes
were misty as she lifted her head and looked at him. "I
kept thinking if only I'd had sex with you, then maybe
you wouldn't have turned to someone else. But we were
so young—I didn't think either of us was ready for that
kind of relationship. I mean, yes, it might have drawn
us closer, but it also would've added more stress."

His hand moved from her shoulder to her face, where
he traced the tips of his fingers along her cheekbone.
"Oh, Lord, Grace, I hate that I hurt you. I hate that I
wasn't mature enough or wise enough to understand
what my lies would do to you. As for us having sex,
you were right. We were too young. For that and all the
other adult responsibilities being thrown at us back then.
And I'm sorry I made such a mess of things—for you,
for the both of us."

Maybe a part of her should have been glad to learn
he'd not left her for another girl. But in many ways cheat-
ing on her was easier to accept than hearing he'd deliberately conjured up a story to end their relationship. If
he lied to her once about something so important, might
he do it again?

Not wanting to dwell on such a dubious thought, she
shook it away and gave him a wan smile. "I accept your
apology, Mack. But I—"

"No, Grace," he quickly interrupted. "Don't start

giving me reasons we should stay apart. I believe we can start over. I want for us to start over."

She started to tremble. Not only from his words, but also from the look of longing in his eyes. "I doubt you're aware of what you're saying, Mack."

"I know what I'm saying," he murmured. "But it might be more convincing to show you what I'm feeling."

All at once his face was descending toward hers and she watched in fascination until his lips fastened over hers in one hungry swoop. And then nothing else mattered except meeting his kiss with the same gnawing need she'd been feeling ever since he'd walked into her clinic several weeks ago.

As his hard lips rocked over hers, she registered the faint taste of coffee mixed with something dark and masculine and ever so erotic. Desire washed over her like a sudden downpour of rain and she moaned faintly as she opened her mouth to invite him to deepen the kiss.

He responded by slipping his arms around her shoulders and pulling her close to him. The contact with his hard, warm body sent her senses flying and she was almost overwhelmed when her arms curled around his neck and his tongue pushed its way between her teeth. Glorious pleasure was pouring through her, awakening all those parts of her that had lain dormant for so long.

"Grace. Grace." He murmured her name softly as his lips moved against her cheek and over the bridge of her nose. "I never thought it could be this way for us again. We've both had other people in our lives. We have children. So much time has passed. You'd think that would be enough to make us forget. But I never forgot."

Tears burned her throat. "I never forgot, either," she whispered.

With his hands cradling her face, he kissed her forehead and then captured her lips once again.

Grace responded hungrily, and for the next few moments she was totally consumed in the melding of their lips and the circle of his arms holding her tight, filling her whole body with delicious warmth.

Then, just when she thought she was going to lose her breath completely, he lifted his mouth and eased his head back from hers.

"I, um, hate to say it, but I came close to forgetting about the kids," he said huskily.

Breathing deeply, she ran the tip of her tongue over her swollen lips. "I came close to forgetting, too. And they could walk in any minute."

He straightened away from her and wiped a hand over his face. "If they found us kissing it might be hard to explain to them."

Grace wasn't sure she could explain it to herself, much less to Ross and Kitty. "I imagine both of them understand that adults kiss each other."

"Just not their mom or dad," he said with a dose of wry humor.

"No. Just not us," she replied, while thinking she was playing with fire. He said he wanted them to forget the past and start over. But start what? As passionate as it might be, she couldn't have an affair with Mack. It wouldn't be enough. No more than a sweet, but safe, romance would be. She'd already had one failed marriage. She wasn't sure she was ready to try again. And even if she was ready, Mack's long years of bachelorhood proved he wasn't the marrying kind.

She rose from the couch, walked over to the fireplace and stood facing the low flames. As she stared into the crackling fire, she imagined how it might be if she was Mack's wife, and as the evening came to a close and the children were snug in bed, they could climb the stairs together. They could make love. Not just for one night, but for the rest of their lives.

Would she be crazy to think such a thing? Much less hope it could come true?

She was trying to answer her question when Mack walked up beside her and wrapped an arm around the back of her waist.

"I've made you angry, haven't I?"

Surprised by his question, she looked at him. "I'm not angry. Why would you think so?"

"I'm not sure. Except that I can feel you pulling away from me."

She reached for his hand, lifted it to chest level and smoothed her fingertips over the weather-roughened skin on the back, then traced a path down each long, strong finger.

"I'm not pulling away, Mack. I'm thinking how very close I feel to you at this moment." She lifted her watery gaze to his and smiled. "And how very glad I am that you're home again."

"Grace."

Her name floated out on a whisper and then he pressed

a soft kiss to her cheek. "Uh, what do you say we go check on our children?"

Our children. Would there ever come a day when Kitty and Ross would be *their* children? Probably not, Grace thought. But just for tonight, it was a very nice dream.

She found his hand and squeezed it. "Yes. Let's go."

The following Monday afternoon Mack had been working his way through a waiting room full of patients when Eleanor informed him he was needed on a house call. After learning it wasn't an emergency situation, he'd decided to send Oren to take care of the task.

Now, as the two men stood inside the supply room, Mack gave his assistant instructions while he gathered the necessary medicines.

He retrieved a big brown bottle of antibiotics from a refrigerator and handed it to Oren. "When you get to Mr. Pollock's farm find out if he's milking more than one nanny. If he is, then you'll need to give all of them the antibiotic. More often than not, the bacteria spreads from one animal to another. So be sure and tell him he needs to keep everything extra clean when he's milking. Do you think you can gauge the nannies' weights?"

"Sure. Dad used to raise goats."

Mack walked over to a wall lined with shelves and plucked up a large plastic bottle filled with intramammary solution. "Good. Then you can calculate how much antibiotic to inject. Once you get that finished, then wash their udders and smear this topical solution on them. Be sure and tell Mr. Pollock the solution needs to be applied twice a day. So leave the bottle with him. And take plenty of needles and syringes."

"What about the antibiotic? Leave it with him, too?"

"He's experienced with animals. I'm fairly certain he's capable of injecting the goats, so, yes, leave the medication with him. Because the nannies are going to need shots for the next four days, at least." He looked at his assistant. "Think you can handle this on your own, Oren? If not, I'll tell Eleanor to delay the rest of my appointments here at the clinic and go with you."

Oren scowled at him. "Heck yeah, I can handle it. That's what you pay me for, isn't it? If I can't take care of a few nanny goats with a case of mastitis, then you ought to fire me."

Actually, Oren was turning out to be an even better assistant than Mack could've ever hoped to find. He came early, stayed late and never shied away from any task, whether it was mundane or serious.

After handing him the bottle of solution, Mack fondly swatted his shoulder. "Oren, I think it would take a lot more than that for me to ever fire you. In fact, I thank God every day that you applied for the job."

A sheepish grin on his face, Oren shook his head. "Aw, Mack, don't be heaping any praise on me. It'll make me look worse whenever I do mess up."

"We all mess up, Oren. Some of us just mess up more than others."

And he'd messed up royally all those years ago when he'd broken up with Grace. Sure, after a few weeks, he'd recognized he'd made a mistake, but not until he'd confessed to her the other night after dinner had he realized just how deeply his deception had hurt her. And him.

She'd said she'd forgiven him. But Mack's real worry was that she might never be able to forget. His lie might always be a wall standing between them.

"Dang, Mack, you don't have anything to worry about. You never mess up."

Chuckling, Mack started out of the room. "Good thing I have you fooled." He glanced over his shoulder. "Better take the Jeep. The road out to the Pollock farm gets treacherous this time of year."

Oren gave him a thumbs-up. "Don't worry. I'll call if I need you."

Mack went on out the door and walked down the hallway to the front of the building, where Eleanor's desk sat behind a tall counter with a glass window that slid open and closed.

Eleanor was in her midsixties and her shoulder-length, salt-and-pepper hair resembled that of a front man of a 1980s hair band, but the style matched the colorful outfits she wore to work every day. The woman brought a bit of cheer to the clinic, and he was grateful. Not to mention she was an expert at juggling appointments and dealing with calls from harried pet owners.

Eleanor was in deep concentration as she studied the appointment book lying in front of her, when Mack knocked lightly on the door facing.

"You're going to hurt yourself thinking that hard, Eleanor," he teased.

Glancing up, she shook her finger at him. "Yes, and it's all your fault, Dr. Mack. You try to do too much."

He walked into the small workspace and peered over her shoulder. "That's what a veterinarian is supposed to do. Have you scheduled anything else after the dog spay?"

"No. I figured it would be closing time by then. Guess you're planning to keep the little lady here over night? I'm asking because the owner is asking."

"If the owner— What's her name?"

Eleanor checked the appointment book. "Cheryl Montgomery."

"If Ms. Montgomery can keep the dog quiet and secure in some place where she'll be warm and in no danger of falling, then she can take her home after a few hours. But the dog will be drunk from anesthesia for most of the night. It would be better if she left her here at the clinic. Two cats will remain in recovery overnight, so Ira has already offered to stay and keep a watch over them."

"Okay. I'll explain the deal to her."

She scribbled something on a notepad and Mack started to leave the room, but Eleanor waved a hand at him.

"Wait a minute—there's something else. You had a phone call from Cord Hollister. He's part of the family who has Stone Creek Ranch, isn't he?"

Just hearing Grace's family mentioned put his attention on high alert. "Yes. Is something wrong at the ranch? If there's an emergency—"

"I would've told you instantly," she interrupted, then raised her chin as though she resented his questioning her judgment. "He only said he'd like to talk with you whenever you have a free moment. He didn't mention a problem with any of the livestock, so I assumed it was something personal. You do have a private life, don't you?"

Mack glanced out toward the waiting room, where three people sat with pet carriers at their feet. Even though the closed window made it impossible for them to hear his and Eleanor's conversation, they were no doubt wondering why he wasn't tending to the business of taking care of his patients.

Turning his back toward the waiting area, he rolled his eyes at Eleanor. "Who's been talking to you? Ira or Oren?"

"Ha! Those two men are as blind as bats. They couldn't tell me if it was night or day."

"I thought you had an eye for Ira. Guess I was wrong," Mack said coyly.

Eleanor sniffed. "You're changing the subject. Anyway, Ira is always talking about the redheaded checker at Weston's Grocery. He thinks she's beautiful."

Mack tried not to laugh. "He's only trying to make you jealous."

"The old fool," she muttered under her breath, then leveled a pointed look at Mack. "In case you're interested, Ira and Oren haven't mentioned you cooking dinner for Dr. Hollister the other night. Little Kitty told me about it. She said you held Dr. Grace's hand and I could tell that made your daughter happy. Made me happy, too."

Mack frowned. On some weekdays after school, he would let Kitty stay at the clinic rather than take her to the day care. As long as she didn't get in anyone's way or venture outside. But this was only Monday. Eleanor couldn't have seen Kitty here at the clinic. "How could you have talked with Kitty?"

Eleanor pointed to the cell phone lying to one side of the counter. "Kitty likes to talk and I told her she can call me anytime. I think she sort of thinks of me as a grandmother figure. Which is just great with me. My only grandchild has grown up and moved away."

"Just don't let my daughter make a pest of herself," he said, then glanced at his watch. "I'm waiting on the anesthesia to take effect on Mr. Douglas's cat. I'll give Cord a call."

As Mack walked back down the hallway to his office, he spotted Ira coming out of the recovery room. He motioned for the man to join him.

"You need me, Mack?"

"Yes. The cat I have on the table in the operating room should be asleep, or close to it. There's a large cyst on its back that I'm going to open up and clean. I want you to shave that whole area with the clippers. You've seen me do it before, haven't you?"

"Sure. A military cut—right down to the skin."

"Exactly. And make sure any loose pieces of hair are brushed away. Okay?"

Ira gave him a confident grin. "No problem. I've got it. Is that all?"

"No. Before you shave the cat, you can go to the waiting room and get the little dachshund. He's here for his vaccines. Get those out of the supply room and have those ready for me. I'll take care of him before I start on the cat."

Ira made an a-okay sign with his thumb and forefinger. "Eleanor thinks I'm too old and helpless to find my way home. That woman doesn't have a clue."

Giving Ira a crooked grin, he shook his head. "In a few months I'll have turned you into a regular vet tech. What's she going to think about you then?"

Ira snorted. "Who can ever tell what a woman's really thinking, Doc?"

Not waiting for an answer, the older man hurried away and Mack went inside his office. Not bothering to make himself comfortable, he stood at the side of his desk and punched in the number Eleanor had jotted on the sticky note.

Grace's brother answered on the second ring. "Hey, Mack. Thanks for calling."

"Eleanor just informed me you'd called. Sorry I didn't think to give you my private cell number when I was out at Stone Creek on Thanksgiving. Having a problem?"

Surely if something was wrong with Grace, someone would've let him know before now. Or would they? Unless Grace had mentioned it to her family, none of them knew he was trying to insert himself back into her life.

Is that what you call it, Mack? Or is it more like trying to lure her into your bed? Why don't you be honest with yourself? You don't want to be married. Even to someone who makes you feel as good as Grace does.

Sickened by the cynical voice in his head, he determinedly pushed it aside as he waited for Cordell to explain the reason for his call.

"I'm hardly an expert on equines, so I'm only guessing that this situation might turn into an emergency, Mack. One of our mares foaled an hour ago. The foal seems perfectly healthy, but the mare hasn't completely expelled the afterbirth. She's one of our older mares and I was hesitant to do anything without talking with you first."

"Good man. Other than making sure she or the foal doesn't trip on the membrane, don't do anything to her. If she doesn't pass it in the next couple of hours, I'll have to take care of it. Horses are very different from cows when they give birth. Dangerous problems can ensue for a mare if she doesn't shed the membrane right away."

"You don't think I could help her pass it—to save you the long trip?" Cordell asked.

"I'd rather you didn't. If something went wrong she could hemorrhage to death."

Cordell whooshed out a heavy breath. "Oh, Lord, then I'll definitely wait for you."

"I have a couple of minor surgeries to deal with here and then I'll drive out," Mack told him, while thinking ahead to Kitty. He'd have to ask Eleanor to pick her up from school.

"Listen, Mack, if it's going to throw a burden on you, I'll call the other vet in town. He doesn't do much in the way of large animals anymore, but I could probably persuade him."

"Cord, I told you if you ever needed help, I'd come," he said firmly. "So I'll be there."

"I appreciate this, Mack. So will the rest of the family. I'll be with the mare at the main barn."

Mack hung up the phone and quickly headed out of the office.

Much later that evening, as the sun was fast disappearing over the western ridge of mountains, Mack gave the chestnut mare an affectionate pat on the neck and was rewarded with her turning her head and pressing her muzzle against his cheek.

Standing a few steps away, Cordell chuckled. "Sissy is a loving little flirt. She's thanking you for making her feel better."

"Best payment I've had all day." Mack stroked the mare's nose, then crossed the stall to finish packing away the medical supplies he'd used to treat the Hollister mare.

Cordell moved over to where Mack was standing. "I'm grateful to you, Mack. We've had Sissy since she was a baby, so we're all pretty fond of her. You did a great job of caring for her."

Mack let out a weary breath as he lifted his hat from his head and raked a hand over his hair.

"Everything worked out well. But do keep an eye on her—to make sure she doesn't start running a temperature. I've injected her with long-acting antibiotics, so I don't foresee her developing an infection. But watch her just the same."

Cordell looked at him with concern. "You're dog-tired. Let's drive over to the big house. I can assure you Mom will have a pot of coffee made and a pie just pulled out of the oven. You can rest a bit before you drive back."

"Sounds great, Cord, but I have to pick up Kitty. After the staff closed up the clinic this evening, Eleanor was kind enough to take Kitty home with her. Plus, I have a bunch of chores waiting on me at the ranch."

Cordell eyed him curiously. "Do you have any hands helping you on the Broken B?"

"A couple of guys. But they only work every other day. However, if things stay this busy at the clinic I might have to put them on full-time."

"Plenty of work at the clinic?"

He picked up the metal case he used for carrying his supplies. "Running out my ears. I never expected business at the clinic to take off so quickly. I have an assistant and another older gentleman who's also helping, but I need another assistant."

"You're in the same boat as Grace. She rarely has time to take a deep breath. She needs a PA to help her with the patient load. But she'd expect the PA to be as meticulous and thorough as she is and I'm not sure she could find anyone that dedicated. But Grace needs more than a PA. Her and Ross shouldn't be living alone." He grimaced, then shook his head. "Sorry. I'm probably making you feel uncomfortable with this kind of talk. But I know you've always cared about Grace and she's had to go through some mighty rough patches."

Cordell's remarks weren't making him feel uncomfortable. They were reminding him how much he wished he could see her again, hold and kiss her again.

"Dad told me that Grace's husband got killed in an automobile accident. She must have been devastated."

Surprise flashed in Cordell's eyes before he glanced

away. "Yeah. It was a bad time. But that personal stuff she went through—it's something she needs to tell you about. Not me."

But what more could there be about Grace's marriage? The man had been killed and she'd been left alone with a toddler. Surely that was all of the bad part. Or was it? Had something happened in the marriage that was too painful for her to talk about? Most widows held onto their married names, Mack thought, but for some reason she'd returned to using her maiden name. Not only that, she'd also changed Ross's name to Hollister. Yes, the name carried weight, but was that her only reason for dropping her husband's name?

Mack would be lying if he said he wasn't curious about the man she'd loved enough to marry and father her child. But he'd stopped himself short of asking her. He'd been hoping she might want to share that part of her life with him. Especially after he'd told her all about Libby and how Kitty had been conceived. But apparently she didn't want to reveal those private parts of her life to him.

Stepping over to the mare, he gave her one last pat on the neck, then moved to the stall gate to let himself out.

"I'll see you later, Cord. Call me if you need me."

Cordell slapped a hand on the back of Mack's shoulder as he followed him out of the stall. "Thanks again, Mack. And if I don't see you before, I hope you and your daughter have a merry Christmas."

"Same to you and your family, Cord."

With a backward wave, he walked out of the barn and into the falling twilight. Beyond the hill to his right, the big house would be lit up with strings of colorful lights, while inside, decorations would brighten each room. Hadley would have a fire going in the den, and that coffee and pie that Cordell had mentioned would be passed around and enjoyed over small talk.

It would be that same way on Christmas Day, Mack thought. Only there'd be more food and family. More talk and laughter. Grace and Ross would no doubt be spending the special day with all the other Hollisters. And for the first time in their lives, Mack and Kitty would be totally alone. His father wouldn't be there to celebrate the blessed day with them.

The holiday wasn't going to be a happy occasion for him this year. But for his daughter's sake, Mack would put a smile on his face and hide the loneliness in his heart.

Chapter Seven

Four days later, Grace picked up Ross at Birdie's house and was driving the two of them home when Ross suddenly popped a surprising question.

"Mom, do you think we could get a Christmas tree in the back of our SUV?"

Grace frowned. "Whatever for? We just put up our tree two nights ago. We don't need another one. Why do you ask? Does Birdie need for us to haul a tree to her house?"

"No. She and the twins have already put a giant tree in their living room. I'm thinking about Kitty. She doesn't have a Christmas tree. And it's making her sad. Really sad."

By now, Grace had reached her own house and she pulled the SUV halfway up the concrete drive before she braked the vehicle to a halt and looked over her shoulder at Ross.

"How do you know Kitty doesn't have a tree?"

He said, "Because she told me. She calls me and we talk on the phone."

This was news to Grace. She didn't allow Ross to have a cell phone, so apparently the times she'd seen him talking on the landline he'd been visiting with Kitty. "You mean those calls you've been getting are from Kitty? Does she have a cell phone?"

"No. Her dad is like you. He says Kitty can't have a phone until she gets a whole lot older. She calls me on their landline at the ranch house."

Mack had told Grace that the cell signal on the Broken B was often spotty, so he kept the landline for a backup. As for Grace, she held on to her landline for times when the weather or other factors knocked out cell service. Obviously, the children were making use of the phones.

"I see," she said to Ross. "I thought you were talking with Bobby or Trevor."

"Sometimes I talk to them. But I mostly talk to Kitty. 'Cause she don't have anybody, you know. Bobby and Trevor have brothers and sisters they can talk to."

And Ross and Kitty didn't have any siblings, but in their minds they had each other. Yes, Grace could see how and why the children were getting attached to one another. And the truth of the matter left a hollow space in her heart. She didn't want to think she'd let down Ross by not giving him a father or siblings. No more than she wanted to believe Mack had fallen short in giving his daughter the family she needed. But Grace and Mack had fallen short in many ways and the fact bothered her greatly.

"I see," she said thoughtfully. "So Kitty and Mack haven't done any decorating at their house?"

"Kitty says her dad has been too busy taking care of animals and at night he only sits in his chair and stares at the wall. That's not fun, Mom."

The image of Mack in a melancholy state of mind bothered her greatly. "No, staring at the wall isn't fun anytime of the year, son."

A week had passed since Mack had cooked dinner for the four of them. During that time she'd received two very short text messages from him. The first to thank her for coming to dinner. The second message simply said he hoped her week was going well. Nothing about him being tired or overworked. But that was hardly a surprise. He wasn't a whiner. Even so, she'd been disappointed that he'd not mentioned wanting to see her again, or anything about missing her.

Maybe the man doesn't feel the same as you, Grace. Just because you're aching to see him, to kiss and hold him close, doesn't mean he's longing for the same thing.

But he could be longing for those same things, she mentally argued with the voice in her head. He'd told her he wanted them to start over and he'd shown her how much he'd meant those words with kisses that had scorched her lips. Maybe he was waiting on her to show him that she was truly interested in starting over.

"Don't you think we should do something about it, Mom? I saw some trees in front of Weston's Grocery.

We could buy one of those. And we have some leftover decorations we can share."

Grace smiled slyly. "You have this all figured out, don't you?"

He gave her sheepish grin. "Well, you always tell me how Christmas is the giving season. So I think we ought to give Kitty and Mack a tree."

In spite of Grace's long, tiring day, just the thought of being with Mack and his daughter lifted her spirits.

"Okay. Let's go change our clothes and then we'll be on our way."

"Yay, Mom! C'mon, let's hurry!"

It took more than a half hour to get everything ready and the tree securely strapped to the top of her SUV, then another thirty minutes to drive the long dirt road to the Broken B Ranch house.

"You should've called before we started out here, Mom," Ross said as they rattled over the last pipe cattle guard before they reached the house. "Kitty and her dad might not be home."

"Normally I would have called. But I wanted to surprise them. If no one is home, we'll leave everything on the porch with a note."

"I guess that'll work. But I want to help Kitty put on the decorations. That's the most fun."

"Yes, it would be more fun to help with the decorating," Grace said in agreement. "So let's cross our fingers and hope we'll find them home."

Five minutes later, Grace steered the vehicle around a short rise and Ross let out a joyous whoop at the sight of the two-story house with lights glowing through several windows.

"Oh, boy, they're home! Do I have to wait on you to go knock on the door?"

Keeping her eyes on the road, Grace smiled to herself. She'd heard so many anguished and sad stories of children who refused to accept their parents desire to date or marry again. Which clearly wasn't the case with Ross. In fact, he was on the opposite end of the spectrum. He was constantly asking his mother when she planned to see Mack again. Most of that could be because anytime Grace and Mack got together, Ross would get an opportunity to spend time with Kitty. But for the most part she could tell her son thought Mack was a super guy.

"Of course, you don't have to wait," she told him. "You can be the one to surprise them."

When they reached the parking area in front of the yard rail fence, Grace braked the vehicle to a stop and Ross instantly disengaged his seat belt and took off in a fast run to the covered porch that ran the entire width of the house.

By the time Grace had pulled on her coat and scrunched her way across the snowy ground to the porch, Mack had already opened the door and stepped outside to greet him. But not before Kitty shot past her father and gave Ross an excited bear hug.

"A Christmas tree!" Kitty yelled. "Look, Daddy! They brought us a tree!"

"I see," he replied in a slightly stunned voice, then

moved away from the door just in time to meet Grace on the steps.

Grace's heart skipped a beat as he reached for her hand and slipped his fingers around hers.

"Surprise!" She laughed lightly. "Don't you just love it when someone barges in on you after a hard day at work?"

Squeezing her fingers, he smiled at her. "I'm thrilled to see you. And very surprised."

"Well, I apologize for showing up without warning. But I wanted to surprise you. I realize it's already getting late in the evening, but it was well past clinic hours when we finally shut the doors."

He chuckled. "Welcome to the club. I've only been home a short while. Just long enough to do the barn chores."

She looked at him. "Are you finished with those? I can help, if there's something else you need to do."

"Thanks for the offer, but we've finished taking care of all the animals in the barn."

"Great. Then I hope you and Kitty haven't yet eaten. I took it upon myself to bring some takeout from the Wagon Spoke. Lasagna was the special today."

He gave her a grateful grin. "We've not eaten and lasagna would definitely hit the spot. But you shouldn't have gone to so much trouble, Grace."

She squeezed his hand. "It's no trouble. Ross says giving and sharing is fun and he's right."

He surprised her by tilting his head and pressing a quick kiss on her forehead. Apparently, he didn't think it would hurt for the children to view the little display of affection. Was this the beginning of them starting over? The idea filled her with hope.

"Give me a moment to get my jacket and I'll carry in the tree before we dig into the food," he told her, then turned to Kitty. "Come on, Kitty. You need to put on your coat."

In a matter of minutes, the four of them had the tree and decorations, plus their dinner, transferred to the house. While Grace stored the food in a warm spot in the kitchen, Mack leveled the bottom of the tree trunk with a handsaw and fastened it into a sturdy stand.

"Now it's time for the big question," he said once he had the tree standing securely upright. "Should we keep the tree here in the living room or put it in the den?"

"Here in the living room," Ross answered first. "'Cause that's where the fireplace is and Santa comes down the chimney to put gifts under the tree."

Kitty was clearly impressed with Ross's logic. "Yeah! Santa might not find the tree if we put it in the den."

Mack looked over the children's heads to give Grace a wink. "And that would be tragic if Santa didn't leave your gifts. So I think Ross has a good idea. We'll leave the tree in here. How about over by the windows? That way any cows moseying by can see the pretty lights."

Giggling, Kitty clapped her hands with glee. "Oh, yes! And the goats would like to see them, too."

Mack positioned the eight-foot spruce over by the window, then stepped back to eye the whole image.

"Looks straight, don't you think?" he asked Grace, who was standing a few steps away.

Tonight she was dressed casually in blue jeans that

flared over a pair of red cowboy boots. A thin red sweater was tucked into the waistband and the long sleeves pushed up on her forearms. She looked twenty-three instead of thirty-three. She also looked like the woman he'd never been able to push out of his mind.

"As an arrow," she agreed. "And it smells heavenly."

"Let's start putting the decorations on, Daddy. Can we?" Kitty implored. "Ross says they bought bubble lights. I've never seen those before."

"They look really cool," Ross said to Kitty. "Just wait 'til you see them."

"Sorry, kids, but we're going to eat first," Mack announced. "Then you can start with the decorations."

Ross turned a pleading look on his mother. "Aww, Mom, I'm not hungry right now."

"Me, neither," Kitty added with an emphatic shake of her head. "I don't wanna eat."

Grace gave both children a stern look. "I'm fairly sure that once we all sit down at the table, you two will be able to eat. If not, you'll have miss out on the decorating. So you two go to the bathroom and wash up."

Kitty and Ross exchanged hopeless glances, then decided that eating wasn't such a bad idea after all.

Ross said to Kitty, "Maybe we'd better go to the bathroom and wash up for dinner. Mom always means what she says."

As the pair of youngsters scurried out of the room, Mack gave Grace a lopsided grin.

"Thanks for backing me up. I hate to be a scrooge, but Kitty is so excited she'd go to bed without even knowing she hasn't eaten."

"They're both excited." She shot him an impish grin. "Ho ho ho! Haven't you heard that Santa is on his way?"

"I'm beginning to get the feeling," he murmured as he slipped an arm around her shoulder and pulled her toward him.

Her heart pounding, she rested her palms against the middle of his chest and lifted her gaze to his brown eyes. They were soft and inviting, and her throat thickened with emotion. "You might not have guessed, but I've been missing you."

"Probably not as much as I've been missing you." Angling his head, he placed a brief, but very thorough, kiss on her lips, then with a rueful sigh eased away from her. "I expect the handwashing is going to be superfast."

She chuckled softly. "I think I already hear footsteps heading this way."

He curled an arm around her waist and urged her on toward the kitchen. "Let's go dig into the lasagna. I think we're going to need some extra energy tonight to keep up with our kids."

Our kids. There, he'd said it again. And though she tried to tell herself he didn't mean the term literally, she wanted to think he did. Just as much as she wanted to believe his kiss had said she was becoming important to him.

For the children's sake, Grace and Mack kept the mealtime as short as possible and decided to have dessert of cookies and hot chocolate later in the living room after they finished decorating the tree.

More than an hour passed as strings of lights, silver garland, ropes of red beads and an assortment of colorful balls were slowly and surely transferred from boxes to the branches of the spruce. With the adults working on the top half, and Ross and Kitty dealing with the lower limbs, the spruce began to evolve into a fully decorated tree.

When Mack eventually placed an angel on the tip-top of the tree, he and Grace took seats on the couch and left the children with the task of draping icicles on the branches they could reach.

"I thought those two would be slowing down by now, but they're still going strong," Mack said.

Kitty and Ross were chatting and giggling as they circled the tree and admired their handiwork. Even if their Christmas Day turned out to be a bit lonely, Mack was very glad his daughter would at least have this night to enjoy the thrill of preparing for the coming holiday.

"Ross was so concerned about Kitty not having a tree," Grace said. "He kept insisting we needed to bring her one."

"I was planning on getting a tree." He cast her a sheepish look. "But…well, I've been so busy at the clinic. That's no excuse, though. I shouldn't have kept putting it off."

"I understand, Mack. Really, I do. With you just getting your practice started, it makes things even tougher." She slanted a curious glance at him. "Did you know they talk on the phone? I didn't, until Ross told me about it earlier this evening."

Mack groaned. "No. I had no idea. I only learned a few days ago that she calls Eleanor on a regular basis.

Sometimes I think I need an extra set of eyes and ears to keep up with my daughter."

Yes, there was no doubt Kitty needed a mother. A mother like Grace. She was doing a great job with Ross and he had no doubt she would treat Kitty as her own daughter. She'd give her discipline and guidance and, best of all, love. But he was letting his thoughts run away with him. He and Grace were just now getting to know each other again. She wasn't thinking about marriage. Not with him. And even if she was, what made him think he could ever keep a wife? So far in his life, he'd lost everyone he'd ever loved.

"At times, I think the same thing. Ross needs a father. But I'd never marry just for that reason."

He couldn't think of a safe reply to her comment and after a long stretch of awkward silence passed, she cleared her throat and changed the subject completely.

"I heard you made a trip out to Stone Creek a few days ago. Mom said everyone was very grateful to you for taking such good care of Sissy."

"Cord actually called me this morning to let me know the mare and colt are doing well. I'm glad." He shifted on the cushion so that he was facing her. "And speaking of calls, several times this week, I picked up the phone to call you, but each time I was interrupted."

Her gaze dropped to where her folded hands were resting on her thigh. "I thought about calling you, too," she said. "But I've been busy, too. And I didn't want to be a…bother."

A bother? Oh, heck. Didn't she know what she meant to him? What she'd always meant to him? No. How could she? A few kisses were hardly enough to tell her what was in his heart.

He wrapped his hand around her bare forearm, and for a moment the soft warmth of her skin made him forget everything he was going to say.

"You could never be a bother, Grace," he finally said. "In fact, I've been wondering if you might like to go out to dinner. Some place nice and quiet. Just the two of us."

She looked at him and the eagerness he saw in her eyes struck a spark of hope in him.

"I'd like that very much, Mack."

Joy spurted through him as he gathered her hands between the two of his. "Tomorrow is Saturday and I'm closing my clinic for the weekend. How does tomorrow night sound to you?"

Her green eyes glowed as a smile curled the corners of her lips. "Perfect. I'm not working tomorrow, either. I made sure Harper didn't schedule any Saturday-morning appointments because I wanted to give my staff a whole weekend off. For the first time in a long time."

"Great," he replied. "Now if I can just find a sitter for Kitty. The day care does stay open on Saturday evenings, but only until nine. I don't want to cut our dinner short. I suppose I could ask Eleanor. She and Kitty have already become fast friends."

Grace quickly shook her head. "No. Don't do that. I'm sure Eleanor would be great with Kitty, but I have a better idea. I'll call Mom. She and Dad would love to have the kids out to the ranch to spend the night with them. And I'm sure Kitty and Ross would have a fun time."

Surprised by her offer, he said, "Kitty would have a blast. But I wouldn't want to take advantage of your parents. Maybe if I paid them—"

"Not on your life!" she interrupted. "You'd insult my parents for even suggesting such a thing. Trust me, Mack, they won't feel used. In fact, they've been scolding me because I haven't let Ross come out to stay here lately. Besides, everyone should get to do fun things now and then. Including you and me."

After a moment's consideration, he said, "All right— as long as your parents are enthusiastic about the idea. I certainly wouldn't worry about Kitty. Not with Claire and Hadley watching over her."

Beaming a smile at him, she rose to her feet. "I'll call Mom right now. You can have the pleasure of telling the kids our plans. But before you do, you might want to put in some earplugs. I have an idea you're going to hear some loud squeals of joy."

She started to turn away, but he grabbed her hand. She paused and cast him a questioning look. "Is anything wrong?"

He grinned. "No. I only wanted to tell you that you've made me happy."

Moving closer, she whispered in his ear, "You've made me happy, too."

Everything inside Mack wanted to pull her down on his lap, so he could wrap his arms around her and cradle her head against his shoulder. But that would have to wait until they were alone.

He released his hold on her hand, and as he watched

her walk out of the room, he felt as if he'd been waiting most of his life for Grace.

The next day, beneath a weak wintery sun, Grace
made a trip to Canyon Corral, a charming boutique
where her sister Beatrice worked as a salesclerk. Located on a corner a few blocks away from Grace's medical clinic, the business was housed in an old, two-story
building with natural, wood-shingled siding. A pair of
large, plate glass windows bracketed the entrance and
as she drew near the door, she paused to take a look
at the clothing and footwear displayed among festive
holiday decorations.

When she stepped inside the store, the jangle of an
overhead bell mixed with the sound of country music
playing in the background. The faint scents of apples
and cinnamon hung in the warm air that filled the long
room and drifted upward to the high, raftered ceiling.
Several women were browsing among the racks of
clothing. And there were tables and shelves filled with
merchandise, ranging from scented candles to granite
coffeepots and cups.

As Grace walked toward a group of dresses, a couple
of the women spoke to her in passing. Grace acknowledged them before turning her focus on a ring of hanging garments.

"Grace! This is a surprise!" Beatrice exclaimed as
she rushed to her sister's side. "Tell me you're here
to buy your twin sisters something cute and sexy for
Christmas gifts!"

Grace chuckled slyly. "Maybe. But I certainly won't

do it while you're around to see what I'm buying. Need I remind you; Christmas gifts are generally kept secret until they're opened."

Beatrice let out a playful wail. "I'll hide my eyes while you're at the checkout counter."

"Sure you will."

Giving Grace a little hug, Beatrice asked, "Seriously, are you shopping for yourself or someone else?"

Grace hesitated. Then, realizing her date with Mack was hardly a secret, she said, "For myself. I'm going out to dinner tonight."

Beatrice's eyebrows shot upward. "A date? For real?"

She lifted a red knit dress from the rack and held it up for closer inspection. "Yes, for real. Why, is it hard for you to believe a guy wants to take me out?"

Frowning, Beatrice answered, "Of course not. It's just that you never— I can't remember the last time you've been on a date!"

Since her divorce, Grace had only gone on a few casual outings with men. All of them had been in the medical profession and none had interested her romantically. After her divorce from Bradley and his subsequent death, she'd hoped she might meet a man who'd make her pulse quicken and her heart soar up to the clouds. She'd wanted to find a man who could make her forget the miserable mistake of her failed marriage and fill her with an eagerness to try again. Instead, she'd had to fight off yawns. Then Mack had come home to Beaver and suddenly everything about her life felt different.

Grace hung the dress back on the rack and proceeded to push the plastic hangers back and forth as she searched through the garments. "I've not wanted to go on any dates," Grace said, then added with a clever smile, "Until now."

Beatrice's expression suddenly turned smug. "It's Mack Barlow, isn't it? Ever since he and his daughter had Thanksgiving with the family, I've been wondering if you two might be getting together. Guess this dinner date explains everything."

"I don't know your definition of *getting together*, but we've seen each other a few times—whenever our jobs allow."

"So what about Ross and Mack's little girl. Are they going along with you?" Beatrice asked.

"No. We had a special time with the kids last evening trimming a tree at Mack's house. Late this afternoon, we're taking them out to stay with Mom and Dad. They're planning on roasting hot dogs in the fireplace. Are you going be home? If so, you might give Mom an extra hand if she needs it."

Beatrice's smiled suggestively. "I have a date. We're going to Cedar City and catch a movie and dinner. But don't worry—Bonnie will be around to help Mom and Dad."

Beatrice sighed. "Mack is one hot dude. I can see why you've forgiven him for throwing you over for another woman. But something like that would be a little hard for me to forget. Aren't you worried he'll do it again?"

Grace glanced over her shoulder to make sure there weren't any customers in the boutique within earshot. "No. I'm not worried about Mack's faithfulness. We were both nineteen years old... Well, you might say twenty, when he broke up with me—far too young."

"You weren't too young to fall in love," Beatrice aptly pointed out.

The whole family often teased Beatrice about being man-crazy and walking around in a romantic fog. But in this case, her sister had put her finger directly on the sore spot.

"True. But falling in love isn't the same as growing and nurturing it into something long-lasting," Grace said defensively. "Anyway, Mack didn't throw me over for another woman. There wasn't a woman."

Beatrice's eyes grew wide. "I don't understand. If—"

Shaking her head, Grace interrupted her. "It's a long story and this is hardly the place to talk about what happened. So help me find a dress. I want to look nice, but not like I've tried too hard. You know what I mean?"

"Sure. You want to look effortlessly gorgeous and sexy."

Grace let out a short laugh. She hadn't been intimate with a man since she and her husband had divorced more than five years ago. She'd practically forgotten how it felt to feel and think of herself as a desirable woman.

"Something like that," she said. "Cleo tells me you have a denim midi dress that she thinks is made just for me. Do you still have it in my size?"

"Yes. But, sissy, it's not nearly sexy enough," Beatrice protested. "You need to look beautiful and sultry!"

"I'm neither of those things, but show me, anyway."

Beatrice looped her arm through Grace's and urged her forward. "Right over here are the latest things we've gotten in. And if you want my opinion, you should get something in green to go with your eyes. He won't be able to tear his gaze away from your face."

Grace cut her sister a crafty glance. "You think it's my face I want him to notice?"

Beatrice stared at her a moment, then giggled and waggled her eyebrows in a suggestive way. "I'm shocked. My big sister has a naughty streak." She rifled through the garments on the rack in front of them until she reached a winter white dress. "So you need something like this to lure his eyes downward. It wraps across your body and has a slit up one leg. Add a pair of tall fashion boots and a pair of dangling earrings, and Mack will think you're smoking hot."

Grace rolled her eyes. "I'm not so sure about the smoking part. But—"

Beatrice interrupted by thrusting the dress into Grace's hands. "No *buts*. Go try it on while I check on the other customers."

Mack had always thought Grace was beautiful. No matter if she'd been on her knees pulling weeds from her grandfather's rose garden, or all dressed up for Sunday church services, her tall, regal stature, honey-blond hair and sparkling green eyes had always awed him. But tonight she seemed even more lovely and he was trying to decide if it was a result of the sexy white dress she was wearing, or the alluring little smile on her lips.

"Do I have lipstick on my teeth or something?" she asked. "For the past five miles you've been giving me odd looks."

Twenty minutes ago, they'd dropped off Kitty and Ross with her parents at the main ranch house on Stone Creek. Now, as Mack maneuvered his truck over the last of the rough dirt road leading off Hollister land, he glanced over at Grace and thought how incredibly glad he was to be with her like this. With no kids to interrupt, or her family surrounding them, or their phones jingling with calls from patients.

"Your lipstick isn't out of place. I'm giving you odd looks because I'm trying to figure out why you look so extra-beautiful tonight. Did you spend part of the day at the spa or take a long beauty nap?"

Her warm laugh made him smile.

"If only I had time for such things." She leveled a provocative smile at him. "I just cleaned up a little better tonight. That's all."

With a negligible shake of his head, he turned his eyes back on the road. "Grace, sometimes you give me the impression that you think of yourself as plain or undesirable. Hell, even saying the idea out loud sounds ridiculous. But that's the feeling I get from you."

From the corner of his eye, he could see her turning her face toward the passenger window. "I'm not in my twenties anymore. Those years are gone. I'm a mother and a doctor. And I look the part. But I don't fret over that. I like myself as I am."

"I like you as you are, too," he said gently. "No, let me change that. I like you better as you are now, Grace. Older, wiser, sexier. Yes, and even prettier."

Turning her head, she studied him thoughtfully for

a moment and then she reached across the console for his hand.

"If you want the truth, I like you better now, too. So I suppose the years have been kind to us. And in spite of them, we're together...again."

He squeezed her hand. "That's the nicest part of all."

She fell silent after that and Mack wondered what she was thinking. Was she having reservations about being with him? Was she thinking they shouldn't be more than friends?

Hell, Mack, why are you worrying? She agreed to this date. She's holding your hand. She's looking at you with a warm light in her eyes. What more do you want?

He couldn't answer the taunting voice in his head. Not exactly. Except that maybe he needed to hear Grace say, in spite of all the passing years, she'd always held him in a corner of her heart.

He cleared his throat and asked, "Where would you like to eat? We can drive down to Cedar City if you want. We'd have more restaurants to choose from."

"Let's not waste time driving. Anyway, there are plenty of good places to eat in Beaver. Even the Wagon Spoke."

"Yes, the food is delicious there. But—" He was thinking of some place with dim lighting and soft music. Someplace quiet, where they wouldn't likely be interrupted by persons wanting free medical advice. "I was thinking we might enjoy Ten Pines. It's a bit out of town, but the view is beautiful."

She slanted him an amused look. "Every view in

Beaver County is beautiful. But Ten Pines will be a treat. I've not been out there in ages."

"Neither have I, so it will be a treat for both of us."

The restaurant called Ten Pines was located about two miles from town, perched on the side of a foothill overlooking the west end of the valley. During the summer months, most of the diners vied for a table on the terrace, but at this time of year, the icy winds whipping through the canyon kept the outdoor dining closed.

Still, Mack and Grace managed to snag a table next to the plate glass wall that partitioned the indoor seating from the terrace. From their vantage point, they could see the lights of town below and watch the snowflakes drift past the window and settle on the planked flooring of the deserted deck.

"Too bad the weather isn't warm enough to go out on the terrace," Mack said.

Before Mack had sat down at the table, he'd removed his hat and leather jacket, and now, as the two of them sipped wine and waited for their meal to arrive, Grace tried not to stare at the way his dark hair waved loosely back from his rugged features and tickled the collar of his white shirt. She tried not to notice the way his broad shoulders flexed as he reached for his glass, or the way his brown eyes warmed in the glow of the single fat candle in the middle of the table. But drinking in his image was like a balm to her scarred heart and tonight she couldn't seem to get enough of it.

"It's pretty with the snow falling," she told him. "And the quietness is lovely. I'm glad you thought of this place."

A wry smile slanted his lips. "We came here together once before. Remember? It was right before you left to go to college in Salt Lake City. I wanted to do something nice for you. But I barely had enough money to pay for our meal."

Her gaze roamed his face. "Yes, I remember. When you mentioned eating here tonight, I wondered if you'd forgotten that time."

He reached across the table and she gladly placed her hand in his.

"I don't think I've forgotten anything about us," he said quietly. "The things we did…how we felt. Time blurs some memories, but not all of them."

How well she knew, Grace thought. Even when she'd been married to Bradley, there had been countless times that Mack had drifted into her thoughts. Had he finished his veterinarian schooling? Had he married a woman he was wildly in love with? And had she made him happier than Grace could have ever made him? Merely asking herself those questions about Mack while she'd been Bradley's wife had made her feel guilty and ashamed. Yet now she understood that, right or wrong, the human heart couldn't be controlled.

"You know what I think?" she asked softly. "We're making even better memories now—tonight."

"Even better. Yes, I like to think so, too."

He'd barely finished speaking the words when the waiter arrived with their meal. Grace reluctantly drew her hand from his and forced her attention on the food, but all during the meal, she could feel some invisible something drawing them together. And Mack must have been feeling it, too.

As soon as dinner was over, they didn't linger. Mack took care of the bill and they left the warm confines of the building. His hand held hers tightly as they walked across the parking lot to his truck, and once they reached the passenger door, he didn't say a word. He simply pulled her into his arms and fastened his mouth over hers.

Grace had no idea she could feel such heat while standing in subfreezing temperature, but she was quickly learning it was possible. Mack's hungry kiss was making her whole body feel as if it was glowing and melting right there in his arms.

Their passionate kiss continued until footsteps crunching against the snow and the low exchange of voices could be heard at the opposite side of the parking lot.

With a reluctant groan, Mack pulled away from her and opened the door. "Let's get out of here," he murmured.

"Yes."

The one word was all she said as he helped her into the truck and quickly took his place behind the steering wheel.

Once he'd started the engine and driven out of the parking lot, he looked over at her.

"Where would you like to go now?"

If she wanted to play it safe, there were many places she could have told him to take her. But Grace had played it safe for far too long. For the past few years she'd felt as if her life had been hanging in limbo and she'd been waiting for something, or someone, to come along and push her on a forward path.

"To my house," she answered. "Where we can be alone."

Chapter Eight

Mack had never been inside the redbrick house Grace called home and normally he would've asked her to show him around the place. But once they'd removed their coats and were standing in the middle of the living room, he didn't give her time to switch on the overhead lights. Instead, he snagged an arm around her waist and pulled her close.

"Don't bother with the lights," he whispered against her lips. "We don't have time for anything…but this."

With a tiny groan of pleasure, she parted her lips beneath his and wrapped her arms around his neck.

The movement caused the front of her body to arch into his and he closed his eyes at the undulating pleasure of having her breasts pressing into his chest, her legs brushing against his.

Somewhere across the room he heard the ticking of

a wall clock, and outside, the sound of a car faded into the distance. The quietness reminded him that they were truly alone, and for one split second the reality shook the floor beneath his boots.

Lifting his head, he gently cupped his hand beneath her chin and lifted her face toward his. "Grace, what if this is a mistake? What if you regret making love to me?"

Her gaze remained riveted to his. "What if *you* regret it?"

He smoothed the pads of his thumbs over her cheeks. "You're not supposed to answer a question with a question."

A tiny smile tilted the corners of her lips. "And you're not supposed to question anything that feels like this. Unless…you're not feeling what I'm feeling."

The low, seductive sound of her voice caused something deep in his gut to do a somersault and he slipped his hands to her back and pulled her even tighter against him.

"Oh, I'm feeling it, all right," he muttered helplessly, then dropped his mouth back down to hers.

This time the kiss they shared was hot and hungry, and in a matter of seconds, desire flooded his body and robbed the last bit of breath in his lungs.

Forcing his head up, he gulped in a ragged breath. "Maybe we ought to go to your bedroom so I can show you exactly what I'm feeling."

She reached for his hand and as she led him out of the shadowy room and down a long hallway, he wondered if he might be dreaming and in the next few moments he'd wake up and find himself pitching hay to cattle on the Broken B, or treating a sick dog at the clinic.

But as she guided him through an open door and over to a queen-size bed covered with a white comforter, everything suddenly became very real. After switching on a tiny lamp near the head of the bed, she turned and began releasing one snap after another on the front of his shirt. As the fabric parted, her lips pressed against the heated skin of his chest and the intimate contact caused him to suck in a harsh breath and anchor his hands on the tops of her shoulders.

"Grace, do you know what it means to me—having you touch me like this? Want me like this?" he asked hoarsely.

A coy smile curved her lips. "As a doctor, I'd say your body is reacting to stimuli and what you're feeling is a mix of chemicals rushing to your brain, telling the part of it that registers pleasure that you want me."

He growled a gentle protest. "Take off your lab coat, Doc. There's more than my brain at work here."

"Yes," she whispered. "There's something magical. Something that time can't erase."

Dropping his head, he buried his face in the side of her neck and breathed in the sweet scent of her skin. "Mmm. You taste so good. Feel so good in my arms."

As he pressed a trail of kisses beneath her ear and onto her jaw, she groaned with gratification. At the same time, her fingers curled into the flesh of his bared chest.

"I've been dreaming of this," she said thickly. "For far too long."

Lifting his head, he spoke against her lips. "This is where the dreaming stops and the real thing begins."

"Show me, Mack. Show me."

He shrugged out of his shirt and tossed it aside, then reached for the knotted tie at the side of her waist. Once he'd worked the two sashes free, the front of her dress fell apart to reveal a skimpy set of lingerie. The lace was very nearly the same color as her skin and at first glance she appeared nude.

Easing slightly back from her, he made a slow perusal of her womanly curves. "I would've never guessed a doctor dressed like this," he said with a lusty growl.

Laughing softly, she reached out and smoothed her hands over his muscled chest and down the length of his strong arms. "You might not know it, but some of us doctors are even born naked."

"Scandalous," he murmured before pressing his grinning lips to hers.

As he kissed her, he pushed the cream-colored dress off her shoulders and it fell to the floor not far from where his shirt was lying. With the dress out of the way, he removed her bra and then her panties. Once she'd stepped out of them, he pulled her into his arms, deliberately squashing her breasts against his bare chest.

To have her soft flesh molding to his, to be able to glide his hands over her hot velvety skin, was almost more pleasure than Mack could bear and he knew it was going to be a fight to hold himself together.

A groan of pleasure rippled from her throat as she slipped her arms up and around his neck. The arch of her slender body lured his hands down to the curve of her buttocks and, cupping his fingers around their fullness, he tugged her hips into his.

The contact sent a shaft of heat straight to his loins and his teeth snapped together as he tried to fight off the urge to toss her onto the bed and drive himself into her warm womanhood.

Tearing his mouth from hers, he lowered his head and slid his lips over the mound of one breast. "Grace, I think this is…too good. I—"

Before he could go on, she pushed her hands into his hair and urged his head back up to hers. "I think it's time you take off these jeans," she whispered urgently. "Before I melt right here in your arms."

The need in her voice matched the desperation that was twisting his insides into helpless knots and his hands shook as he sank onto the edge of the bed and tugged off his cowboy boots.

When the second boot fell with a clunk to the floor, Grace planted a hand in the middle of his chest and pushed him backward against the mattress.

"Save your strength," she told him. "Let me finish this for you."

Bending over, she grabbed the hems of his jeans and as she pulled them down over his feet. Mack's throat tightened with emotions that seemed to rush at him from every direction and confuse the circuitry in his brain. This wasn't a time to be feeling with his heart, to be getting sentimental, he thought. This was all physical. Nothing more.

After she'd put aside the jeans and slipped off his

socks, she crossed the room, shut the door and turned the lock.

"Are you expecting company?" he asked.

She walked back to the side of the bed and Mack pushed aside his wayward thoughts as he watched her naked body move with lithe elegance and her gold-blond hair swing against the top of her shoulders.

She switched off the lamp by the bed to leave the interior of the room a mixture of gray and black shadows.

She said, "No. I just want to feel as though we're truly alone. That we're in this closed room where no one can part us."

Mack linked a hand around her wrist and pulled her down next to him. "I like your way of thinking. Because right now if the roof was on fire I don't think I could leave you or this bed."

She rolled into him and he sighed with pleasure as she slipped her arm around his side and snugged the front of her body next to his.

"Mmm. That might make for some extremely hot lovemaking." She kissed his cheek, then traced the line of his jaw with her fingertips.

A coarse chuckle rose from deep in his throat. "We don't need a fire on the roof for that. We can make plenty of our own heat."

Tilting her head back, she looked into his eyes and the warm gentleness he saw in the brown depths caused his throat to grow even thicker.

"Oh, Mack, I never thought this would happen for us. I feel like I'm in a dream. I'm afraid if you don't hold me tight it will all end."

Sliding his hand in her silky hair, he cupped the back of her head and drew her lips to his. "My sweetheart, I'm not going to loosen my hold on you. I promise."

A tiny moan vibrated past her lips and then she began to kiss him with a hunger that made him forget everything, except taking what she was so generously offering and trying to give a part of himself back to her.

With his hands roaming over heated skin, his lips tracking kisses and nibbles across her breasts and belly, the desire burning in Grace grew to such mammoth proportions that she was fairly certain her body was going to split apart. Was that possible? Was it possible for any woman to feel as she did at this moment?

The questions were rifling through her mind, when he finally eased away from her and leaned over the edge of the bed to reach for his jeans.

"What's wrong?" she asked.

"I have a condom in my wallet," he explained.

"There's no need for that." She placed a hand on his upper arm and urged him back to her. "I'm protected with the pill. And I've not had sex in…well, in five years."

The look of faint surprise that danced across his face was swiftly followed by a rueful smile. "This is kind of embarrassing to admit, but I've not had sex since… Kitty. She's five years old. Now you're thinking I need a therapist, not a condom."

"Then you must be thinking the same thing about me," she said.

"No," he said with a tiny shake of his head. "I'm believing that all we need is…each other."

Wrapping her arms around him, she tugged him toward her and he quickly positioned himself over her. Instinctively, her thighs opened to allow him entry, and as he lowered his body down to hers, she gripped his arms and whispered, "Love me, Mack. Now."

And always.

Her heart was crying out the last two words as he entered her, but she didn't give voice to them. No. Talking about the future could wait until later. Until she was sure he wanted them to have a *forever* together.

And suddenly any thought of the future was wiped from her mind as the incredible sensation of having him inside her—moving, gliding, teasing her with more and more—overwhelmed her senses.

Somehow she'd always known that making love to Mack would be unlike anything she could've ever imagined. And she'd been right. Her whole body was glowing with intense heat and a pleasure that was so splendid, she couldn't believe her heart could continue to beat, that her lungs could maintain the ability to draw one breath after another. Yet it wasn't just her body that was receiving an overload of gratification. Her thoughts were strolling through the Milky Way, hanging from a star and jumping over the moon. She was on a trip she never wanted to end.

She was gulping for air, wondering how much longer she could keep going, when she felt his strokes quicken and his hands slide beneath her buttocks to lift her hips upward. With her legs wrapped around his, she strained to give him more, while searching for the relief she desperately needed.

His mouth found hers, his tongue dipped between her teeth and then suddenly he was driving into her at a frantic pace.

Grace's breaths became nonexistent, but the lack of oxygen hardly mattered. She heard his low grunt of satisfaction and then she was floating in a dark, endless sky, where Mack had her safely anchored in his arms.

Long moments passed before the undulating waves of pleasure finally ended and she was able to open her eyes. Yet even then, the room seemed to be in a lazy spin. Her lungs were fighting for oxygen as the weight of Mack's body crushed her deep into the down comforter.

His face was buried in the curve of her neck and she could feel his warm breath brushing across her skin. Next to her breast, his heart was pounding wildly, matching the frantic pace of hers.

Exhausted, yet feeling more replete than she could ever remember, she lifted a hand and smoothed her palm over his damp back.

He groaned and shifted his weight to one side, while keeping his arm tightly anchored around her waist. She snuggled her cheek to the middle of his chest and drew in the masculine scent of his skin.

"I hope you don't want to move," he said. "Because I want to keep you here—just like this—for as long as I can."

"Mmm. Don't worry. I couldn't move right now even if I wanted to."

His voice was low and raspy, and the sound of it caused the skin on her arms to erupt in tiny goose bumps.

He moved his head so that his forehead was touching hers. "There's nothing I can say to you right now, Grace, that wouldn't sound trite. So I'm not going to bore you with words like *wonderful* and *incredible* or *amazing*."

Her lips tilted upward. "How do you know they'd bore me?"

Chuckling, he dropped his face to the curve of her neck and began to plaster kisses over the soft skin.

"Oh, Grace, to me you're all those things and more," he whispered.

She tenderly trailed her fingers up and down the ridges of his backbone. "Have you ever thought you might be all those things to me and more?" she asked.

Easing his head back, he used his fingers to comb her tangled hair away from her face. "You deserve someone better than me. That's why I believed it was right for me to let you go all those years ago. So you could find someone who could give you financial security as soon as you married. But since then, especially now that I've come back to Beaver, I've learned something about myself."

Her eyes searched his face. "What have you learned?"

His lips formed a lopsided grin. "That I'm selfish. I don't want some other guy to have you."

In so many ways his words thrilled her, yet a part of her couldn't help but wonder how long he would want her solely for himself. Once before she'd believed the two of them would always be together. Would she be a fool for believing it now?

He touched a forefinger to the spot between her eyebrows. "There's a little line right here that wasn't there a moment ago. Did I say something wrong?"

Nothing was wrong, she thought. Except that when she looked at the future, uncertainty swirled through her. But she'd done her part in luring Mack back into her life. Now wasn't the time to start getting cold feet.

"Not at all. I was just thinking—" With a long sigh, she glanced across the darkened room. "There's something I should've already told you—about my marriage."

Frowning, he eased back, then propped his upper body on one elbow. "Your marriage? Oh, Grace, I don't need to know about that part of your life. Especially not tonight."

"Yes, tonight is the right time. Because I believe you have the wrong idea about…things. I've gathered from some of your comments that you think I'm a widow. But I'm not, Mack."

His jaw dropped. "Not a widow? Are you trying to tell me that Ross's father isn't really dead? If that's true—"

She clasped a hand around his forearm. "No. Bradley was killed in an auto accident. From what I was told, he'd received an emergency call in the middle of the night and was hurrying to the hospital to perform surgery. Another driver ran a red light and smashed into his vehicle. He died at the scene. But you see, when the accident occurred, we'd already been divorced for a few months and at that time Ross and I were living in an apartment far from Bradley's house. In fact, I was in the process of packing everything to be moved here to Beaver."

His expression turned thoughtful. "Divorced," he repeated. "Dad told me your husband was killed. I suppose he didn't know you were divorced. And no one else told me differently."

Grace rested the back of her head against the mattress and stared up at the dark ceiling. "With us living in Salt Lake City, not too many people knew about it. Some didn't even know I was married. See, Bradley only visited Stone Creek Ranch once and that was for one short day. He wasn't an outdoor person, at all."

"Hell."

He grunted the one word and she sighed with regret.

"You don't have to say it. You're wondering why I ever married such a man in the first place. Believe me, I asked myself that same question many times. My only explanation is that I wasn't seeing things as they really were. Yes, he was a successful surgeon and he could easily support me with a cushy lifestyle, but I wasn't concerned about any of that. I thought he loved me and he was very persuasive. He even agreed to move to Beaver with me and base his surgical practice here, or in Cedar City. It made me happy to think how much good we both could do by providing health care for the people in this area."

He smoothed his fingers down her arm. "What happened? Let me guess. He didn't think you or Beaver was enough to lure him away from a profitable practice in Salt Lake?"

Long ago, Grace had accepted the fact that she'd

been foolish to ever marry Bradley, but not until tonight, until she'd actually explained it out loud to Mack, did she understand just how much she'd gone off track and set herself up for a collision course.

Nodding, she said, "When I finally received my license to practice medicine and started making plans to move to Beaver, that's when he started balking. After that I tried. I kept hoping he'd have a change of heart. If anything, he began to show his true colors. And he finally admitted that he wasn't working sixteen-hour days because he wanted to save lives. For him it was all about the money and he couldn't make money living and working in a one-horse town."

"What about Ross? He must have been a baby at that time. Didn't your ex-husband care anything about his son?"

Closing her eyes, Grace tried to swallow the bitterness rising up in her throat. "His attitude toward Ross is the worst part of the whole ordeal. During the days after I'd given birth to Ross, Bradley put on the act of a proud father. But after a few weeks he didn't bother. He rarely took time to acknowledge his son. He wasn't really interested in being a father."

She opened her eyes to see Mack's expression had turned hard and resolute. "What a first-class ass."

Grace grimaced. "When I told him I was getting a divorce he made noises about a custody fight. But I didn't take it seriously. I knew it was only talk. He didn't want to be bothered with a child."

His sigh was rueful. "Ross is such a fine boy. I hope he never learns how his father felt about him."

"He'll never hear it from me," Grace said. "That's why, as soon as the divorce was final, I had mine and Ross's last name changed to Hollister. I didn't want either of us to have any lingering connection to Bradley and I especially wanted Ross to have our family name. He asked me once why his name wasn't the same as his father's and I simply told him that with his father dying so long ago it was better this way. In years to come, he'll probably ask deeper questions. But I'll deal with those as gently as I can."

"Does Ross have other grandparents? Or aunts and uncles on the paternal side of his family?"

She shook her head. "Bradley's father died from cancer when Bradley was just a baby. Later when he was about ten, his mother died from a brain injury she suffered during a freak fall. After her death, an aunt and uncle in Seattle finished raising him. But once he was old enough to be on his own, he didn't stay in touch with them."

"That's rough," he said.

She grimaced. "Yes. But Bradley never was a family-oriented person. I found that out too late."

Silence fell between them for a moment and then Mack said, "There's no point in me acting like I'm shocked to hear your ex-husband's attitude about life and what he considered important. Because I'm not. Maybe I'm jaded, but I've seen firsthand how money means everything to some people." Lowering his head next to hers, he stroked his fingertips against her cheek. "Even me, Grace. And I'm sorry about that. Truly, truly sorry."

Stunned by the anguish in his voice, she shifted onto her side and looked into his eyes. "What are you talking about, Mack. Money has never been your motive for becoming a veterinarian. Even though we've been apart for a long time, I don't have to wonder what pushes you to work. It's always been about the animals."

The corners of his mouth turned downward. "Yes. But when we were young I let money stand in the way of us being together. I thought...hell, I wanted everything to be perfect for you. I wanted enough money to be able to give you the best of things. For most of my mother's life, I saw her do without. Not that she was unhappy. She wouldn't have changed anything about her life, but I wanted more than hard work and making do for you. And then when I realized it would be years before I'd be making a decent income, I—"

"Made up the story that you'd found someone else to love," she said flatly, then shook her head. "Mack, there's a huge difference in wanting money to help others and wanting it for yourself. But...you were wrong, anyway."

"Thanks," he said, then to soften the sarcasm in his voice, he turned his head and pressed his lips to her forehead. "I guess I needed to hear you set me straight."

Curling her hand over the ridge of his shoulder, she urged him closer. "What I'm trying to say is that all I ever wanted was you. That's all I needed to make me happy."

"And now?"

Snaking a hand at the back of his neck, she pulled

his lips down to hers. "You've made me very happy," she whispered.

"Grace. My darling. It's always been you. Only you."

Her heart full, she turned in his arms and wrapped her lips over his.

The following Monday afternoon, Mack was finishing suturing a wound on a horse's shoulder when Oren strolled into the treatment area wearing a red Santa's cap and a goofy grin on his face.

"Ho ho ho!" he proclaimed. "Thanks to Eleanor and Ira we now have a Christmas tree in the waiting area. With blinking lights, candy canes and the whole works."

Mack focused on tying a knot in the surgical thread and clipping the end. "That's nice. But I hate to think how long the tree might last if a cat or dog gets lose from its leash or carrier."

"Aw, Mack, don't be a humbug." Oren pulled off the cap and levered his black Stetson onto his head. "No pets have gotten loose yet. And it's nice for our clients. Besides, it's time you showed a little excitement. Or could be you're worried you've been too naughty to get any gifts."

Mack had already been given a gift, he thought. When Grace had invited him into her bed two nights ago, she'd given him more than he could have ever hoped for. Throughout the whole weekend, he'd been walking around in a blissful fog. But coming to work this morning had jerked him back to reality and the more he thought about Grace, the more he wondered what she wanted from their relationship or where she expected it to go. Not once that night, or even yesterday before they'd parted, had she mentioned anything about having a future with him. And more importantly, she'd not so much as hinted that she was in love with him.

Saturday night, after they'd had sex a second time, he'd come close to telling her that he had no intention of ever letting her go. A part of him had wanted to confess that she already owned a major part of his heart. But that would've been the same as saying "I love you." And he wasn't at all sure that she wanted to hear something that serious from him. After all, he'd sworn he'd loved her before and then let her down badly. Now, if he spoke the words to her, he wasn't sure she'd believe him. And he couldn't blame her.

"I don't imagine I've been any naughtier than you," he told Oren, while trying to keep a note of frustration from his voice. It wasn't his assistant's fault that he didn't have the courage to simply take Grace in his arms and tell her how much he loved her. How much he wanted her and Ross to make their home on the Broken B with him and Kitty. "And right now I'm not worried about Christmas gifts. I'm worried about keeping up with all the appointments and walk-ins we're getting. How many are left in the waiting room?"

"Five, I think. Three dogs and two cats. Uh, better make that six—there's a rabbit."

Mack painted the horse's wound with an antibacterial medication, then carefully covered the top part of the sewn flesh with a bandage.

"Okay. I'm finished here. Would you take Peanut back to a recovery stall?"

"Aren't you going to cover the whole thing?" Oren took a closer look at the injury on the buckskin's shoulder, then glanced at Mack. "This will get dirty, won't it? Sorry. Who am I to question a vet?"

"You can't learn without asking questions. And since you weren't here when the horse was brought in, a bull gored him. The wound is fairly deep, so it's going to need to drain for several days." Mack removed his latex gloves, then pointed to a spot where the sutures stopped. "See—I purposely left this area open for that purpose. Otherwise, the shoulder would swell up like a balloon. Didn't your prior boss do things like this?"

Shaking his head, Oren said, "I recall him putting in drain tubes. To tell you the truth, he didn't do much with big animals. His practice was mostly cats, dogs, some birds and reptiles."

"Well, in this case, a tube isn't feasible. Give Peanut about two minutes and he'd wrap his teeth around it and then you'd find the darned thing stomped in the ground." Mack patted Oren's shoulder. "You're learning. That's good. Now, what do you know about treating a cow who's lost her cud?"

Oren said, "Enough to know it can be complicated to treat her."

"Okay. When you get Peanut settled, join me in the cattle pen and maybe you can learn something else today."

Leaving Oren to deal with the horse, Mack quickly strode down the hallway to his office to fetch his jacket and cell phone. After jerking on the denim ranch coat, he grabbed the phone from the corner of the desk and, in the process, spotted a text message on the screen. A quick glance revealed it was from Grace and he paused to read the short note.

Ross has a small part in a school play tomorrow night— 7:30. If you're not too busy we'd love for you and Kitty to come. Let me know.

Because they'd spent most of the weekend together, Mack hadn't been expecting to hear from her anytime soon. The fact that she was already reaching out to him was enough to push away the doubts that had been circling around in his head.

Time, he thought. That's all he needed to convince Grace that this time around he'd not leave her for any reason. In time, she would begin to see how much he wanted her to be his wife and Kitty and Ross to be their children, not just his daughter and her son.

Quickly, he typed. Barring any emergencies, we'll be there.

After pushing the send arrow, Mack slipped the phone into his coat pocket and hurried out to the cattle pen, where Oren was waiting to help him treat the cow.

The next evening cold wind was whipping across the school parking lot as Grace hurried her son toward the building. In spite of the weather being frigid, the numerous parked vehicles were a sign that the auditorium would be filled with parents and friends waiting to see the children's play about a fantasy trip to toy land.

Ross's head swiveled back and forth as he peered at

the rows of cars and trucks. "Mom, are you sure Mack and Kitty are coming? I don't see their truck anywhere in the parking lot."

Grace tried to reassure him. "Unless there's an emergency Mack has to deal with, I'm sure they'll make it. Right now you've got to think about getting into your costume and going over your lines to make sure you remember them."

"Gosh, Mom, I only have three lines."

"And you don't want to blow them."

His chin lifted to a confident angle. "I won't forget. You just watch. Kitty says I'll be the best elf of the whole bunch!"

Smiling, she playfully ruffled the top of his head. "You're always my best elf. And Kitty is right. You're going to do great."

As they neared the entrance of the building, Grace glanced over her shoulder to give the parking lot one last scan. There was still no sight of Mack's black truck, but there was still plenty of time for him and his daughter to get here before the play started. She didn't want to think about how disappointed Ross would be if they didn't s show up. But he wouldn't be the only one. Grace was more than eager to see Mack again.

Making love to him had shaken her from a long sleep and she felt as if she was just now able to see the world around her and experience the pleasure of really living. Now the sun seemed brighter, food tasted better and even the pop music Harper had been playing over the clinic intercom made her want to hum along to the tunes.

Perhaps she was being foolish to think that having Mack in her bed for one night was enough to bind him to her. Especially when he hadn't mentioned anything about love or the future. But her heart wasn't in any shape to listen to reason. It was too busy shouting that she loved him. That she would always love him.

Inside the building, Grace left Ross in a room full of energetic children and several teachers dealing with costumes and final instructions, then made her way to the lobby of the auditorium to wait for Mack and Kitty.

Twenty minutes later, the seats were beginning to fill with people and there was still no sign of Mack and Kitty. She was checking her phone to see if she'd received any messages from him when she spotted her mother and the twins emerging through a pair of double doors that made up the entrance to the auditorium.

As soon as they spotted Grace, they waved and headed toward her.

"Yay! We're not late," Bonnie exclaimed as she planted a sisterly kiss on Grace's cheek. "Mom nearly skidded off the road twice trying to get us here before the curtain rose."

Claire said, "Bonnie is exaggerating. I only fishtailed the truck one time. And that was because the road is slick, not because I was speeding."

Grace greeted each of the women with an appreciative hug. "I wasn't expecting you to be here."

Claire looked at her with faint amusement. "Then why are you standing out here in the lobby? Weren't you were waiting for us?"

Grace felt her cheeks turning pink. "No. Mack and

Kitty were planning to be here, but so far they've not shown up."

Beatrice shook her head. "I wouldn't hold out much hope on seeing them, sissy. I passed Mack's clinic less than an hour ago and the parking lot looked more like a car dealership than an animal hospital. Most likely he's still working."

Sunday, after she and Mack had picked up the children from Stone Creek, he'd taken them by his animal hospital and given Grace and Ross a tour of the place. She'd been very impressed with the facility and how much effort he'd put into place. Getting a view of his workplace had also given her a glimpse of how serious he was about his veterinarian practice and she was pleased that his business was thriving. He deserved the success. But just for tonight, she wished he could be here with her and Ross.

Grace tried to hide her disappointment from her mother and sisters, but she knew she must look crestfallen. "Oh," she said, "well, that's the way it is for a doctor. Even an animal doctor."

Claire patted her shoulder. "Don't let it get you down, sweetheart. You of all people should understand. But I wish you would've said something earlier—we could have picked up Kitty and brought her with us."

"It's okay, Mom. There will be another occasion. And it's so nice of all three of you to take time out to come tonight. Ross will be glad you're here," Grace said. Then, with the cheeriest smile she could muster, she glanced toward the open doorway leading into the auditorium. "I think I hear the music starting. We'd better find a seat."

* * *

Much later that night, as Mack tucked his daughter in bed, he could hardly bear to look at the tears running from the corners of her eyes.

"You can't keep crying, Kitty," Mack said gently. "You'll make yourself sick and then you really won't be able to see Ross. You'd have to stay in bed."

Her bottom lip quivered as she scrubbed her eyes with a pair of closed fists. "But he's going to be sad, Daddy. He wanted me to be there to see him in his elf suit. And we didn't go!"

Yes, Ross probably was sad, Mack thought dismally. The two children were growing closer every day and Mack regretted letting them down. Yet he felt even worse about disappointing Grace. Sure, it wasn't like the play was a major event, but it was important to Ross and Grace. Still, she was a doctor and she understood how it was to be overrun with patients or faced with emergencies. But understanding didn't take away the fact that he'd failed her.

Bending over the bed, Mack stroked his daughter's mussed hair away from her forehead. "I'm sorry. I've tried to explain I couldn't leave the animals sick and hurting. What if Mildred and Morris were hurt? Or if Rusty was sick? You wouldn't want me to leave the goats or the dog, would you?"

She pursed her lips as she considered his question, then reluctantly she shook her head. "No. I'd want you to make them all better. But I wanted to see Ross!"

Seeing another spurt of tears rush from her eyes, Mack decided now wasn't the time to remind Kitty that there would be more occasions like tonight, when she'd have to sacrifice because of her father's profession.

When he was working for the KO Ranch in Nevada there were times he'd had to work late, or climb out of bed in the middle of the night to tend to a horse or cow in distress. At times, he'd promised to do special things with Kitty, only later to be forced to postpone them. Yet the responsibilities he had on the KO hadn't included dealing with a demanding public. A public he now depended on to make a living for himself and his child.

But what did a little five-year-old girl know about responsibilities? he thought ruefully.

"You can call him tomorrow after school and explain what happened." He pressed a kiss to her damp cheek. "Now go to sleep, sweetie. It's well past your bedtime."

He turned off the bedside lamp, then, leaving the door ajar, slipped out of the bedroom.

As he started down the stairs, he realized the hour was too late to call Grace and the short text he'd sent her earlier tonight to let her know he was going to have to miss the play hadn't explained that he'd been overrun with patients at the clinic. In fact, he'd been so busy throughout the whole day that he'd not had a chance to eat anything since an early breakfast. Thankfully, while he'd been bogged down with dogs and cats, Eleanor had collected Kitty from school, kept her busy in the receptionist's office and had a to-go meal from the Wagon Spoke delivered to the clinic for his daughter's evening meal.

In the kitchen, he turned on a light over the cookstove, then rummaged around in the refrigerator for something to eat.

He found a plastic container of leftover spaghetti and meatballs along with a bottle of beer. Without bothering to heat the food, he grabbed a fork and sat down at the table to eat.

Halfway through the meal, the cell phone he'd slipped into his shirt pocket earlier began to vibrate. He was so dog-tired that for a moment he considered ignoring the phone. But it had been late when Oren had left the clinic for his long commute to get home and to make matters worse another round of snow had set in for the night. If Oren had any sort of trouble on the road, he might need Mack's help.

After a long swig of beer, he pulled out the phone and was totally surprised to find a text message from Grace.

Are you still up?

Mack didn't bother answering with a message. He punched her number and she answered after the first ring.

"So you haven't gone to bed," she said. "I was afraid to call. I didn't want to wake you."

Just hearing the sound of her sweet voice made everything more bearable. "I'm just now eating."

"Since lunch?" she asked with dismay.

"No, breakfast," he answered. "Working sixteen hours on toast and scrambled eggs isn't easy."

"It isn't good for you, either."

Closing his eyes, he swiped a hand over his face.

Thank God she didn't sound angry. Mack didn't think he could bear having her angry with him. "I was afraid you'd probably gone to bed. I planned to call you tomorrow to explain—"

She interrupted before he had a chance to say more.

"No need for explanations. I got your text shortly after the play started. And Beatrice had already told me the parking lot at your clinic was overrun with vehicles. It was easy to figure out you were bogged down with patients."

He sighed. "It's been one of those days. Everything from the mundane to extremely serious. On top of that, someone found a stray kitten that had been struck by a vehicle and brought it in thinking I might be able to save it."

"Tell me you managed to save it."

He used his thumb and forefinger to massage his closed eyelids. "I had it in surgery for about a half hour. One of its legs was broken and it suffered some serious facial lacerations. I had to sew a part of its ear back on. But when I left for home, he was alive. If he survives, I've decided I'm going to give the little fella to Kitty for a pet she can keep in the house. Once she learned Ross has cats in the house, she wants one, too."

"Aw, Mack. You're going to make me cry."

Another sigh slipped out of him. "Please don't. Kitty was still in tears when I left her bedroom. She's very upset with me. Which is bad enough. But letting you and Ross down is making me feel like a heel. I hope he wasn't too angry with me."

"Ross was disappointed, not angry. He might be only

seven, but he understands adults have lots of responsibilities. Anyway, Mom and the twins were there and
you'll never guess who else showed up to support his
little nephew—Flint. We were already seated and the
curtain had just gone up when he slipped into a seat
behind us. He surprised us all."

Grace's younger brother worked as a deputy sheriff
for Beaver County and his job schedule made Mack's
look like child's play. In fact, Thanksgiving Day on
Stone Creek was the first time Mack had seen the man
in months, unless he counted the few times he'd spotted
him driving down the street in a patrol vehicle.

"Wow. Flint has really made me look bad."

She said, "Not hardly. It was pure chance that his
shift happened to end in time for him to stop by the
school and join us. As for Dad and my other brothers,
they were all too tied up with work on the ranch to attend. You know how it is at this time of year."

Mack took another long swig of beer and stared
across the kitchen to a door leading out to the back
porch. Next to the door, a wall rack made from deer
antlers held one of his work jackets and an old felt hat
he wore while working here on the ranch. For years, his
father had always hung his work gear on the same rack.
A plaid wool coat, the red and brown colors faded to
melon and rust. A brown felt hat with the brim split in
the center from being tugged too many times. Those
things were no longer hanging next to Mack's and the
empty spaces on the rack made him realize he missed
his father, now more than ever. He needed Will's quiet

strength and sage advice. Even more, he needed his father's love. Something little Ross had never known.

Pulling his thoughts back to the present, Mack said, "Yeah, I know how it is, so I'm glad some of your family was there. But let me try to make up for my absence. What about the four of us meeting up to have hamburgers or something at the Wagon Spoke tomorrow night?"

There was a slight pause and then she said, "I'd love that, Mack, but unfortunately, I have a meeting at the hospital tomorrow night with some of the other local doctors. Something about the town's emergency-management readiness."

"Okay, then what about the night after that? Hopefully, on my end of things, there won't be a flood of desperate patients show up at quitting time."

"I'd like that very much. I'll tell Harper to keep my appointments as light as possible that afternoon." She paused and then her voice grew softer. "I can't wait to see you again, Mack."

He groaned as the need to be close to her very nearly overwhelmed him. "Grace, I've had hell trying to keep my mind on my work these past couple of days. Even when I close my eyes, I see you wherever I look. We need to be together again. Alone. But...after the mess I've made of tonight, we can't leave the kids behind Thursday night. They'd never forgive us."

She sighed. "Naturally, we can't leave the kids behind. You and I will have to wait. Maybe we can find time just for us this weekend?"

The thought of being in her arms again, kissing her, holding her warm naked body next to his was enough to cause his loins to tighten with need. "Yes," he said thickly. "We'll try to figure something out when we take the kids to the Wagon Spoke. How does that sound?"

"Wonderful," she said softly. "And until I see you, give the little stray kitty some extra love from me, will you?"

"Softie," he teased. "You'd never make it as a doctor."

Her laugh was low and knowing. "I'll try to harden my heart."

"Don't you dare. I want your heart just as it is."

There was a long pause and then she whispered, "Good night, Mack."

"Good night."

She ended the connection and Mack set aside the phone to finish his meal. But instead of digging into the container of spaghetti, he sat gazing around the empty kitchen. Would he ever see Grace sitting here as his wife? Or had he already made too many mistakes with her to even hope she might come to love him that much?

Chapter Nine

The next two days turned into a whirlwind for Grace and the whole staff at Pine Valley Clinic. Along with the emergency-management meeting, which had taken up her entire Wednesday evening, the clinic had been bombarded with flu cases. She'd seen patients as young as toddlers all the way up to folks in their nineties, one of whom she'd had to hospitalize with severe lung congestion.

Now, as the day progressed into the late afternoon, the waiting room was still filled with coughing, feverish patients, waiting for Dr. Hollister to give them some sort of relief.

After tossing a wooden tongue depressor in a trash receptacle, Grace peered into the ears of an eight-year-old boy, then fastened her stethoscope and listened to the child's lungs.

"Do you think he needs a shot, Dr. Hollister?"

The middle-aged mother had finally taken a seat in the corner of the examining room, only after Grace had insisted she needed more working space around examining table.

Grace said, "No. In this case, he doesn't need an injection."

The woman sniffed. "Well, my sister says the only way you can get over this crud really quick is to get a shot. Not to waste time on a bunch of pills."

And who exactly is the doctor here? Grace wanted to ask the woman. Instead, she bit down on her tongue and was drawing in a weary breath as the young patient began to bang the heels of his athletic shoes against the end of the gurney table.

"Don't tell her that, Mom!" he loudly complained. "I don't wanna shot!"

"Now, Barry, don't give me, or Dr. Hollister any trouble. If she says you need a shot, you'll get one!"

Grace mentally counted to three before she removed the stethoscope from her ears. "Believe me, Mrs. Willard, a round of oral antibiotics will take care of your son's illness. He's fortunate. His case is mild."

The woman looked outraged as she scooted to the edge of the plastic chair and stared at Grace. "Mild! How can you say that? My son has been coughing his head off! And—"

"Excuse me, Mrs. Willard, I'll be back in a minute."

Not giving the woman a chance to reply, Grace hurried out of the room before she lost her temper and said something she'd later regret.

Out in the hallway, she met Cleo headed in the direction of the waiting area. The weary nurse was carrying a mop and bucket and her ever-present smile.

"What are you doing with those things?" Grace asked. "We don't have time for cleaning!"

"Someone vomited in the waiting room," Cleo explained. "I can't leave the mess in the floor!"

With a helpless groan, Grace asked, "Where's Poppy? I need some help."

"Taking a patient's vitals."

Grace grabbed the mop and bucket from Cleo's hands. "Right now, I'd rather deal with the vomit. Take a flu instruction sheet to exam room two and give it to Mrs. Willard. Tell her that Barry's prescriptions will be called in to her pharmacy."

Cleo darted her a concerned look. "So you're finished with them?"

More than finished, Grace thought. Then, feeling a bit ashamed of herself, she said, "Yes. And please go over the instruction sheet with the woman before you let them go. Not that she'll listen, but give it a try."

"Right." Cleo turned to go, then paused. "Uh, when you get finished with the floor, your next patient is waiting in exam room three."

"I'll be there as fast as I can," Grace assured her.

Forty minutes later, Grace could see that meeting Mack for dinner at the Wagon Spoke was going to be impossible. Between patients, she hurried to her office and rang his cell phone to give him the disappointing news.

When he failed to answer, she left a message in his voice mail explaining the situation and promised to call him as soon as she could.

* * *

The next day Mack didn't get a call from Grace. But shortly after lunch, he did receive a text message saying she'd been bombarded with flu patients and this evening she was going to have to make hospital rounds.

He was trying to decide how to reply when Eleanor walked into his office with a small note in her hand.

"A rancher by the name of Rollins just called. Says he needs your help—pronto. Do you think you can work in a house call today? Or should I try to put him off."

"What sort of problem is he dealing with?"

"The way he put it, he has a bunch of snotty-nosed cows and you'd know what he meant."

"Yeah. He needs help," Mack said as he raked a hand through his hair. "What do I have left on the appointment book for this afternoon?"

"Two cat neuters and a dog spay. The rest are annual vaccines for a couple of dogs and three cats."

"I'll take care of the neuters and spay. Call Rollins and tell him I'll be there in a couple of hours. Oh, and when Ira gets back from lunch, tell him I want him to handle the vaccinations, because I'm going to need Oren with me. And don't worry about Ira—I've been teaching him how to do the shots. He can handle it."

"I got it," she said with a nod, then added, "Oh, and some lady has a lizard she thinks is sick. I told her you don't do reptiles and suggested she take it down to the vet in Cedar City. The one Oren used to work for."

"Good girl, Eleanor. Have I told you today that you're brilliant?"

She gave him a cheeky smile, then winked. "No. But you might tell me now."

Rising to his feet, he slipped the phone into his shirt pocket and reached for his hat. "You're brilliant, Eleanor. I'll let you know when we're leaving for the Rollins ranch, but I have no idea when we'll get back. So you and Ira close up shop at regular office hours."

"Will do." She started out the door, then turned to cast a shrewd glance at him. "Uh, what about you and Grace? Remember, I kept this afternoon purposely light so you could get out of here in time to meet her for dinner."

He fought off the curse word he wanted to spit out. Eleanor didn't need to know just how thin his patience was wearing over his efforts to be with Grace again.

"No need to worry about that now," he said flatly. "Grace is tied up. To hear her tell it, half the town is down with the flu."

Eleanor grimaced. "Grace is right. Everywhere you go people are sick. So you just get that sulky tone out of your voice. I imagine she's had very little rest or sleep. Keeping herself and her little son healthy is what you ought to be worried about."

"Damn it, Eleanor, I agree with what you're saying. I am worried about her not getting enough rest. Of being exposed to all that sickness. All I'm asking for is a chance to see her. Is that asking too much?"

"Maybe it is. If I remember correctly you missed going to her son's little Christmas play. But that was different, right?" she asked in a sweetly mocking voice.

With a helpless groan, he walked over to where she

stood in the open doorway. "Did I just say you were brilliant?"

She gave him a smug smile. "You did."

He patted her cheek, then moved past her and said over his shoulder, "Well, I was right. You are."

With a little wave, she headed back to her office and as Mack strode on to the surgery room, he reminded himself that Eleanor was being sensible and right. All that mattered was Grace and Ross's well-being. Seeing her again would have to come later. He only hoped the wait wouldn't be too much longer.

The next week passed with Grace and Mack playing a game of tag as they both tried to catch up to each other. Her patient load at the clinic was beginning to taper off, but she still had patients in the hospital, where she visited twice daily. Once in the early morning before her clinic opened and in the evenings after it closed.

She'd finally managed to speak with Mack in person yesterday, but only for a couple of minutes before an emergency had forced him to hang up. To be fair, he'd also been overrun with work at his animal hospital. To make matters worse, one of the hands who worked on the Broken B had come down with the flu and Mack was forced to also take care of the extra chores on the ranch.

In spite of their chaotic schedules they had been talking on the phone late at night. But by that time of the evening, she could hear the sheer exhaustion in his voice. Along with a dose of frustration. He wanted them to be together and so did she. Yet each time they planned to meet, something happened to squash their plans.

Yes, Grace understood the situation. In fact, each day that passed brought a clearer picture of the problem. She and Mack were far too busy to have a personal life. Even if he did love her, when would he ever have the time or energy to show her that love? And she was just as guilty. When would she be able to give him and Kitty the love and attention they deserved?

Along with exhaustion, she was beginning to feel hopeless and defeated, but she was doing her best to hide it from Ross and her staff.

"Grace, you have an hour before your next patient. Mr. Thompson just called and canceled," Harper said as she stood in the doorway of Grace's office. "Why don't you get out of the clinic and have a nice lunch."

Cleo pushed past the receptionist and jerked Grace's coat off the rack. "Harper is right. Get out of here while you can. Go to the Wagon Spoke and have a nice hot meal—forget about this place for a bit."

Even as Grace shook her head, Cleo took hold of her arm and tugged her up from the executive chair.

"I have test results to go over and—"

"You need to eat," Cleo firmly interrupted. "No arguments, please."

The nurse tossed the coat around Grace's shoulders and practically pushed her out of the office.

"Okay. I get the message," Grace said with a groan of surrender. "You all want me out of here."

Outside, a cold wind whipped Grace's hair across her face as she walked to her car. High gray clouds promised more snow to come and with Christmas being only three days away, she figured the holiday would most likely end up being a white one.

Or more like a blue one for her, Grace thought dismally. For a while, after Mack had spent the night with her, she'd been making all sorts of plans in her head for the four of them to celebrate a special day together. But now, she had no idea what Mack was planning, or even if he'd be available to spend part of the holiday with her and Ross.

As for Ross, he'd been complaining every day about not seeing Kitty, and for the past several evenings she'd overheard him talking to her over the phone. Once when she'd passed by him, he stopped in midsentence, as though he didn't want his mother to hear what he was saying to the girl. Grace figured both children had been complaining to each other about their parents and she could hardly blame them. They'd both been neglected.

With the Wagon Spoke located only three short blocks from the clinic, Grace was there in less than two minutes. In spite of it being the middle of the afternoon, the place was still full, but she managed to find a table in the middle of the room.

Several diners, most of them working cowboys, were sitting at the bar that stretched along one wall of the café. Behind the counter, Rita, a redheaded waitress, was serving them coffee from a glass carafe. Music from a radio was playing in the background, while around her people were talking and chuckling over plates of home-style food.

The sights and sounds made Grace glad she'd listened to Harper and Cleo. It was nice to see happy people who weren't coughing or holding handkerchiefs to their noses.

"Dr. Hollister, this is a surprise," Laverne said as she approached Grace's table carrying a menu and a glass of ice water. "You've not been in to eat in ages!"

Grace gave the waitress a friendly smile. "Unfortunately, no, Laverne. I've been busy. This flu season has been especially bad."

The woman placed the glass of water and the menu directly in front of Grace. "Tell me about it," she said with a shake of her head. "Several of the waitresses have been out. I had to pull a few double shifts. But we're managing. You want a minute to look at the menu?"

"No. I want the special and about a gallon of coffee. It might keep me from falling asleep in my plate."

"Gotcha," she said with a wink. "And if you don't mind my saying, you look just as pretty as ever, Doctor. It amazes me how you've kept some man from snatching you up."

It was easy, Grace thought dismally, when the man she wanted in her life was too busy to do any snatching.

"I haven't found one who can keep up with me," she joked.

Laverne laughed. "I'll be back in a minute with your coffee."

A few minutes later, she was digging into the meal and sipping hot coffee when a male voice sounded directly behind her.

"Hey beautiful, mind if a hungry man shares your table?"

Glancing over her shoulder, she was more than surprised to see her brother Hunter. The wide grin on his face was just the dose of medicine she needed to lift her flagging spirits.

"Hunter!" Jumping to her feet, she hugged him tightly. "When did you get back to Beaver County?"

He kissed her cheek, then took a chair opposite from hers. "Last night."

Grace sank back into her seat and leaned eagerly toward him. With Hunter being on the road most of the year with his rodeo company, the Flying H, he was rarely home long enough to visit with his parents and siblings. "Seen Mom and Dad yet?"

He nodded, then removed his gray Stetson and placed it in the empty chair next to him. As the firstborn child of Claire and Hadley, Hunter was about to turn forty. Tall and husky with dark hair and blue eyes, he resembled their father more than any of the eight children.

"I stopped by this morning before I drove into town. They look great. Mom is chattering nonstop about the upcoming holidays and you know Dad. He opens up his wallet and lets her do whatever she wants."

Smiling wanly, Grace picked up her fork. "It makes Dad happy to spoil Mom and she adores pampering him."

"Yeah. Guess it's always been that way with them. Even way back, when times were lean, they never lost faith in each other. That's special, you know?"

Oh, yes, Grace knew. Long ago she realized how rare it was to find such a unique bond with another person. She'd believed she'd found it with Mack, especially after the two of them had come together after so many years apart. But now she was beginning to wonder if she was the only one holding on to the tenuous bond between them.

"We both know how special," she said quietly.

Laverne's sudden arrival at the table prevented Hunter from making any sort of reply and as he gave the waitress his order, Grace wondered exactly how much her brother thought about his ex-wife. Willow had been a lovely woman and, in spite of her being somewhat of a loner, she'd seemed proud to be a part of the Hollister family. Everyone had been stunned when she'd simply packed up and left without a word of explanation. Now the majority of the family believed Hunter was still pining for the woman. But Grace wasn't so sure he was pining. She'd always had the impression he was quietly seething over Willow's desertion.

"How long are you planning to be at home this time?" Grace asked.

"Until after the first of the year. Then we'll be going down to Texas and over to Louisiana."

She couldn't help but frown. "So far away? I was hoping you'd get to hang closer to home this coming year. Maybe get to know your siblings again?"

He slanted her a wry smile. "I have to follow the money, dear sister. Competition is stiff for rodeo companies. Especially smaller ones like mine. I'm grateful for the committees that offer me a contract."

"I understand. But we miss you."

Laverne arrived with a cup of coffee and a thermos-type pitcher so the two of them could help themselves to warm-ups. After she departed, Hunter eyed her thought-fully as he sipped his coffee.

"Mom tells me you've been working practically non-stop for the past couple of weeks. But don't tell me you're doing it for money. Like me."

Her lips pressed to a thin line as she glanced across the table at him. "Who are you kidding? You don't do what you do just for the money. You love producing ro-deos. And I doctor ailing folks because—" She paused as she realized there weren't enough words to explain why she'd devoted herself to caring for the health of her fellow man. "Well, it's my calling. Although, I have to admit, this month my job has been rather taxing."

Laverne appeared with Hunter's food and as Grace eyed the mountains of cholesterol and carbohydrates, she considered asking him if he was trying to eat his way to a heart attack, but kept the question to herself. This was the first time she'd seen Hunter in weeks and she wanted him to see her as a sister, not as a nagging doctor.

"The twins tell me you have a boyfriend," he said as he started to eat. "Or maybe I should've said you're back with your former boyfriend."

The fact that her younger sisters were spreading such news hardly surprised Grace. Both of them seemed very keen on the idea of Grace and Mack being together.

"Mack and I have been seeing each other. Or trying to see each other," she added. "We've both been tied up with our jobs. I imagine you've noticed the new animal hospital he's opened here in town."

"I have. I'm sure he's an excellent vet. Actually, I'll

probably be using him from time to time with some of my stock. And I've always liked Mack."

"I hear a *but* in your voice. You have reservations about him and me being together?"

He chewed a bite of the chicken-fried steak before answering. "I didn't say I have reservations."

"No. You didn't have to."

His fork paused midway to his mouth as he looked at her. "Okay. I'll be frank. I think you'd be better off finding someone else."

Finding? She'd not been looking for a man. He needed to understand a person didn't necessary search for love. It just happened. Like a star colliding with earth.

"You know, Hunter, I happened to believe a person can have more than one love in his or her lifetime. But only one will be the deep kind that roots down in your heart and stays there forever."

One of his eyebrows arched ever so slightly. "I'm hardly a romantic like you, Grace, so I'm not an authority on the subject. I only know that Mack hurt you terribly once. Why give him a chance to hurt you again? Besides, you have a good career and a wonderful son. Why take a risk on Mack?"

She could see where Hunter was coming from. Willow, his ex, had stabbed him right through the heart. He couldn't think about love without feeling the pain. But love was worth the risk, wasn't it? And since she and Mack had reunited, she'd come to realize more than ever how much she wanted to be a wife and a mother to more children. But how could she be those things and a doctor, too? Moreover, how could she ever expect to have a family with Mack when he barely had time for a phone call?

Sighing, she shook her head. "Maybe I'm crazy, Hunter. But I am sure about one thing. Mack is my one love. He always has been."

And that left a major question for Grace to answer. What did she intend to do about him and making the four of them a family?

"Daddy, why can't we go by and see Ross before we leave town? It's been days and days since I got to see him!"

As Mack steered the truck onto the highway that led out of town, he glanced in the rearview mirror at his daughter belted safely into the back seat. Her lower lip was sticking out a mile, and from the shaky sound of her voice, he expected tears to start any minute now.

"I realize that, Kitty. And I'm sorry it's been this way, but—"

"You're always saying you're sorry, Daddy! When are you ever gonna say 'okay—we'll go see Ross'?"

She was practically shouting at him, something she normally would never do. Her rebellious attitude jolted him. Mostly because he knew he was at fault. Damn it. He wasn't just ruining everything between him and Grace. He was making a mess of his relationship with his daughter.

Sometimes he wondered if he'd been wrong to ever insinuate himself back into Grace's life. Yes, he loved her. And without a doubt, he always would. But how could love fix their problems? Huge sacrifices would have to be made for them to ever be a real family of four. Would Grace be willing to make them? Would he?

"I don't know, sweetie," he said honestly. "I had hoped we might drop by Grace and Ross's tonight. But Seth is sick. So whenever we get to the ranch all the livestock in the barn will have to be fed and watered. Think you can help me with the chores?"

Her image in the mirror didn't look the least bit enthusiastic, but she let out a loud sigh of surrender. "I guess so."

"That's my girl."

A stretch of silence passed and Mack desperately wished he could say something to make her smile. But making her promises he might not be able to keep would only make the situation worse later on.

"Daddy, Christmas is going to be in two days. Are we going to be alone?"

A lump of emotion balled in his throat. Grace had promised to contact him as soon as she could to finalize their plans for the four of them to have Christmas on Stone Creek with her family, but so far today she hadn't called. And Mack was beginning to wonder if she'd changed her mind or something had happened to alter their plans. "I'm not sure. But I can promise you that Santa will deliver your gifts to the ranch on time."

Kitty's loud, sulky voice shot back at him. "I don't care if Santa comes or not! If Ross isn't with me it won't be any fun!"

For a split second, Mack considered pulling the truck to the side of the road and shaming his daughter for her behavior. She needed to understand she couldn't always have what she wanted. He should make the point of how she should be grateful for having plenty, when many little children had so little. But she was only five years old and Christmas was a magic time for her. Besides, how could he scold her when he was feeling just as miserable? As much as Kitty needed Ross to make her holiday a happy one, Mack needed Grace to cheer his heart.

For the remainder of the trip home, Mack didn't mention the upcoming holiday or when they might see Grace and Mack. Frankly, because he didn't have a clue as to what was going on with her. Yesterday, when she'd finally found a minute to call him, they'd only spoken briefly. She'd been apologizing for having to cancel their plans, then he'd been forced to end their conversation and rush to an emergency call. Later, when he'd tried to call her back, all he'd managed to get was her voice mail. Just trying to have a simple five-minute phone call with her was making him as frustrated as hell. Especially when he was just as guilty as her of letting work take precedence.

Nearly an hour later, Mack was pouring grain out for the two horses that sheltered in the barn each night, when he heard the phone in his jacket pocket ding with an incoming text message.

Expecting it to be Ira, who was staying overnight at the clinic to watch a pair of surgery patients, he was totally surprised to see Grace's name above the text.

Hope this finds you home. Ross and I are headed your way.

His mind whirling with this turn of events, he quickly typed two words and pushed the send arrow. We're here.

He slipped the phone back into his pocket and walked over to where Kitty was trying to coax one of the barn cats from behind a stack of hay. Thankfully, the rescue kitten he'd performed surgery on was now thriving. At least he could give Kitty the house cat she'd been asking for, he thought.

"I have a surprise for you," he told her.

Straightening from her crouched position, she put down the bowl of food and cast him a wary glance. Clearly, she wasn't expecting anything good to come out of her father's mouth.

"What kind of surprise?" she asked.

"We're going to have company. Grace and Ross are on their way here."

A look of incredible joy swept over her face. "Really? Right now?"

"Yes, really. And, yes, right now. So let's hurry and finish with things here in the barn."

With a little cry, she flung her arms around his legs and hugged him tightly. And in that moment, Mack was overcome with guilt. His daughter's wants and needs were just as important as his own. At some point during these past hectic days, he'd forgotten that giving her financial security wasn't the only thing his daughter needed.

He gently patted her back and she gave him a wide, beaming smile.

"I'm all finished with my chores," she proudly announced.

"I'm all finished, too," he told her. "Want a piggy-back ride to the house?"

"Yay!"

Five minutes later, he was lowering Kitty to the floor of the front porch when she shouted, "I see the lights! Here they come, Daddy!"

As Mack watched the approach of Grace's SUV, his heart picked up its pace. He couldn't guess what had prompted her to make the thirty-minute drive out here to the ranch tonight, but he was thrilled she was here.

By the time the vehicle braked to a stop outside the yard fence, Kitty was racing off the porch to go and greet their visitors.

Mack followed at a slower pace and while Ross and Kitty hugged and talked in excited spurts, he skirted the hood of the vehicle and met Grace as she climbed out of the car.

"Hello, Grace."

With the car door against her back, she pushed it closed, then stepped toward him. Mack reached for her hand and as she gripped his fingers, she rose up on tip-toes and kissed his cheek. It was all he could do not to jerk her into his arms and smother her lips with his. But the children were only a short distance away, so he had to be content with giving her a brief hug.

"Hello, Mack."

Maybe it was the shadowy lighting or perhaps the long, long days that had passed since he'd seen her, but at this moment, she'd never looked more beautiful to him. And the sight of her lovely face caused an ache to form in his chest.

Clearing his throat, he said, "It's cold out here. Let's go in."

With his arm at her back, they walked slowly toward the house. Along the way, Ross and Kitty ran past them, giggling and shouting until they reached the porch.

She said, "I think those two are happy to see each other."

"Not nearly as happy as I am to see you," he told her.

Even in the semidarkness, he could see her glance at him was dubious.

"Really?" she asked.

He looked at her in wonder. "I can't imagine why you'd even ask that question. Unless—" He frowned. "You aren't glad to see me."

Her sigh was carried away by a burst of cold wind, but Mack didn't miss it and the sound was as chilling as any blast of icy air.

"Of course, I am, Mack. I'm just a bit weary, that's all."

Weary? What the hell did she think he was? He'd been getting very little sleep and meals that were eaten in hurried snatches. Endless responsibilities were constantly pressing down on him. Not to mention the constant longing to be with her. And for the first time since the two of them had gotten back together, he wanted to unleash a string of heated words at her. But that wouldn't accomplish anything. It would only spoil this precious time he had with her.

"I am, too," he admitted. "So we'll be weary together."

When they entered the living room, Kitty was already making a big deal of showing Ross some drawings she'd made at school.

"Would you like coffee? Something to eat?" he asked as he helped her out of her coat. "I'm not sure what we might find in the fridge, but I do remember there's some leftover chicken and rice Eleanor sent home with me last night."

"Maybe some coffee later." She pushed strands of wind-tossed hair away from her face. "Ross and I have already eaten. What about you and Kitty?"

"We had fast food before we left the clinic."

He hung her coat in the hall closet, then gestured toward the couch. "Let's sit in front of the fire," he suggested. "I managed to build a small one before Kitty and I went to do our chores at the barn. Now that you and Ross are here, I'm glad I did."

"Yes, it feels nice. The cold has been especially brutal the past few days."

She eased onto the middle cushion of the couch and he took a seat close to her side. Immediately, her sweet scent enveloped him, while the softness of her arm and thigh pressing against him made it seem as if months had passed since their night of lovemaking. Did she feel the same way? If she did, she certainly wasn't showing any signs that she'd been missing him.

"Forgive my dirty clothes," he said. "I had some nasty jobs at the clinic this evening and I haven't had a chance to change since I got home."

She gave him a wan smile and as he took in the delicate angles of her face, he noticed fatigue had left shadowy hollows beneath her eyes and cheekbones. He didn't like thinking of her pushing herself to the point of exhaustion. But he was hardly in a position to tell her she needed to slow down.

She said, "I'm a ranch girl, remember? I'm used to men having dirt, manure and dried blood, among other things, on their clothes."

Yes, before Grace had immersed herself in her studies to become a doctor, she'd spent time riding with her brothers and helping with ranching chores. But those idyllic days seemed like a century ago. "Sometimes I forget that you were once a ranch girl, Grace. I always think of you as a doctor."

She bit down on her lower lip and glanced away from him.

Mack studied her solemn profile. From the moment he'd met her at the car a few minutes ago, he'd sensed something was off with her. But what?

He was about to prod her for an explanation when Kitty and Ross suddenly approached them.

"Daddy, me and Ross want to go to the den and play a video game. Is that okay?"

"It's okay with me." He glanced at Grace. "What about you?"

Her smile encompassed both children. "It's fine with me."

Mack watched the pair hurry out of the room before he turned to Grace. Now that the children were gone, a dismal look had returned to her face, making it more than clear she was unhappy.

"Okay," he said. "What's wrong? I know you didn't drive for thirty minutes over rough country roads to stare at the fire in the fireplace."

Her eyebrows arched as her green eyes scanned his face. "Did you ever think I might have driven thirty minutes just to see you?"

She didn't exactly sound sarcastic, but there was a tightness in her voice that made him want to reach for her and hold her in his arms until he felt her body go soft against his.

"At this time of night? No," he answered. "It's been days and days since I've seen you. Or have you forgotten exactly how long it's been since we've been together?"

The look she gave him was one of amazement, but just as quickly, her expression was replaced with a rueful grimace.

"How could I forget? We've been playing a game of tag for the past several days. And before you say anything, I'll admit that much of the problem has been my fault. And I feel—" Her voice broke as she dropped her head and pressed both hands to her face. "Lost and lonely and angry and—" She lifted her head and looked at him. "Scared, Mack. I think that's what I am the most. Scared for us. If…there is an *us* anymore."

Her words jolted him, but her demeanor shook him even more. He'd never seen her with such a defeated expression. And he could only think this wasn't his smiling Grace, the strong woman he'd come to know and love.

And he did love her. He supposed he'd always loved her. But what was that going to get him? What had it ever gotten him, except pain?

He gathered one of her hands between his. "What is that supposed to mean?"

"You need ask?" Tears suddenly pooled in her eyes. "Mack, when we were together that night at my house, I was so hopeful. I thought things were going to be different for us this time—better. But now I'm beginning to think…maybe we shouldn't try to have a relationship. Between your clinic and mine, I don't see…well, it's causing us both a bunch of angst we don't need."

Anger and shock hit Mack in rapid succession. He dropped his hold on her hand, then stood and stared down at her.

"Is that why you came out to see me this evening? To tell me it's over?" he demanded. "Apparently the night we spent together meant nothing to you! Except a night of sex."

Her face turned pink, then white. "That's a hell of a thing to say, Mack!"

His jaw dropped. "And you think the things you've been saying to me are acceptable?" he asked incredulously. "I was under the impression that we were starting over. I thought you wanted to be with me and I damned well wanted to be with you. But—"

Jumping to her feet, she interrupted the last of his words. "That's just it, Mack! We can't be together! Not like normal people. Why do you think I'm scared? Why I'm feeling so lost and— Do you think I want things for us to be this way?"

At some point in the past few seconds, the tears in her eyes had fallen onto her cheeks and she swiped at them with angry desperation. Mack wanted to pull her into his arms and kiss the salty drops from her soft skin, but touching her, kissing her, wouldn't fix the problems she was throwing at him.

"Honestly, Grace, I'm beginning to see things more clearly now. If you have to choose between me or your career, I'm obviously going to end up the loser."

For a moment, she looked so stunned and angry that he got the impression she might actually slap him. But suddenly she brushed past him and didn't stop until she was standing on the fireplace hearth.

Mack followed her and she promptly blasted him with a question. "What do you think you're doing, Mack? I couldn't even get a three-minute conversation from you yesterday!"

"I had an emergency!" he practically shouted. "You, above anyone, ought to understand what that means!"

"Exactly. Now you're getting the point." She dropped her head in her hand and spoke in a shaky voice. "This is what I meant, Mack. We're both doctors. We'd have to be crazy to ever expect to have a normal relationship."

His hand closed over her shoulder and the warmth of her flesh made him ache with longing. Not just to hold her close, but to hear her say "I love you, Mack." To hear her promise to always be at his side. But nothing close to those words was coming from her mouth, much less her heart.

"So you want to just throw up your hands and quit?" he asked softly. "You want us to go our separate ways and pretend we're happy and better off for it? Hell, Grace, I need you and you need me. If I didn't believe that I'd tell you to leave this ranch right now."

Her green eyes stared at him in wonderous disbelief.

"I'm supposed to believe you need me, when I've not seen you in days? I'll be the first to admit I'm gullible at times. But not enough to believe I'm a priority to you."

Seeing their argument was going around in a circle to nowhere, he tugged on her shoulder and she teetered toward him, then landed awkwardly against his chest.

"Since you don't believe my words. Maybe you'll believe this," he murmured.

He fastened his lips over hers and relief rushed through him when she didn't reject the contact. No, her mouth opened to his like a blossom to the sun and he kissed her hungrily, desperately.

In a matter of seconds, her arms lifted and wrapped tightly around his neck. With a grunt of triumph, he crushed her to him and tried to let his kiss convey how much he needed her.

Desire began to boil in his loins and the image of carrying her up to his bedroom and making long, passionate love to her began to burn in his brain.

And then somewhere in the distance, he caught the sound of a door opening and closing. Or was it a footstep?

The kids!

Chapter Ten

Mack had become so lost in their kiss, he'd forgotten all about Kitty and Ross being just down the hallway, in the den.

Putting a few inches between himself and Grace, he glanced over his shoulder at the doorway leading out of the room. "I thought— Did you hear something?" he asked in a husky whisper."

Appearing a bit dazed, she shook her head. "No. Do you think the children saw us kissing?"

"I don't know. Let's go to the den and look," he said.

They walked down a short hallway, then entered a long room furnished with comfortable furniture, an entertainment center and, in one corner, a simple desk and chair. The gaming controls had been put away, but the TV was still on, along with the overhead light. However, the children were nowhere in sight.

"They've probably gone to the kitchen," Grace said. "Unless you think they went upstairs to Kitty's bedroom. From what Ross says, she has stacks of books. She might've wanted to show them to him."

"Let's go look in the kitchen first," Mack said. "They probably got hungry."

"And came to the living room to ask if it was okay for them to eat something," Grace added with a groan. "They probably saw us in a clench."

He glanced at her pale face. "And what would be so awful about that? They need to understand we're... together."

She didn't say anything to that and Mack figured her silence was better than her disputing the situation.

Farther down the hall, they made a left turn into the kitchen and when they saw the room was also empty, they exchanged uneasy glances.

"No kids here. But we still have upstairs," Mack said with a thoughtful frown. "Unless you think— Do you think they might've gone outside?"

Grace shook her head. "Ross wouldn't go outside after dark, unless he asked permission."

"Neither would Kitty." He walked over to the baker's rack, where he normally stored any leftover desserts or packaged cupcakes. As he sifted through the bread and boxes of treats, he said, "Nothing here looks like it's been disturbed. I guess we'd better head upstairs and make sure those two are okay."

"Mack! Look at this!"

The panicky sound to her voice had him whirling around to see her reading from a small square of paper.

"What's that?"

Lifting her head, she shot him a terrified look. "The children have run away!"

He was at her side in two strides and she handed him the note.

Ross had printed in bold letters: *Me and Kitty are going to somewhere better. So we can be brother and sister together.*

Tossing the note to the cabinet counter, he looked at Grace's anguished face. "Oh, God, what have we done?" he said quietly.

She was shaking her head, and close to sobbing, then seemed to catch herself, and she squared her shoulders. "They must've overheard us arguing. Oh, we've made a huge mess of things, Mack. That's what! We have to find them quickly! It's cold and dark and—"

"And anything might happen." He grabbed her shoulder. "Come on. Let's get our coats. They've obviously left the house. I don't think they've had enough time to get very far walking. At least, let's hope not. And with any luck, we can spot them."

Moments later, after Grace and Mack had jerked on their coats and collected a pair of flashlights, they searched both front and backyards without any luck.

As each second ticked by, Grace was close to panicking, yet she tried her best not to show it. Mack hardly needed a hysterical mother on his hands. She had to be strong to be of any help in finding the runaways.

"I'm thinking we should probably call the sheriff's office for help," Grace said as she opened the back door on the SUV to make sure they weren't hiding inside the vehicle. "Flint will alert the family. They'll all come over to help us hunt."

Standing a few steps away from her, Mack rotated the beam of the flashlight in a wide circle. "We might have to resort to calling your family, but I'd rather not panic them needlessly. Especially your parents. The kids couldn't have been gone long. And—" He paused and she saw that he was looking at little boot tracks heading off in the newly fallen snow. "Look, Grace! We're on their trail."

The tracks guided them directly to the inside of the barn. However, when Mack turned on the overhead lights, there was no sign of the children or Rusty, their Collie.

In a hushed voice, Grace said to him, "They could be hiding in here."

"If they were hiding in here, Rusty would be barking to tell us."

"I don't see a dog," she said. "Does he usually stay here in the barn?"

"He roams around during the day, but at night he always stays in the barn with the rest of the animals," he told her. "The dog is obviously gone with the kids."

"Oh, God help us."

As she murmured the short prayer, Mack flashed his light to the far end of the barn and immediately spotted a gate hanging open on one of the horse stalls. "Look, Grace! They've taken a horse."

Grace gasped. "Mack! On a horse—in the dark! This is awful!"

They hurried down to the stalls and found Kitty's pony, Moonpie, still safely latched in his stall, but Mack's horse was missing.

"Why wouldn't they have taken the pony? How could Ross saddle your big horse, much less the two of them get on him?"

The frantic questions were flying from Grace as she quickly followed him to the tack room.

"I don't know. Maybe they thought Moonpie was too small to carry both of them. How Ross managed to make Ghost stand still long enough for the two kids to get on him is beyond me," Mack answered.

Once he'd opened the door to the tack room and rapidly swept the light over the interior, he turned to her. "All the saddles are here. But a bridle that was hanging on the last peg on the wall is missing. Those two are riding bareback. Does Ross know much about riding, or horses?"

She looked at him, her eyes wide with fear. "He's been riding by himself since he was four. So, yes, he's fairly experienced. But is your horse suitable for kids to ride?"

Shaking his head, he took hold of her arm and started out of the barn. "Ghost is a working ranch horse and high-spirited. I've never allowed Kitty to sit on him. But we can't worry about that now. Come on! Let's get the truck, and with any luck, we'll find them riding down the road."

It was simple enough for them to follow the horse and dog tracks down the snowy road. But to Grace's further dismay, after a short distance, something had caused the kids to leave the road and head off into the dark pastureland.

"Oh, God, where could they be going?" Grace said in a stricken voice. "What are they thinking?"

"I'll tell you what's in their little heads," he answered flatly. "They want to be a part of a family. They want to be brother and sister—with parents. They believed we were going to give them those things until…one, or both, of them must have overheard us arguing."

He was right, of course, Grace thought. Recently, Ross had talked more and more about Kitty being his real sister. He'd even asked Grace if she thought Mack would want to be his father. Grace hadn't known how to answer her son. She couldn't make him promises when she had no idea what Mack wanted for his and Kitty's future.

"Oh, Mack, we—we've been so wrong!"

"We've been a whole lot of things," he muttered as he braked the truck to a halt on the side of the road. "From here, I'll have to take after them on foot. The truck would only get stuck out in the pasture."

"There's no way I can just sit here," she told him. "I'm going with you."

Shaking his head, he pointed to the toes of her suede fashion boots peeking out beneath the hems of her jeans. "In five minutes your feet will be soaked in those things."

"I don't care," she argued. "I'm going."

He seemed to realize she would be frantic if she stayed here alone, so he conceded. "All right. Let's go. I'm hoping if they see our lights following them, they'll stop."

"I wouldn't be so sure," she told him. "I've been trying to think like Ross and I have a feeling he's headed to Stone Creek. He's going in the right direction, but he's not thought about crossing all the creeks and a vast arroyo between here and there."

"Yeah," he said grimly. "The kids probably have the idea your parents will fix everything for them."

They climbed out of the truck and began to follow the tracks of the horse and dog. Even with long legs, Grace struggled to keep pace with Mack's strides. The terrain was rough and rocky, with thick clumps of sage making it impossible to walk a straight path. She stumbled several times, but each time Mack reached out to steady her and each time his strong hand wrapped around her arm, she realized she'd been a major fool. She couldn't live without Mack. No more than she could survive without food or water.

"Mack, I'm so sorry," she told him. "This is all my fault. If anything happens to our children, I'll never forgive myself."

Without breaking stride, he frowned at her. "Stop it! This isn't your fault. It's *our* fault. I'm just as guilty and when this is over we're going to have a—"

He broke off in midsentence and swiped the beam of the flashlight up ahead of them. "I thought I heard a horse neigh."

At that moment, Grace caught the flash of something moving and then close by a dog barked.

Grabbing his arm, she pointed to a spot several yards to their left. "If Ghost is a gray, that might be him!" Grace exclaimed. "Should we yell at them?"

"And warn them to go faster?" He shook his head.

"Let's get a little closer before we let them know we're on their tail."

Even at a hurried pace, it took them five more minutes to get near enough for a full view of the children. By then, Grace was winded and, as Mack had predicted, her feet were soaked and so cold she could hardly feel them. But none of that mattered. Her son and his daughter were safe. And Mack's arm was tight around her waist, as if he wanted to keep her safe, too.

When Mack finally called out to the pair, Ross immediately reined the horse to a stop and walked the animal back to where the adults were standing. Rusty circled the whole group with happy barks as if the dog understood the children had been rescued and he no longer needed to guard them.

Grace expected Ross and Kitty to be a little shaken by the wild adventure they'd taken. Or, at the very least, worried about the consequences of being disobedient. Instead, both children looked defiant.

"Mom, am I going to get a spanking?"

Since Grace had never spanked her son, she was surprised he'd even considered she might dole out such punishment.

"No," she told him. "Right now I'm glad we found you and you're both okay."

With her little arms still clinging tightly to Ross's waist, Kitty lifted her chin and looked at her father. "I don't want to go home, Daddy. Not if Ross has to leave."

"We'll talk about all of that when we get back to the ranch house," he told her. "It's going to be okay. I promise."

Grace slipped her arm around Mack's waist and hugged herself close to his side.

"And I promise, too," she said to the children. "From now on, everything is going to be as it should be. With all four of us together."

A broad grin spread across Ross's face, while Kitty suddenly burst into tears.

Twisting around on the horse's back, Ross frowned at her. "Gosh, Kitty, what's wrong? Aren't you happy?"

The girl's bottom lip quivered as she bobbed her head up and down. "I'm happy."

Ross rolled his eyes and Mack looked at Grace and chuckled. "I'm still trying to figure out how the female mind works."

Laughing softly, Grace tightened her hold on his waist. "You'll figure it out after we have another daughter or two."

Some thirty minutes later, with Ghost safely back in his stall, and the children sitting on the fireplace hearth, drinking hot chocolate, Grace sat snugged up to Mack's side.

"Are you getting warm now?" he asked.

Resting her head on his shoulder, Grace purred. "Mmm. Even my feet have thawed."

"That's good." His hand gently smoothed over her forearm. "Because I think it's time we had a talk about our future. You promised the children that the four of us were going to be together."

Raising her head, she looked into his brown eyes. "I'm sorry, Mack," she said without blinking. "But having a wife and son in this house is something you're just going to have to get used to."

His eyes grew soft and then his hand gently cupped the side of her face. "What happened to the woman who said we might as well call it quits? Has she hightailed it out of here?"

Grace sighed as her heart swelled with the love. "She's gone forever, Mack. And I'm sorry I said all those things. These past days I started to feel everything was crashing in on me. The crazy schedule I've had at the clinic and then you being so busy you couldn't get away, or talk. Not seeing you was wearing on me and then I—I'll be honest—I wasn't sure you wanted my love. You've never said—"

His hands were suddenly on her shoulders and the feel of his warm fingers pressing into her flesh was telling her how much he needed and wanted her.

"Grace, I'm the one who should be apologizing. No, let me rephrase that. I should be down on my knees begging you to forgive me for being such a blind fool." A mixture of anguish and hope crossed his features as his gaze continued to search her face. "I've been in love with you for so long, I guess I took it for granted that you knew how I felt about you. I don't know—maybe I thought you would read it on my face, see it in my eyes. If you didn't, then I'm telling you now. I love you. And I always will."

"Mack." His name came out on a broken sob and she pressed her fingers against her eyes as tears began to slip onto her cheeks. "I've been so stupid. I was afraid to tell you I love you—or that I wanted us to be together. You've been single all this time and I didn't believe you'd want to become a married man—not even for me."

His lips twisted to a wry slant. "Why I never married? I thought everyone knew the reason was you. You're the only woman I've ever wanted for my wife. Marrying anyone else never interested me."

A tiny groan sounded in her throat. "These past six weeks… After you brought Kitty to the clinic, there were so many things we should've been saying to each other. Instead, both of us were saying all the wrong things."

"At the wrong times," he added as his fingertips drew precious circles on her cheek. "So hopefully I'm saying the right thing now. Will you marry me, Grace?"

The cold spots in her heart were suddenly filled with the warmth of his love. "Yes. A thousand times, yes."

Smiling now, he pulled her into his arms and she placed a soft kiss on his lips, then nestled her cheek against his.

He said, "We can do this together, Grace. Just like your parents and mine. Just like any couple who are truly bonded with love."

Easing her head back, she looked at him through a mist of happy tears. "Yes. We are truly bonded and I'm going to do my part to make sure that bond is never broken. I can see I'm going to have to make plenty of changes. And I understand they won't happen overnight. Or making them will always be easy. But I promise I will be making them. For you. For me. For our children."

"What sort of changes are you talking about? Because there's no way I'd let you quit being a doctor. Caring for people is who you are. It's one of the reasons I love you."

Smiling gently, she said, "And I'd say the same about you if you ever tried to quit being an animal doctor. No, I'm talking about reasonable changes. Starting with hiring extra help at the clinic. First and foremost, a PA I can trust. I have to learn to cut off appointments at a normal hour each day and to make time for myself and my family."

He nodded. "The same goes for me, Grace. I need more help at the clinic, especially an experienced assistant to go with Oren. I'm going to have Eleanor limit my patients to a more comfortable workload, and trust me, if anyone can do that, it's her. But the changes I need to make don't stop at the clinic. Here on the ranch, I'm going to hire a full-time ranch hand. The end profit for the Broken B won't be as much. But money isn't everything. Being a vet or a rancher isn't everything. What's most important is having the people I love with me."

She groaned with misgivings at the thought of all the mistakes they'd both made and the miseries they'd caused each other and their children. "Oh, Mack, these are the things we should've been saying to each other earlier. Before the children ran away. Why did it take a five-year-old girl and a seven-year-old boy to rip the blinders off our eyes?"

He shook his head with regret. "Because adults get stuck in a rut and close their minds to change. But when I read Ross's note and recognized just how desperate our children were—to run out in the cold night just so they could be a family—I felt like I'd been struck by a lightning bolt. The thought of losing them was more than enough to make me see that you and the kids are all that matters—the four of us together."

A mist of tears glazed her eyes as happiness swept through her. "Yes, it was the same for me," she murmured. "All those years ago we let our determination to become doctors get in the way of our love. But that didn't teach us anything. This past month we were still on that same path. So busy being doctors, we pushed each other aside. But tonight we finally learned a great lesson, don't you agree?"

Wrapping his arms around her, he pulled her into a tight hug. "Yes. And once we get married I have a feeling we're going to be learning more." Easing her head back from his shoulder, her grinned at her. "Right now I'd like to hear more about those daughters you mentioned we're going to have."

She gave him a soft, seductive smile. "So you didn't miss that comment?"

He chuckled as his hands moved temptingly up and down her back. "I was a bit rattled at the time. But I heard you."

"Well, we might have a couple of sons to go along with two more daughters," she said with a promising grin. "That way, we'd have a nice half dozen."

"Hmm. Not as many as Claire and Hadley, but I think an even half dozen will do for us," he told her. "And speaking of children, it looks like our two little trail riders are played out."

Easing away from him, she twisted around on the

couch to see both Ross and Kitty stretched out on the floor in front of the fire. Both had their heads pillowed on their arms as they gazed at the bubbling lights on the Christmas tree.

For the most part, Grace and Mack had decided the children had already gone through enough without adding more punishment for their attempt to run away. Instead of taking privileges away, they'd given the two a long talk about how dangerous their behavior had been and made them promise to never get on a horse without an adult's permission. And thankfully, now that both children could see they were all going to be a real family unit, they appeared to be remorseful for misbehaving.

"Let's go see if we can rouse them," she suggested. "I think it's time they went to bed."

"I do, too." He lowered his lips close to her ear. "Especially when their parents need some alone time."

Leaving the couch, they walked hand in hand over to the sleepy children. When Grace kneeled next to them, Ross looked up with pleading eyes.

"Mom, do we have to go home tonight?"

Grace glanced at Mack, and he answered Ross's question by squatting down on his heels and stroking a reassuring hand over the boy's rumpled hair. "You are home, son. For now and always."

Epilogue

Christmas Day was always a huge event at the big house on Stone Creek Ranch and this year was no exception. Thanks to Claire and the twins, each room was cheerfully decorated and there was hardly a table anywhere that wasn't loaded with homemade candy, cookies and roasted nuts.

In the den, a safe distance away from the roaring fire Hadley had built in the fireplace, a huge spruce was loaded with decorations. Many of the ornaments had been handmade years ago by Grace and her seven siblings and the passing years had left a few of them a bit tattered. But Claire insisted that only added to their charm and each Christmas she made sure they were proudly hung from the green boughs.

A mound of wrapped gifts beneath the tree had been handed out and opened amid surprised gasps, good-

natured groans and loads of oohs and aahs. There'd
been picture taking, holiday music playing on the satel-
lite radio and tons of rich food consumed. As for Kitty
and Ross, they'd brought a few of the toys Santa had
delivered to the Broken B with them to Stone Creek,
and though they'd wanted to bring the rescue kitten
they'd named Lucky, Mack had convinced them the
little cat needed more recuperation before he was ready
to attend a party. So for most of the morning, the two
children had been trying to keep up with their baby
cousin, Bridget. At six months old, Cordell and Maggie's daughter was crawling all over the place and getting into whatever she could get her hands on.

Throughout the merry-making, everyone had been
offering their congratulations to Grace and Mack for
their decision to get married. Not that they'd made any
sort of announcement to the family. Kitty and Ross had
made it for them as soon as the four of them had entered
the door this morning. Now Beatrice and Bonnie were
already pressing her for wedding plans and Cordell was
talking about cleaning out the barn again for another
reception shindig.

Grace was glad to see Mack was taking the happy
mayhem all in stride. Yet as she watched him quietly
taking in the events of the day, she couldn't help but
wonder if being a part of her huge family was overwhelming him.

Now as they sat close together on a love seat in the
den, she reached over and gave his hand a squeeze. "Are
you having a merry Christmas, Mack?"

A faint smile curved his lips. "Very merry. Don't I look happy?"

She nodded. "You do. But I'm sure you must be thinking about your dad and your mother, too. I truly wish they were here. Not just for your sake, but for all of us. Do you think they'd be pleased about us being together again?"

"Mom and Dad would be as thrilled as I am. I don't think I've told you this, but when Dad learned you were single again he held out hopes that the two of us would get back together. I told him he was being foolish. You'd probably never give me a second chance."

Her faint smile was full of irony. "And what did Will say to that?" she asked.

"He didn't think you were a vengeful woman. And you know what? He was right." He clasped his hand around hers. "Him and Mom always wanted to give me siblings— to have a big family like Claire and Hadley's. Since that never happened, I believe my parents are now smiling to see I'm marrying into the huge Hollister bunch."

Grace nodded. "I do, too. And our family has become even more huge since we've learned we're related to the Hollisters down in Arizona. You know, it would be nice if this coming year we'd find out just how the connection with their family came to be. It's clear that Dad isn't going to rest until the mystery of the matter is uncovered."

He turned a thoughtful expression on her. "Earlier this afternoon, I overheard Van telling Hadley she has plans to try and locate Lionel's ex-wife. I won't call her your grandmother because I know none of you and your siblings have ever considered her in those terms."

Grace grimaced. "No. She was never our grandmother. She left the family when Dad was far younger than little Ross—a really heartbreaking situation. But I understand why Van is reaching in all directions to find answers to Lionel's past background. She's rapidly coming to a dead end for answers. And I hate to rain on her efforts, but even if she does locate Scarlett, I don't believe the woman could or would give out information about her ex-husband. Once Scarlett left Stone Creek, that was it. She was never heard from again."

Mack nodded thoughtfully. "I'm afraid I agree. I figure Van's chances of getting help from Scarlett are slim to none. But I understand she doesn't want to give up on solving the missing branch of the family tree."

Grace leaned over and kissed his cheek. "No, darling. Just like we didn't want to give up on each other."

His eyes twinkled as he squeezed her hand. "What do you say the two of us take a little walk around the backyard? I want to have you all to myself for a few minutes."

A short while ago, Hadley and Quint had taken the kids and Maggie's shepherd dogs over to the ranch yard to see a pair of newly born lambs. Now was the perfect chance for Grace and Mack to have a quiet moment together.

"Sounds good." As he helped her to her feet, she glanced out the window. "I'll get my coat and hat. It's starting to snow again."

Once they were both bundled against the weather, they walked through the house and out to the covered patio, which took up only a third of the spacious back-yard. Presently, the winter brown grass was hidden beneath a thin layer of snow, along with the long tarps sheltering the rose garden.

With Mack's arm curled around the back of her waist, they walked to the edge of the brick floor and gazed out at the distant mountains. The peaks were totally white, while down below in the valley floor a herd of black cattle foraged among the thick stands of sage and chapparal.

Sighing, she said, "If it was dark and the evening star was shining down on the valley floor, it would be a perfect Christmas scene."

A clever grin lifted one side of his lips. "Maybe you won't have to wait for dark to see a star."

She arched a playful eyebrow at him. "Oh, you must be going to thump me on the head, or kiss me. If I have a choice, I'd really prefer the latter."

His eyes full of warm desire, he pulled her into arms and kissed her gently and thoroughly.

"Mmm. That was especially nice." She rubbed the tip of her nose against his. "Want to try it again?"

He chuckled. "In due time, sweetheart. Right now I want to give you something."

Grace stared in surprise at the box he pulled from his ranch jacket. The small square was wrapped in silver paper and tied with a golden bow. It had to be a piece of jewelry, she thought. Or a gift certificate to Canyon Corral.

"Mack! You've already given me a gift." She touched the charms on the beautiful bracelet he'd given her earlier this morning. "And you spent way too much on this piece."

"Not nearly enough. Not for the woman who's going to be my wife and the mother of my children." He handed her the box. "The bracelet was a gift for today. This gift is for the rest of your life."

Quickly, she ripped off the paper and stuffed the scraps into her coat pocket. Inside the box, she discovered a smaller velvet box, but before she could open it, he took the case from her and flipped up the lid.

Grace gasped as she stared in stunned fascination at the oval diamond surrounded by a circle of tiny diamonds and set upon a filigree band of white gold. She'd been expecting jewelry, but something like earrings. Not a dazzling engagement ring.

"Mack! This is… It's so very lovely." Her eyes shining with love, she looked up at him. "You've really surprised me. I…well, I took it for granted you'd give me a simple wedding band when we got married. I guess this means we truly are engaged."

"Truly. And from all the hoopla your family is making over giving us a wedding, they aren't going to let us be engaged for long."

She laughed softly. "So you've already figured that out. Will it bother you, Mack, if we have a short engagement?"

"Are you kidding? If it wasn't for robbing your mother and sisters the joy of planning a big ceremony, I'd marry you tomorrow." He took the ring from its velvet nest and slipped it on her finger. "I love you, Grace. Now and always."

With a little cry of joy, she flung her arms around him and for the next few moments she let her kiss show him exactly how much love she planned to give him for the rest of their lives.

The creak of the door behind them opening and closing had them finally easing apart and Grace looked around just in time to see Ross and Kitty barreling toward them with Maggie's Australian shepherds right on their heels.

"Daddy, Daddy! We got to see the baby lambs. And Quint let me hold the girl lamb in my arms. She was wooly and sweet!"

Kitty was practically out of breath with happy excitement and Grace could only smile at the transformation the girl had undergone from the lost and lonely child with tummy aches. Kitty's visit to the clinic that evening more than six weeks ago hadn't just changed Kitty, it had changed all their lives for the better.

"And Uncle Quint says a real sheepherder might be coming to Stone Creek as soon as winter passes," Ross added eagerly. "He says the cowboy will have horses and dogs, and he'll stay in the mountains with the sheep to keep them safe. He said that me and Kitty can ride out with him one day to visit the sheepherder. That's going to be really fun!"

"Yeah!" Kitty exclaimed. "We done told him that we already know how to ride double! And in the dark, too!"

Mack quickly placed his hand over his mouth and Grace knew it was to hide his laughter from the children.

"Sounds like Uncle Quint plans on giving you two

a big treat," Grace said with the straightest face she could manage.

"Yeah, he's pretty neat. All my uncles are neat. But they're not as cool as Mack." To underscore his comment, Ross went to stand at Mack's side. Immediately his hand rested affectionately on Ross's shoulder and Grace's heart swelled at the image they made together. Eventually, the bond between them would be like true father and son. And she had no doubt that before long, Ross would be calling him Dad and looking up to him as his hero.

"Quint named the twin lambs Nick and Noel because they were born on Christmas Eve," Ross went on. "He says Nick can be my lamb and Noel can be Kitty's. But we have to leave them here with their mother."

"But that's okay. Because that's where the lambs need to be," Kitty said, then with a beaming smile, she reached for Grace's hand. "'Cause everybody needs a mommy."

Fearful that Kitty might see her cry, Grace picked her up and held her tightly in her arms. "You are so right, my little darling."

"And there's something else," Ross added proudly. "Grandpa told Kitty that she could call him and Grandma, her grandpa and grandma, too. Isn't that good? Me and Kitty say this is the best Christmas we've ever had!"

Mack looked at Grace and the smile they shared was a promise for a lifetime.

"The best ever," Mack agreed.

* * * * *

SPECIAL EXCERPT FROM

H HARLEQUIN
SPECIAL
EDITION

With the help of an unusual Cupid,
can two friends who've known each other
forever take a chance on love?

Read on for a sneak preview of

Matchmaker on the Ranch
by Marie Ferrarella.

Chapter One

Yesterday had been one of those extremely long days for Rosemary Robertson. She was affectionately known to her family and friends as "Roe," as well as the "youngest triplet" to her sisters because she had been the last one of the trio to make her appearance that fateful evening that her widowed mother had given birth.

Now, exhausted beyond words, Roe had no recollection of even climbing into her bed. One minute she was making her way into her small bedroom, the next minute she had made contact with her pillow.

She was sound asleep probably before her head had hit her pillow.

She didn't even remember lying down. The one thing she knew was that she certainly hadn't bothered getting undressed. The allure of the double bed had seductively called to her, and the next thing she knew was sleep. It was a good thing that her two dogs, Kingston and Lucy, had stayed on the floor; otherwise, she could have very well flattened one of them, if not both, as her body made contact with the bed.

But after living with their mistress for a number of years, the Bichon Frisé and the petite German shepherd had developed survival instincts when it came to being around the town's veterinarian.

The dogs had also developed certain habits when it came to living with their mistress.

One of these habits involved waking her up at a certain time in the morning. The way her dogs went about this was to lick her face—vigorously—until she would finally open her eyes and respond to them.

And that was exactly the way Roe woke up the next morning, having her face bathed by pink tongues, one very small tongue, one rather large tongue, both of which were moving madly along her cheeks. She had fallen asleep on her back, and each dog had picked out a side, anointing her until her eyelashes finally began to flicker and then, at long last, opened.

Roe groaned, shifting on the bed. She did her best to attempt to wave the dogs away from her face.

"Oh come on, guys, just give me five more minutes. Please." She sighed deeply and attempted to wave the dogs away again, but their licking only grew more pronounced and frantic. Roe gave up. "Okay, okay, I'm up, I'm up," she told the dogs, struggling into an upright position.

With another deep sigh, Roe scrubbed her hands over

her now very damp face, doing her very best to try to pull herself together.

It was a slow process, but she was getting there.

Finally fully awake, she looked from one dog to the other. "You know, if you don't change your tunes, I can always find a nice home for you two. What do you think of that?" she asked, attempting to pin the dogs down with a look.

The pets apparently weren't buying it. Kingston, clearly the leader despite his size, began licking her face again and this time, Roe gave up and just laughed at her pets.

"Okay, okay, I know where this is going. Time for your breakfast," she told the dogs. "But first you're going to have to let me get up out of bed." As if by magic—she had trained the two dogs relentlessly when it came to obedience—Kingston and Lucy retreated from her bed. "That's better," she said, praising them.

Roe swung her legs off the bed, searching around with her toes for her shoes. She usually wore boots all day, then pulled them off the moment she walked in the front door and put on her shoes in their place.

Finding her shoes, she slipped into them and then stood up.

"Okay, let's go see about that breakfast," she told the dogs.

Her furry fan club all but hopped around her in a yappy circle, not exactly getting underfoot, but not exactly steering clear of her, either.

Roe made her way into the kitchen and began preparing two bowls of food for the dogs. The bowls each had boiled chicken thighs, a tablespoon of pureed pumpkin sauce, a sprinkling of cheddar cheese scattered on top and just enough dog food to make it an all-around meal for the pets.

Once done, she set the bowls down on the floor and watched the dogs go at it as if they had been starved for days instead of fed midday yesterday when her neighbor had come in to leave dishes for her pets that Roe had prepared.

Roe always got a kick out of the fact that Kingston cleared his bowl much faster than Lucy did, despite their difference in size.

"No picky eaters here," Roe declared happily. They had all but cleared their bowls completely in less time than it had taken her to put the meals together. "Well, I hope you enjoyed that because you're not getting anything more until I get home tonight," she told them as she filled their water bowls. "With any luck, today won't be anything like it was yesterday. I hardly got a chance to take two breaths in succession."

As she spoke, Kingston cocked his head first one way, then the other. The dog she had found stumbling around town one morning eight years ago had become attached to her almost instantly. He'd had a large, fresh gash in his rear right leg at the time. She initially thought she might have to amputate it because it looked as if a serious infection was swiftly spreading through the injured limb.

By working diligently and relentlessly, Roe had managed to save his leg and keep the infection from spreading until she was finally able to eradicate it. But it had been touch and go there for a while.

Initially, she had taken Kingston home to watch over him until he got well. Slowly, eventually, her home became his home.

Permanently.

Lucy had turned up on her doorstep a year and a half after that. If she had ever harbored any doubts about her ability to care for animals, Lucy quickly cured her of them. The frightened dog had been easily won over by her. Roe came to the happy conclusion that she had an affinity not just for caring for animals, but for curing them as well.

She stood for a moment now, just looking at the two dogs that had added so much meaning to her life. Roe could feel her happiness radiating inside of her.

It took effort to draw herself away the pets, but she managed.

The rest of the day was waiting for her to get started.

Roe had just gotten out of the shower and hadn't even had a chance to dry off yet when her cell phone began ringing. She shook her head as, still dripping, she glanced over at the phone she had left on the side of the bathroom sink.

"Looks like it's going to be another wonderful, chock-full-of-patients day," Roe murmured to herself.

Grabbing her bathrobe with one hand, she picked up her phone with the other and put it on speaker. She rested it on the sink as she punched her arms through her bathrobe sleeves. She wanted to at least begin the process of absorbing the dampness from her body, not to mention having something on to cover her.

"This is Dr. Robertson," she told the caller. "How can I help you?" Roe asked, leaning over the receiver as she raised her voice to a more audible level.

"You could try picking up your phone when I call," the voice on the other end said.

A lot of people who interacted with them said that not only did the three Robertson sisters look alike, they also sounded alike as well.

But those who *really* knew the sisters claimed that they could actually tell their voices apart.

"I was in the shower, Riley. What's up?" Roe asked as she quickly toweled her hair dry with one hand. "And although I know I don't have to tell you this, talk fast. I have an early morning appointment with a rancher."

"Hmm. Business or pleasure?" Riley asked. Roe caught the interested note in her sister's voice, but that could just be because Riley was getting married and she was interested in everyone's situation.

Kingston was watching attentively as Roe swiftly finished drying herself off, then stripped off the now-soggy bathrobe.

"Both," Roe answered her sister matter-of-factly. "My business always gives me pleasure."

"Nice to hear. And how do you feel about weddings?" Riley asked her, deliberately sounding vague.

Roe closed her eyes as she hit her forehead with the flat of her hand. "Oh God, the rehearsal. I forgot all about the rehearsal," she cried. She was supposed to be there later today, after her appointment. "I am so sorry."

"Well, despite the fact that I have a spare sister I can always turn to, I do forgive you. But only because I am so very magnanimous and kindhearted," Riley told Roe. "And it's not like you haven't been to a wedding before and have no idea what to expect or do," she added. And then Riley changed her tone as concern entered her voice. "You sound really tired, Roe. Is everything all right on your end?"

"Honestly?" Roe asked, momentarily at a loss.

"No, lie to me," Riley answered cryptically. "Of course, honestly."

Roe sighed, thinking of the possible threat that might lay ahead when it came to the cattle ranch she had been to the other day. "I'm not sure yet, but that's not anything for you to concern yourself about." She grinned as she made her way into her bedroom, carrying her phone with her. "You have a wedding to plan and nothing else should matter right now.

"Speaking of which," Roe said, continuing her train of thought as she opened her closet and took out fresh clothes for the day, debating whether to bring a second set with her to change into later. She decided it wouldn't hurt to toss them into the trunk, just in case. "Are you sure you want me to be your maid of honor? People might get confused. Especially since you're going to have Raegan as your matron of honor."

Riley laughed, dismissing her sister's concerns. "Anyone who doesn't know that I have two sisters who are mirror images of me really doesn't concern me because they're relatively strangers," she informed Roe. "Just as long as you and Raegan don't get your roles confused, that's all that counts," Riley teased, then went on to clarify the roles. "You are the maid of honor and

Raegan is the matron of honor—and Vikki is the flower girl. She is *really* excited about being part of this wedding. When Matt and I asked her to be flower girl, she told me she wasn't able to take part in her mother's first wedding and she is very happy to be able to be part of this one—which I think is adorable."

"You didn't tell her that there wasn't a wedding, right?" Roe asked her sister. "She's a little young to take all that in."

"Vikki is a lot older than the date on her birth certificate claims," Riley answered loftily. "But Matt and I thought we'd save that little tidbit of information for another time just in case after hearing that, Vikki comes up with questions that wind up stumping us."

"Wise decision. What time do you want me at the church since I missed the original run-through?" Roe asked, referring to the original rehearsal.

"Father Lawrence gave me a list of possible times. Barring an emergency, how does three o'clock this afternoon sound to you?" Riley asked. "Whatever you pick, I'll call the others and tell them. Nobody else has any conflicts. I already checked."

"Three o'clock is doable—barring an emergency," Roe echoed her sister's words, although it would have to be a really big emergency to prevent her from getting there.

"Then I'll see you at the church at three o'clock—barring an emergency," both women said simultaneously, their voices blending. The conversation ended with a laugh. "'Bye, Roe," Riley said just before she hung up.

Roe hit the "red" button to end the call. She listened to make sure the call was over, then sighed as she roused herself.

She didn't have time to stare off into oblivion. She had things to do. Not to mention a cattle herd to check out before she could show up at the local church for rehearsal.

There had been an anthrax scare far up north but with any luck, it was either a false alarm or a scare that wasn't going to work its way down to the area surrounding Forever. She had no idea how the local ranchers would respond to that sort of threat if it actually did materialize.

She fervently hoped she would never have to find out. She was perfectly happy to go through life without ever finding out if she was up to that sort of a large-scale challenge. She thought she was, but she would rather not have her abilities tested. Roe honestly felt she was perfectly fine handling mundane things and remaining unchallenged for the entire course of her career.

Dressed in jeans and a work shirt, as well as a denim jacket, and almost ready to leave, Roe came out into the small living room where Kingston was entertaining himself by chasing Lucy around.

"Try not to destroy the house while I'm gone, guys," she told her pets. "I'll try to get home at a decent hour, but I can't really promise anything. Barring any emergency and if the wedding rehearsal goes off on schedule, I'll be able to feed you on time—but don't hold me to that," she said, addressing her words to the lively, fluffy white dog that was busy spinning around in a wide circle in front of her.

She knew it was Kingston's way of trying to entertain her and getting her to stay.

Kingston made a noise, and it was almost as if he actually understood what she was saying to him.

Roe laughed as she petted one dog and then the other. "Glad we understand one another. I will see you two guys later—and remember, you're supposed to guard the house," she instructed.

Not that there was actually anything to guard against, she thought as she locked the door behind her. Forever, Texas, was part of a dying breed: a small, friendly town where everyone knew almost everyone else and looked out for one another to make sure that nothing happened. It was the very definition of the word "neighborly."

There were some exceptions, of course. After all, this was reality and that meant there were people who preferred to keep to themselves and avoid any sort of unnecessary interaction with anyone. But by and large, those people were mercifully few and far between.

For the most part, everyone in the small town knew everyone else and had known them for a very long time. The ones who hadn't been born in Forever had made a strong effort to become part of the town and blend in, often more than those who had been born here.

Roe checked her watch to see how much time she had before she needed to get to the church. Not showing up once was forgivable. Not showing up twice was another story entirely. And besides which, she did want to take part in this. After all, this was for Riley's wedding and she knew how important this was to all parties concerned.

Pacing herself, she paid visits to several of the local ranches to check on how their cattle were doing. Other than a couple of instances—in one case a calf had gotten tangled up in a section of barbed wire and it took a great deal of careful maneuvering to get the animal's horns uncoupled from the fencing—Roe's visits to the ranches were rather uneventful.

She would have never actually admitted it to anyone except for possibly her grandfather, but it was the wedding rehearsal that had captured the major part of her attention.

Because the last ranch on her list was farther away than the other two, it took her a while to get there. Consequently, the trip back took even longer, despite the fact that she hurried and drove her truck faster than normal. It turned out that she was the last one to arrive at the church anyway.

Riley was looking out the church window and was the first to see her coming.

When the front door opened, she greeted Roe, her brown-haired, brown-eyed mirror image with, "Ah, you're finally here. I was just about to send out the search party to look for you."

"Now you won't have to 'cause she's here," Vikki declared happily, a grin encompassing the red-haired little girl's small, beaming face.

"Yes, I am." Roe made her way over to Vikki. "Hi, Angel. How are you doing?" she asked the little girl who was about to officially become part of their family once Riley married Vikki's father, Matt.

"I'm doing fine," the almost five-year-old answered solemnly, as if the question that had been put to her required deep thought. "How are you doing?" Vikki asked, turning the question back on Roe and looking very proud of herself for the accomplishment.

Roe struggled to keep from laughing out loud, knowing it would probably hurt Vikki's feelings. Her exchanges with the little girl always tickled her. She was rather amazed at how well Vikki had learned to cope with her mother's passing.

"I'm doing just fine, now that I see you here," Roe answered.

Her small, smooth brow furrowed as she tried to understand what Roe was saying to her. "You didn't think I would be here?" Vikki asked.

"Oh, but I did. After all, you're the flower girl. I just meant that I was really very happy to see you," Roe explained.

"Oh." Vikki's freshly arranged red hair bobbed up and down as she nodded. "Well I'm happy to see you, too," she told Roe. "How's Kingston? You didn't bring him with you, did you?"

As she asked, the little girl quickly looked around the church in all the places that the dog would choose to hide.

"No, not this time, honey. He's home keeping Lucy company," Roe told Vikki, thinking that was the most understandable explanation she could tell her. "Lucy gets lonely whenever I leave the house."

Vikki thought that over for a minute. "Maybe I could go over to your house and keep her company."

"That's a lovely idea," Roe agreed, but then quickly added, "We'll see. Right now, they need you here for the ceremony."

"Oh, yeah," Vikki agreed, her expression looking almost solemn.

Father Lawrence chose that moment to walk out from his office and into the church proper. He clapped his hands together as he scanned the small gathering before him. It was composed of just the wedding party, not any of the guests.

"Well, it looks like everyone who is supposed to be here is here now," the tall, fair-haired, blue-eyed priest noted. "Shall we get started? Spoiler alert," he said, as if it was meant to be a side comment. "There are no surprises. This is going to be just like the last ceremony I officiated for you, except that it was for Raegan and Alan," he said with a wink. "This time it'll be for Riley and Matthew."

"And me!" Vikki piped up, excited.

Matt laughed and looked in wonder at the daughter he hadn't even known existed such a short while ago. Now her existence filled his heart in ways he couldn't have even begun to imagine. It wasn't until Riley, Breena's best friend, had written a letter telling him about Vikki. He had come to Forever not really knowing what to expect. He certainly hadn't expected to fall in love twice over.

But he had.

"Most definitely you, buttercup," Matt teased, giving the little girl an affectionate hug.

"I'm not a buttercup," Vikki said, pretending to protest. "I'm a girl."

"Yes, you most definitely are that," Matt agreed. Then he flushed and looked toward the priest, thinking the man was waiting to get started and he was interrupting. "Sorry, Father."

"No need to apologize." Father Lawrence nodded toward the little girl. "I find this sort of display very heartening. But, in deference to those here who are on a tighter schedule and would like to get things moving along, I do suggest we get started." Father Lawrence looked around the immediate area. "Any objections?"

Mike Robertson laughed and shook his head. "Not from this crowd, Father," he told the priest.

"All right, then let's begin—I promise this will be fast and painless, especially since we've already gone through it once before," the priest said as he smiled at the people standing around hm.

Vikki frowned as she tried to follow what the priest had just said. "No, we didn't," she protested.

"Father Lawrence is talking about when he married your aunt Raegan and your uncle Alan," Roe told Vikki, whispering into the little girl's ear.

Vikki's face lit up as comprehension suddenly filled her. "Oh, now I understand," she said. "Sorry, Father Lawrence."

Vikki didn't understand why everyone in the church was suddenly laughing at what she had just said, but she politely refrained from asking because Father Lawrence seemed to want to move things along.

Chapter Two

Mercifully, Father Lawrence had everyone go through their paces just once. When the wedding rehearsal finally ended, he smiled and said, "Well, that should do it. Nothing left to do, folks, but have the actual wedding take place," he told the small collection of people, his eyes washing over them.

"Can't we do it again, Father?" Vikki asked, her small voice echoing around the church and challenging the growing silence.

Surprised, Matt looked at his daughter. Kids her age liked to be outside and playing, not stuck indoors and being quiet.

"Why would you want to do it again?" he asked. He would have thought she would be bored by now. For all intents and purposes, she had behaved perfectly and been exceptionally quiet.

Vikki answered the question solemnly, her expression looking like the last word in sincerity.

"'Cause I want to make sure that I do it right. It's important to get it right, isn't it?" she asked, looking from Riley to her father. "This is your wedding and weddings are important," she stressed.

Matt didn't even try not to laugh. Getting down on one knee, he put his arms around the petite little girl and pulled her closer to him. He couldn't believe how lucky he was to have discovered he had a daughter after all this time and that she had turned out to be such a little darling. "Just having you here for the rehearsal is doing it right, sweetheart," he told her.

The puzzled look on Vikki's face testified to the fact that she really didn't understand, but she was not about to question such things in a room full of grown-ups. It was obvious she thought they might laugh at her.

Instead, she merely agreed with what her father had said. "Okay."

That was the moment that Miss Joan, the owner of the town's only diner, chose to breeze into the church. It was apparent by her intense expression that she had timed her entrance.

"Hello, Father," she said, greeting the man she'd known ever since he was a small boy. "All done here?" It was obvious that she thought he was and that she was asking what amounted to a rhetorical question.

"Hello, Miss Joan. Yes, we're all done here," Father Lawrence replied with a wide smile, then decided to compliment the woman. "You timed your entrance quite well, Miss Joan."

She didn't bother denying it. "I do my best," she replied. There was no missing the fact that she was quite pleased with herself. Her hazel eyes swept over the small gathering and she nodded. She saw what she needed to.

"Everyone hungry?" She wasn't expecting anyone to say "No."

"Because if you are," she went on, "there's a wedding rehearsal dinner waiting for all of you at the diner. Just follow your noses." Miss Joan looked amused as she waved her thin hand toward the church's double doors.

The way she worded her invitation, as well as her tone of voice, indicated that not only was everyone welcome to come to the diner, they were actually required to come there. Miss Joan was not accustomed to being turned down or having her invitation ignored, and to everyone's recollection, she really never had been.

Miss Joan was about to turn and walk out of the church when Vikki urgently tugged on the hem of the diner owner's dress. Hazel eyes looked down, pinning the little girl in place.

"Yes?" Miss Joan asked in the same voice she used whenever an adult wanted her attention.

"Will there be ice cream there?" Vikki asked her hopefully.

Miss Joan's expression never changed. "After you eat your dinner, yes, there will be ice cream there."

But Vikki wasn't finished asking questions. "Lots and lots of ice cream?" she asked.

Miss Joan treated the question as if it was actually a serious inquiry. "How much you eat is all up to your father," she told the little girl. And then she fixed Vikki with a look that had been known to make grown men flinch. "But a word to the wise, nobody wants to see you exploding, little girl."

The little girl giggled. "I wouldn't do that," she said, waving away the very idea. "People don't explode if they eat too much.

"Well, I certainly hope not," Miss Joan said. "But you never know. Just remember, if you do explode, then you're going to have to be the one who cleans everything all up." She looked down at Vikki pointedly. "Understand?"

Her eyes met Miss Joan's, and she nodded her head up and down so hard, her red hair bobbed almost frantically now.

"I understand," the little girl echoed in a serious tone.

For one of the few times in her life, Miss Joan actually found herself struggling to keep the corners of her mouth from curving upward. There was no doubt about it, the woman got a huge kick out of the little girl, far more of a kick than she had gotten out of a child in years.

Against all odds, she succeeded in keeping any hint of the smile from her face. Only then did she speak, declaring a single word, "Good," and accompanying the single word with a nod of her head. And then, for good measure, she looked around the small gathering. "All right, everyone, get in your vehicles and come on down to the diner," she instructed.

With that, Miss Joan turned on her stacked heel and walked out of the church.

With a laugh, Roe looked in Matt's direction. "You

know," she commented, "I think Miss Joan had to have been a general in her previous life."

Absorbing every word that was being said around her, Vikki's mouth dropped open in total awe. "Really?" she cried, her eyes huge. She looked from Roe to her father, as well as at several other faces. The little girl appeared to be utterly captivated by this newest piece of news.

Riley made no effort to keep from laughing. "I think your aunt Roe is teasing you," she told the little girl.

Hearing the comment, Vikki shook her head. "She's not my aunt yet. She won't be my aunt until after the wedding."

Amazed, Matt was beginning to think that it was going to take the combined efforts of all the adults gathered together in the church at this very moment to stay one crucial step ahead of his bright little girl.

"You're absolutely right," he told his daughter. "Tell me, how did you ever get to be so very smart?"

Vikki never even blinked. "I was born that way," she informed him proudly. "Mama said so."

Riley tilted her head slightly, trying to keep the tears from falling from her eyes. Breena would have been so proud of Vikki. Riley could swear she could hear her late best friend's voice talking to the little girl, patiently teaching her things. Breena never talked to Vikki as if she was a child, treating her instead like an adult waiting to happen.

Turning to look at her, Matt thought he saw the glimmer of tears in Riley's eyes. "Are you all right?" he whispered to the woman he was going to make his wife.

Recovering, Riley got hold of herself and flashed

a smile at Matt as she took Vikki's hand in hers. "I'm just fine, Matt."

Roe looked on, feeling more than a little envious. She dearly loved both of her sisters and was very happy that Raegan had found someone to love and that Riley had as well, but there was a part of her that was envious of the fact that both of her sisters had found what amounted to their "other halves" while she felt unattached and in all probability would continue to feel that way for possibly the rest of her life.

Oh well, Roe thought philosophically, she had signed on to do her very best to take care of the animals who came her way and that was turning out very well. That was what she needed to focus on, not on what she didn't have.

She got into her own vehicle at the same time that everyone else was getting into theirs. Roe decided to turn on some music to drown out any sad, interfering thoughts that might wind up distracting her. She turned the volume up high and drove herself over to Miss Joan's diner.

Miss Joan wanted this to be a pre-celebratory party, and Roe wasn't going to allow any sober thoughts to get in her way and bring her down.

This was definitely not the time to feel sorry for myself, Roe silently lectured.

This was about Riley and Matt and the sweet little girl who was officially going to become part of their family once Riley and Matt said "I do." Anything she could do to help that happen was absolutely perfect in her book.

* * *

When Roe arrived at Miss Joan's diner, she half expected to see a notice on the door declaring that the diner was closed for a private party. But there was no such notice. Miss Joan was apparently juggling both the rehearsal dinner and her regular customers with both hands. She had a section cordoned off so the wedding party, along with Father Lawrence, who had been included in the invitation, were able to sit together while Miss Joan's regulars still had tables available for coffee and their meals as usual.

Vikki gleefully found herself smack dab in the center of the wedding party's seating arrangement. It was obvious to anyone who looked that the little girl loved being the center of attention. She talked up a storm. Riley and her entire family loved Vikki dearly.

"Smile, Roe," Raegan ordered her sister as she came up to join her. "Otherwise, those furrows in your brow are going to be permanent."

Roe had no idea she had been frowning. She flushed. Then, instead of making up excuses about why she looked that way, Roe told her sister honestly, "I'm just worried."

"Well, that certainly narrows things down," Riley said flippantly. "Look, we just came through a history-changing drought and managed to survive just fine, thanks to some of the precautions that our team made. Everything else just naturally winds up taking second place," Raegan assured her.

Roe knew that Raegan knew what she was talking about. Raegan and her husband, along with several of the men he had brought into the project, were responsible for saving Forever from suffering a really terrible fate, possibly a permanent one. They had managed to build a reservoir and also drill for water, bringing it to the all-but-dried-out area and eventually reviving it.

"Not everything," Roe murmured almost to herself.

Raegan was immediately alert. "Would you care to elaborate?"

Roe realized that her sister had heard her. She most definitely didn't want to elaborate. "I don't want to get ahead of myself," Roe told Raegan.

"Oh no, you don't get to toss out unnerving statements and then retreat as if you hadn't said anything at all. Now out with it, Roe. Is there something we should all be bracing for?" Raegan asked.

Before Roe had a chance to come up with an acceptable answer, Riley leaned over and got into the discussion. "What are we talking about and why does my matron of honor look as if she's just bitten into a sour piece of fruit?"

Roe decided to quickly wave away the question. "Nothing to concern yourself about," she told her sister firmly, flashing a smile at Riley. "I told you, all you're supposed to be focused on is your bridegroom, your adorable imp of a daughter, and the upcoming wedding. Everything else is just everything else."

"You know, I'd really feel a lot better about it if you weren't such a terrible liar," Riley told Roe.

"I'm not lying," Roe told her, trying to look like the absolute soul of innocence. "What I am is exhausted," she emphasized. "I got about twelve minutes of sleep last night and just when I was finally drifting off, I was awakened by two madly moving little tongues washing my cheeks and doing their very best to wake me up. Apparently, they thought it was time for breakfast."

Riley looked at Raegan dubiously. "Do you believe her?" she asked the first triplet to exchange marriage vows.

"I'm not all that sure if we have much of a choice. Our sister can be pretty closed-mouthed when she wants to be," Raegan complained.

Roe had had enough. "Stop interrogating me. This is supposed to be a party," she reminded her sisters. "If you're not careful, Miss Joan is going to come over and start asking questions. And you *know* she's not going to retreat until she's satisfied that she managed to get the truth out of us."

Riley looked up as a shadow was suddenly cast over her. "Speak of the devil," Riley murmured under her breath.

"You're not calling me the devil, are you?" Miss Joan asked Riley, coming up behind the two young women and putting an arm around each one of them with just enough pressure exerted to make them realize she had overheard them.

"Oh no, we wouldn't dream of doing that, Miss Joan. Everyone knows you're the very opposite of the devil," Riley told her solemnly.

Miss Joan gave the bride-to-be a very penetrating look. "You're just afraid that I'm going to make you wash all the dishes on this table once everyone is done eating," the woman quipped.

"I can wash them for you," Vikki piped up, happily volunteering her services. The little girl bobbed her head up and down in assurance as she added, "Mama taught me how."

This time Miss Joan actually did laugh out loud, tickled. "I'll keep you in mind if my dishwasher breaks."

Vikki obviously thought that Miss Joan was talking about a person, not a machine. "Do people break?" she asked, wide-eyed.

"Not usually, little one," Riley told Matt's daughter. She pointed to Vikki's dinner plate. "Eat up so you can have dessert," she coaxed.

Picking up her fork, Vikki did as she was told, applying herself diligently to the contents of her plate and quickly making what was on it disappear.

Before she made her way over to the other guests seated in the diner, Miss Joan paused to bend toward Roe. "Before you leave my establishment, I'd like a word with you, missy," she told her.

Roe felt her stomach tightening. This sounded serious. "About?" she asked Miss Joan, the word all but sticking in her throat.

"You'll find out when the time comes and I tell you, won't you?" Miss Joan asked Roe cheerfully. With that, she turned on her heel and made her way to the other guests at the table and then, to the ones in the diner.

Roe sat and watched the woman go. She was afraid to hazard a guess as to what Miss Joan wanted to talk to her about.

Chapter Three

As it turned out, Roe was destined to wait until everyone included in the wedding party finally walked out of the diner before Miss Joan turned her attention to her.

Coming her way, Miss Joan frowned as she looked at Riley's maid of honor.

"You know, you look like you're waiting for the executioner to come your way and throw the fatal switch, electrocuting you," the diner owner commented. Her eyes met Roe's. "I'm not as scary as all that, am I, girl?"

There was no point in trying to bluff her way through this or denying what the woman had just said, Roe thought. And there was certainly no point in lying to her. Miss Joan had a way of seeing through everything.

Roe's eyes met Miss Joan's. Very briefly, she thought of denying it, and then she admitted, "Sometimes."

Contrary to what she expected, Roe's answer seemed

to amuse the woman. Miss Joan allowed a glimmer of a smile to pass over her lips before she finally told Roe why she wanted to see her. "Well, honey, the reason I called you over is because, quite frankly, I was worried about you."

"You were worried about me? Why?" Roe asked, confused. Why would Miss Joan even say something like that? She had absolutely no idea where this was going.

"Yes." Miss Joan circled around to where Roe was seated, looking at her critically. "You look like death warmed over, girl." The diner owner studied her more closely, as if she expected to see the answer to her question in Roe's eyes. "You getting enough sleep?"

The answer was no, but she wasn't about to admit that to the owner of the diner. Instead, Roe gave the woman an indirect answer. "I plan to get some tonight. I'm going straight home from here, feeding the dogs and then crawling into bed." She waited to see if that satisfied the woman.

Miss Joan looked knowingly at the girl she had helped bring into the world. "It might help you get that extra sleep you need if you remembered to close your bedroom door at night."

Roe read between the lines. She had no idea how Miss Joan had guessed that her dogs were responsible for waking her up way too early in the morning. But she had made her peace with the same fact as everyone else did. This was Miss Joan and that meant somehow, the woman always seemed to know everything.

So rather than protest, or agree to the idea that she

was going to lock her pets out, Roe merely just agreed. "Sounds like a good idea."

Miss Joan snorted as she looked at the vet knowingly. "But you don't plan on doing it, do you? You do know those dogs aren't going to get insulted if you bar them from your bedroom, especially for your own survival." And then the diner owner shrugged, her thin shoulders moving up and down. "But you do what you feel is best."

Finished with her commentary, Miss Joan leveled a piercing gaze at her. "Now go home, girl," she ordered. "I don't want to hear about you falling asleep behind the wheel of your truck and landing in some ditch when I get up tomorrow morning."

"Yes, ma'am," Roe agreed contritely. She gathered her things together and got up from her seat.

The thing about Miss Joan was that beneath all that surface bluster, she knew the woman actually cared. And that, in the long run, was all that really mattered.

Roe didn't quite remember the drive back to her home, but not for the first time, she was really grateful that she lived in town and not on her grandfather's ranch the way she and her sisters had for all those years growing up. The way she felt right now, Roe knew she might have been in real danger of actually falling asleep behind the wheel the way that Miss Joan worried she might.

Falling into a ditch was another matter, though. There weren't all that many ditches to fall into in and around Forever.

She congratulated herself when she pulled up in front of her house.

The moment Roe unlocked her front door, she was immediately greeted by almost nonstop barking. The dogs, she had long ago concluded, were expressing their joy at having her come home. Kingston was racing around her, creating a fluffy white circle until Roe finally bent down to slow him down and run her hand over his fur to pet him.

As if sensing what was going on, Lucy gave the smaller dog a moment to bond with his mistress, then nosed the little guy out of the way so she could have her turn with her mistress as well.

"Yes, yes, I missed you guys, too," Roe laughed despite herself. As she petted each dog, she said, "But you have to promise to be good tonight She rose then and went into the kitchen.

Opening the refrigerator, she began preparing food for Kingston's and Lucy's evening meal. "I'm going to feed you and then I'm going to bed," she informed the dogs, talking to them as if they were absorbing her every word. "Thanks to you guys and your morning alarm system, Miss Joan commented on the fact that I look like I am dead on my feet." She frowned and shook her head. "You can imagine how well that went over."

Their barking grew louder, as if they were expressing their opinion on that.

Roe placed servings of chicken, a sprinkling of cheese and the all-important spoonful of ground pumpkin in each bowl, then brought the bowls over to their feeding spot.

She was convinced that Kingston was going to sprain a least one paw if not two by dancing around her, salivating madly.

"Miss Joan said I should lock you guys out of my bedroom if I want any peace and quiet, but I'm not going to do that—if you two promise to behave yourselves and be good. Do you?" Roe asked, eyeing her two pets as if she expected an answer from them. She placed the bowls of food on the floor. She turned and went to fill up their water bowls.

The dogs lost no time in scarfing up their dinner. Roe had a feeling that, left to their own devices, the dogs would go on eating until they wound up exploding. She was going to need to keep an eye on them, she decided. She definitely didn't want them overeating.

But that was something she would look into tomorrow, she told herself. Tonight was meant for sleeping—which she was going to do immediately.

Roe fell asleep the moment her head hit the pillow. So fast, in fact, that she didn't even notice the blinking light on her answering machine.

The following morning for once, she woke up herself, without the dogs anointing her cheeks in an effort to rouse her from sleep. She had slept later than usual and felt both grateful and a little bit guilty for leaving the dogs to their own devices like this—but mainly she felt grateful.

She stretched, feeling like an entirely new person from the one she had been yesterday morning. She walked over to the door and opened it, then quickly got back into her bed a hair's breadth ahead of the dogs. Sitting up, she patted the place beside her and was instantly rewarded with not one but two dogs bounding over to sit on either side of her.

Their expressions all but said, "Weren't we good? Aren't you proud of us?"

Roe laughed. "Thanks, guys," she told them. "I really needed that sleep. To show you how grateful I am, I'm going to get your breakfast and put it out *before* I take my shower this morning."

As Roe walked into the kitchen, she saw the landline blinking. Whether it had been doing that last night or someone had called earlier yesterday, she had no way of knowing. She was going to need to hit the "play" button to find out.

But that was for after she prepared breakfast for the dogs. She quickly did a repeat of last night's meal, then set both bowls down on the floor.

"Eat up, boys and girls. Today feels like it's going to be another busy, long day. I've got several appointments coming into my office, not to mention a maid of honor dress to pick up. You wouldn't know about being a maid of honor, would you?" she asked with a laugh as the dogs paused to cock their heads at her, as if they were waiting for her to elaborate. "Trust me, it's a big deal in the human world," she told them. "Anyway, I'll probably be late coming home tonight so I'll leave you a lot of water to tie you over until I can get back."

Finished with the dogs, Roe stretched and yawned, then went back into the bedroom. She was going to postpone finding out who had left the message on her landline until after she had taken her shower.

But as usual, her curiosity got the better of her.

Hopefully, whatever it was could be quickly handled with a "yes" or "no" answer, she thought. Those were few and far between, but they did exist on occasion, Roe told herself, crossing her fingers.

She pressed the "play" button as she held the receiver to her ear.

Roe knew that her friends had far more sophisticated devices when it came to communication, but she tended to gravitate toward more old-fashioned things. She liked those better. There were times when she felt that the world was moving much too fast for her.

"Dr. Robertson," the deep voice on the other end of the call began, "This is Christopher Parnell. I don't know if you remember me or not, but I think I might need your help."

Remember him? Roe thought, amused by his choice of words. She might not have spoken to him for a number of years, but she certainly remembered him. She vividly remembered him from a time when there was no need to refer to her as "Dr. Robertson."

They had gone to school together, with Chris being a couple years ahead of her. At the time, she had had a giant-sized crush on him.

Actually, if she thought about it, Roe mused, a part of her still did, more or less. More than less, she amended. The very thought of seeing him had her blood rushing rather madly through her veins in anticipation.

She could remember watching him in a rodeo competition one summer. The competition involved his coming in first riding his palomino, Big Jake. He had also taken third place in a bronco-busting event, which she had found even more impressive. Roe could recall him looking absolutely magnificent on the back of that horse, hanging on tightly as the horse did his best to buck him off.

But then Chris had graduated high school and, with everything she had been involved in, Roe had lost track of him. She did remember hearing that he had applied to college and was accepted and she had thought that was that. But the following spring, his father had died. The question of who would take care of the ranch came up, but his older brother, Pete, didn't want to be bothered with it. Pete had other plans for himself. He just wanted to sell his share.

Chris didn't want to see the ranch falling into the wrong hands, or actually into any other hands, so he had scraped together as much money as he could and bought his brother out. What he wasn't able to come up with, he borrowed and made arrangements to make regular payments on the property, which he did, although it wasn't easy, until it finally became his free and clear.

She knew all this and admired it. She admired other things about Chris as well, she thought, smiling to herself.

Roe listened to the rest of the message on the machine. The Chris Parnell she recalled from high school had been a happy, fun-loving guy. The voice on her answering machine sounded as if all the fun had been summarily drained out of him.

All he had said was he thought he might have a problem, adding that he never thought he would ever wind up calling her for help. Yet, that was exactly what he was now doing.

He left his number and asked her to call him back at the first chance she had.

Roe really wished she had seen his message earlier, but there was no going back to rectify that error, she thought. All she could do was move forward and do things in the present.

She replayed the message, listening more closely and jotting down his phone number. Roe planned on calling Chris the moment she finished showering and getting dressed.

Fifteen minutes later, she was dried off and dressed and dialing the number she had jotted down.

Instead of getting him, she found she was listening to a recording.

"This is Chris Parnell. I can't answer my phone right now. Leave me your name, your number and a message and I'll get back to you as soon as I can. I'll be branding my cattle in the north forty, so it might be a while before I can get back to you."

The call abruptly ended.

Roe frowned at the receiver in her hand. She really didn't have time to play phone tag, she thought, hanging up the landline receiver. She supposed she could try calling him again later, but this "phone tag" could very well go on indefinitely, and there was something in his voice that made her think he was really worried. She wondered if there was a problem with his cattle.

She remembered him as a far more upbeat guy and not a worrier. Things had obviously changed.

She caught the bottom of her lip between her teeth, and worked it, thinking. He said he was going to be branding cattle in the north forty. She was basically familiar with where that was on his property.

Never one to put things off, Roe decided she could easily ride over to his ranch to see him and get to the bottom of whatever was bothering him. She had to admit that her curiosity was definitely aroused.

Grateful that there was no wedding rehearsal scheduled for today, Roe finished getting dressed. She pulled on her boots and took off the moment she was ready. She made a mental note on the way over, to call the animal owners who had appointments in her office today and push those appointments up by an hour or so, citing a medical emergency that required her attention.

She smiled to herself. It occurred to her that the people of Forever were basically a very understanding lot. Thank goodness for that.

Don't miss
Matchmaker on the Ranch *by Marie Ferrarella,*
available August 2023 wherever
Harlequin® Special Edition books
and ebooks are sold.
www.Harlequin.com

COMING NEXT MONTH FROM

HARLEQUIN®

SPECIAL EDITION™

#3001 THE MAVERICK'S SWEETEST CHOICE
Montana Mavericks: Lassoing Love • by Stella Bagwell
Rancher Dale Dalton only planned to buy cupcakes from the local bakery. Yet one look at single mom Kendra Humphrey and it's love at first sight. Or at least lust. Kendra wants more than a footloose playboy for her and her young daughter. But Dale's full-charm offensive may be too tempting and delicious to ignore!

#3002 FAKING A FAIRY TALE
Love, Unveiled • by Teri Wilson
Bridal editor Daphne Ballantyne despises her coworker Jack King. But when a juicy magazine assignment requires going undercover as a blissfully engaged couple, both Daphne and Jack say "I do." If only their intense marriage charade wasn't beginning to feel a lot like love...

#3003 HOME FOR THE CHALLAH DAYS
by Jennifer Wilck
Sarah Abrams is home for Rosh Hashanah...but can't be in the same room as her ex-boyfriend. She broke Aaron Isaacson's heart years ago and he's still deeply hurt. Until targeted acts of vandalism bring the reluctant duo together. And unearth buried—and undeniable—attraction just in time for the holiday.

#3004 A CHARMING DOORSTEP BABY
Charming, Texas • by Heatherly Bell
Dean Hunter's broken childhood still haunts him. So there's no way the retired rodeo star will let his neighbor Maribel Del Toro call social services on a mother who suddenly left her daughter in Maribel's care. They'll *both* care for the baby...and maybe even each other.

#3005 HER OUTBACK RANCHER
The Brands of Montana • by Joanna Sims
Hawk Bowhill's heart is on his family's cattle ranch in Australia. But falling for fiery Montana cowgirl Jessie Brand leads to a bevy of challenges, and geography is the least of them. From two continents to her unexpected pregnancy to her family's vow to keep them apart, will the price of happily-ever-after be too high to pay?

#3006 HIS UNLIKELY HOMECOMING
Small-Town Sweethearts • by Carrie Nichols
Shop owner Libby Taylor isn't fooled by Nick Cabot's tough motorcycle-riding exterior. He helped her daughter find her lost puppy...and melted Libby's guarded emotions in the process. But despite Nick's tender, heroic heart, can she take a chance on love with a man convinced he's unworthy of it?

YOU CAN FIND MORE INFORMATION ON UPCOMING HARLEQUIN TITLES, FREE EXCERPTS AND MORE AT HARLEQUIN.COM.

HARLEQUIN
PLUS

Try the best multimedia
subscription service for romance
readers like you!

Read, Watch and Play.

Experience the easiest way to get
the romance content you crave.

Start your **FREE TRIAL** at
<u>www.harlequinplus.com/freetrial</u>.